Sergeant Simpson's Sacrifice

NICHOLAS RHEA

Sergeant Simpson's Sacrifice

ROBERT HALE · LONDON

© Nicholas Rhea 2005
First published in Great Britain 2005

ISBN 0 7090 7829 3

Robert Hale Limited
Clerkenwell House
Clerkenwell Green
London EC1R 0HT

The right of Nicholas Rhea to be identified as
author of this work has been asserted by him
in accordance with the Copyright, Designs and
Patents Act 1988

2 4 6 8 10 9 7 5 3

Typeset in 10/13pt Monotype Bembo
by Derek Doyle & Associates, Shaw Heath.
Printed in Great Britain by
St Edmundsbury Press Limited, Bury St Edmunds, Suffolk.
Bound by Woolnough Bookbinding Limited.

CHAPTER 1

IT was inevitable that discovery of the man's body in Latima Park would drastically change the rest of Sergeant Simpson's life but he wondered if it would help or hinder the preservation of his deep family secret.

At the time and with only eighteen months until he could retire with a modest pension, Sergeant Richard Simpson was patrolling the streets of Hildenley. In uniform, he was the supervisory officer for the late shift and was the most senior police officer on duty in the small town.

It was Thursday 27 October, 1960; his shift was due to finish at 10 p.m. and he would be pleased when it was over. Throughout that day's work, he'd been feeling excessively tired, an increasingly worrying condition which he'd endured for several months. He told friends and family it was a combination of advancing age and many years of shift work but in truth he thought there was something more seriously wrong. A friend had died from leukaemia after showing very similar early symptoms and the sergeant wondered if he had the disease. He had never voiced his real worries, however, and, like so many men, had not consulted a doctor nor had he taken sick leave – that would have meant getting a doctor's certificate. He did not want people to think he was sickly. In spite of a good ill-health pension if he had to finish his working life, he had no wish to be declared an invalid.

His personal pride would not allow it. It was his ambition to complete his police service. He had no wish to unduly alarm his family either – whatever the cause of his constant weariness, he would tolerate it and he could complete his patrols if he took things easy with frequent rests.

In spite of his tiredness that October evening he had periodically visited all five constables on duty in the town to talk about current professional commitments or even family matters, to advise them in their investigations into minor local crimes or to discuss any other matter they wanted to raise, including any personal issues they might wish to share. Family happiness and security meant a lot to Sergeant Simpson, both personally and for his subordinates.

During that evening's patrol, he'd considered visiting his son, Ian, but he would be at evening class until nine-thirty or so. Ian had his own flat in town and Sergeant Simpson would often pop in while on duty, just for a chat or a cup of tea; it was a private place where he could sit down when he felt very tired. It kept father and son in touch too, and showed Ian that he cared.

With only a few minutes before the conclusion of his shift, it was time for Sergeant Simpson to make his way back to the police station. There he would record the safe return of every constable as they booked off duty – if any was missing or late without explanation, it could indicate a problem. Checking them in was not a matter of trust or distrust, it was a matter of accounting for their safety and then, before going home, he would update the incoming night-shift sergeant who would then assume responsibility for law and order until six o'clock the following morning.

As the little town came to life the following morning, hopefully with no overnight crimes or dramas, traffic would increase, factories would open, people would scurry to work, shops and offices would prepare for business and the townspeople would bustle about their daily routine. Anything more exciting rarely happened in Hildenley; it was that sort of place. Things just went along as they always had, nice and peacefully.

Against this background of small town life, Sergeant Simpson made his way back to the police station, torch in hand. It was in Keld Rise, fairly close to the town centre, the bus station and the railway terminus. Known for his calmness, his friendliness and his ability to communicate with children, young people and adults of all ages, the sergeant was liked and respected by everyone. His stolid and sturdy appearance exemplified all that was good about the British police service – honesty, reliability, friendliness, efficiency and security. Sergeant Simpson, Dick to his colleagues and friends, was one of the old school, strict but fair, honest and friendly, yet no fool. Dark-haired with a round, smiling clean-shaven face, good teeth, twinkling grey eyes and a rather rosy complexion when he was not so tired, he bore a look of perpetual cheerfulness. His physical appearance was not outstanding and although he seemed rather slow and ponderous at times, he possessed a fine brain, one which, in all probability, was under-used. Out of uniform, he was not the sort of person who would dominate a room or be noticed in a crowd. He was not particularly tall or heavily built, nor was his facial appearance overtly attractive although he did exude a positive aura of quiet strength and reliability.

Everyone who met him, young and old, felt he could be trusted in every way. Most found it impossible to imagine Hildenley without his reassuring presence.

Just before that final stage of his tour of duty, he had spoken to PC Harry Stead. That was just before 9.30 p.m. while Harry was making a conference point at the telephone kiosk known as West End kiosk. Policeman made 'points' at telephone kiosks every half hour at pre-arranged times in case the office wanted to contact them. With several constables patrolling at any given time, it meant a beat constable could be contacted around the clock. A simple but very effective system.

Patrol sergeants would visit constables at these 'points' too, to ensure they were patrolling their beats and that they were safe – just as Sergeant Simpson had done that evening. His visit to PC Stead had actually been at 9.25 and they had chatted for a few minutes. Before they parted at 9.30 p.m., Sergeant Simpson had initialled Stead's pocket book to confirm the time and place of their conference (this was known within the service as a 'chalk'), and Stead had done likewise in the sergeant's book. Sergeant Simpson had then told Stead he would make his way back to the police station via Latima Park and would check the park *en route* – that meant Stead need not include it in the final minutes of his own patrol. Stead thanked him and said he would complete his duty by making an official visit to The Black Lion around 9.45 p.m. before heading via Fern Lane towards the police station. Like all the constables reporting in, he would time his walk so that he arrived at the police station at 10 p.m. precisely, not one minute early and not one minute late.

When Sergeant Simpson left PC Stead, he walked from West End kiosk down Scrivener Street and turned along Park Road as he headed for the park gates. It was a ten minute walk from West End kiosk to the first of the park gates, but slightly longer if you stopped for a chat or checked lock-up properties along the way. On that short journey, Sergeant Simpson did check the doors of one or two shops and spoke to several people, townspeople who were homeward bound or just enjoying a late walk in the brisk fresh air of autumn, and who bade the popular sergeant goodnight. He didn't stop for a long chat with any of them nor did he note their names because he was anxious to complete his check of the park and not be late booking off duty.

There was some light traffic on Park Road, cars mainly, and a couple of buses groaning along, stop by stop. Give or take a minute or two, he reached the first of the park gates about 9.45 p.m. just in time to notice a male figure hurriedly leaving by the next gate, a hundred and twenty yards or so along the road. The street lights were switched on but their glow was insufficient for Simpson to identify the person, save to say it was a young male in dark clothes. He was hurrying out of the park with his head down and, apparently, with his hands over his cheeks or ears. The gait of the man was familiar. It looked like Ian. Wondering if he was in distress of some kind, Simpson called out but the hurrying figure did not respond; in fact, the shout apparently made him hurry away with greater speed. That made it all the more likely that something was wrong. But had he heard the sergeant's call? Or had the noise of that bus drowned it? Indeed, was it really Ian?

The fleeing figure broke into a fast trot, quickly distancing himself from Sergeant Simpson who then pointed his torch at him and switched on the beam, but it made no difference. He was too far away for the torch to be effective and within seconds, the man had vanished into the shadows as the road curved away. That minor incident had taken just a few seconds. While Sergeant Simpson paused with a high degree of puzzlement, he realized another man was walking towards him, slightly dazzled by his torch. He switched it off. The man had been close to the wall of the park, moving towards the sergeant in the shadows of overhanging trees, but now he halted. He had a small black spaniel on a lead; it was sniffing the scarce vegetation which grew along the edge of the pavement at the base of the park wall.

He might have seen or heard the departing youngster, reasoned the sergeant. Man and dog were between Simpson and the gate through which the mystery man had appeared. In the glow of the street lamp, he recognized the newcomer.

'Hello, Sergeant Simpson. Working late?' Geoffrey Stalker asked in a friendly way.

'Good evening, Mr Stalker,' responded Simpson. Stalker was a local solicitor. 'Yes, it's my week for late shift, but I'm nearly finished. Just a few more minutes to go.'

'Bed's calling me too, I'm homeward bound, but as you know, I do enjoy a late potter around the park. The fresh air's a real tonic before I turn in.'

You could almost set your watch by Geoffrey Stalker – he came this way every night at the same time with his dog. Quarter to ten on the dot.

'Just think, I get paid for walking in the park!' joked Simpson. 'It always makes a pleasant end to my shift whatever time of day that happens to be. I'm ready for bed now though, I'm shattered! I'm getting too old for this sort of life! But talking of walking in the park, did you see who that young man was? The one I tried to spotlight just now, dressed all in black. He rushed out of that gate just behind you.'

Using his torch, Sergeant Simpson indicated the gate further along the road.

'No, who? I saw you flash your torch and wondered why, but I didn't notice anyone. He must have been some way behind me; the darkness can play tricks and those street lights aren't much help being so far apart.'

Mr Stalker turned around to look in the direction of Simpson's torch beam but the footpath was completely deserted. Whoever it was could have crossed the road to disappear among the houses opposite but that was unlikely – Simpson would have seen him do that. He could have gone back into the park by a gate further along or simply continued along the parkside in the shadows to disappear around the bend in the road. Ian's flat was along that way too, beyond the western boundaries of the park so had it been him heading home? If it had been Ian, it was odd he'd not responded to his father's shout. Probably it wasn't Ian after all.

None of the park gates was locked at night – in fact, they weren't normal gates, they were more like kissing gates which would admit a person or a dog but not a cyclist. Their purpose was to deter cars and motor bikes too but they permitted pedestrian access at any time of the day or night. The fellow, whoever he was, could have been running for fun and gone back into the park further along.

'He seemed in rather a hurry,' Simpson explained. 'I thought he was in some distress but he didn't stop when I called so I can't be sure who it was. If there was a problem, there's nothing I can do now. It's probably nothing to do with me anyway. Mind you, I'll keep my ears and eyes open as I go through the park.'

'Well, I've just been walking around the west end and never saw anyone but it is dark and full of shadows,' admitted Stalker, waving his hand to indicate the area of the park he had visited. 'Sooty never barked either; he usually does if he hears unusual noises or comes across some-body unexpectedly. I came out of the far gate, the west one, but I didn't hear you call to the man.'

'A bus went past just as I shouted, it might have drowned my voice. It's probably nothing to worry about, someone rushing home from the pub, trying to get home before his wife or mother starts to grumble! Well, I must be getting along. I want to check the museum to see if it's OK, then a quick tour of the park benches and shelters to check for vandals or people sleeping rough. I can just fit that in before I knock off at ten.'

Stalker and his dog continued their way as Sergeant Simpson looked along Park Road to see if the hurrying youngster had re-appeared but he had not. If he was to finish duty on time, the sergeant had no time to visit Ian's flat to see if he was all right and he knew the lad would contact him if he needed any kind of help. Feeling there was no cause for alarm or concern, he entered Latima Park by that first gate, No. 1 Gate or the East Gate as the park authorities termed it.

There were lots of paths within the park. It was a veritable maze to someone unfamiliar with them, criss-crossing and inter-linking in what appeared to be a haphazard fashion along the kidney-shaped site. The park was on a south-facing slope about a third of a mile long from east to west. Some of its paths had steps and some were without, some passed through cultivated gardens while others crossed lawned areas or wove among rockeries and borders. One led past the goldfish pond and another extended to the Latima Museum, tucked away in the eastern top corner. The museum was a small building containing local exhibits and there were other paths leading to seats and shelters where people could sit and admire the flowers, shrubs and trees or merely enjoy the views across the town.

Lots of work-people came here at lunchtime to eat their sandwiches or read their newspapers. At night, the park was illuminated by Victorian-style decorative street lamps but because they cast a lot of shadows among the trees and shrubs, some people wouldn't venture there during the night-time hours. Nonetheless, at night from the upper reaches of the park there was a wonderful view of the low-lying areas of the brightly-lit town and, according to police records, there had never been any assaults or serious crimes in the park. It was undoubtedly an asset to Hildenley and a wonderful oasis of solitude for those who sought it.

Especially at night, Hindenley's police officers routinely checked the seats and shelters for vandals, people sleeping rough, drunks and courting couples. Sometimes they had to search for runaway children or individuals who had left home, hopefully to start a new life, only to arrive here without a bed or roof over their heads.

In spite of these minor wrinkles in the town's night-life, a regular police presence maintained the aura of peace in the park even though the shadows of night, along with thick shrubs and leafy trees, concealed a great deal. Many an illicit courtship had been conducted here, and among the regular visitors were lonely people, sad people, the bereaved and people with overwhelming worries, some of whom liked nothing better than a chat with a friendly policeman who might be able or willing to help. Sometimes, a policeman was the only sensible and impartial person available.

Tonight, as always, Sergeant Simpson would undertake those dutiful chores. He would check the museum to ensure the doors and windows were locked, and to ascertain that no one had broken in or harmed it in other ways. Crimes like attempted arson or acts of malicious damage such as throwing a stone through a window could happen even in Hildenley; even here, some people were likely to do that sort of thing. Bored youngsters might set fire to the contents of dustbins, push lighted papers through letter boxes, toss stones through windows or use sheltered doorways as toilets – but not if Sergeant Simpson was around. The town's youngsters knew and respected Sergeant Simpson; he was regarded as a firm but fair policeman.

As the time ticked away, it would take only a few more minutes for Sergeant Simpson to complete his rounds; his torch removed the need to walk to every bench or shelter. He knew his way through the maze of footpaths and made good use of its powerful beam to check from a distance the interiors of several shelters or for occupancy of the benches.

A torch with good batteries was a bonus, as it saved a lot of time and leg work. During his tour, all he found in his sweeping arc of light was a courting couple huddled together for warmth on one of the benches at the western end; Mr Stalker hadn't mentioned them. The girl wore a heavy black coat and the young man had his left arm around her shoulders. That was the extent of their intimacy in this public place but he shouted an apology for disturbing them.

Then he directed his torch elsewhere and headed for his final check – the museum and a nearby shelter. The museum was fairly modern and of modest size, a plain, single-storey, stone building with a flat roof. It was jokingly known as 'The Shoebox' due to its long, narrow and rather low uninspiring shape. It had been constructed to the memory of Alberto Latima, a local benefactor who had made a fortune from the manufacture of refrigerators. It housed a variety of local artefacts which spanned the ages from the first living inhabitants of this region until the second World War; entry was free and the building also accommodated various group meetings, including the Hildenley Literary and Philosophical Society and Hildenley Art Club. As Sergeant Simpson walked around its exterior, shining his torch on all the windows, the rear door and the large solid front door on its western front, he found everything correct. He tried the doors and both were locked. Behind the building were a couple of box-like public toilets, male and female. He checked them too, announcing his presence before entering the ladies. Both were deserted. Sometimes, people slept there, or even fell ill. Checking such places was one of the many unseen duties undertaken by the police.

In his official notebook, he would make an entry to record those visits when he returned to the police station. Now for his final task – checking the bench in the shelter which stood at the top of the grassy slope about twenty yards below the museum, the one on the top edge of a splendid rockery containing a host of specialist plants. That would be his last job before emerging from the park by its south gate. The police station was only about five minutes walk away.

And close to that bench is where he almost stumbled over the man's body.

CHAPTER 2

THE dim glow from street lamps just beyond the park was barely strengthened by the decorative lanterns among its autumn tinted trees, and in the poor light Sergeant Simpson immediately thought this was a drunk who had fallen off the bench while asleep. It took only a few moments for him to realize he was wrong. As the beam from his powerful torch played across the still form, he could see blood, lots of it; some had stained the concrete where the man lay, with more about his face and neck and soaking his upper clothes, his shirt collar and jacket lapels.

Even so, it was remotely possible the man might have rolled off the bench and smashed his nose on the concrete. That could produce a lot of blood, but as Sergeant Simpson absorbed the sight with his customary calmness, it was increasingly evident this was something far more serious. It looked like a particularly vicious attack with some kind of heavy weapon. Without wasting a second, Sergeant Simpson knelt beside the man, spoke to him and allowed the beam of his torch to move slowly across the motionless face – and it produced no response from eyes which stared from a mass of blood and gore. Pieces of smashed bone were protruding from the indented skull and from a cheek bone; the blood was everywhere, all wet and sticky but not yet congealed. He hadn't been here very long, that was evident. Minutes even. Due to the injuries, the man's face was almost unrecognizable, but in spite of that, he looked familiar. Simpson felt sure he knew him. He frowned as he tried to identify the face beneath all that blood and damage but positive recognition was far from easy.

Even so, that battered face jolted faded and unpleasant memories from the past. Age had drastically altered the fellow's appearance but the realization that this man was continuing to haunt Sergeant Simpson sent a shiver down his spine. Certainly it looked like Swainby. Edward Albert Swainby. But was it really him? After all this time? If so, why had he come back to Hildenley?

But there was no time for those questions. His duty came first and his duty right now was to save life, whoever the man was. That's if he wasn't too late. Already, Sergeant Simpson's hands were sticky with blood, his trouser knee was wet where he had knelt in a sticky pool and his uniform was coated where he had instinctively wiped his hands down his tunic and trousers. Then he touched one of the man's hands, the left one. It lay on the ground, warm and flexible as he felt for a pulse but there was none, not the faintest sign. He leaned closer to the face and listened for sounds of breathing or the tiniest touch of breath on his own cheek, but there was none. And as the sergeant's trained eyes absorbed more of those terrible injuries, he knew they could not have been accidental. They *might* have been the result of an accident if this man had fallen head-first from a very high cliff or bridge, but they could not have occurred by falling just a few inches from a park bench. This man had been brutally attacked with some kind of blunt instrument; that he was dead was almost a certainty. But he must not let his personal knowledge of this man influence his actions, he must give him a chance of life. That was a police officer's duty – the preservation of life. Urgent medical help was required. There was no time to lose. He needed a doctor, an ambulance and police assistance.

He could not – must not – presume the man was dead. People *could* survive this kind of attack even if they appeared to be dead . . . and after all, he was not a qualified doctor. He *was* a very experienced policeman, however, one who had seen death and near-death on many occasions. But Sergeant Simpson was alone in the park and there were no telephone kiosks. Where was the nearest phone? West End? The police station?

The police station was nearest but that was several minutes away, at least five minutes when walking fast. Two or three minutes while running? The museum was closed and locked but he did not think he could or should break in to use its telephone. In those days, police officers did not have the benefit of personal radios but even though help was urgently needed, he couldn't leave the scene. More important than the scene was the fact he could not leave this man alone. Kneeling at the man's side, Sergeant Simpson hauled his police whistle from his breast pocket and blew it as hard as he could. Would PC Stead hear it? Or any of the other officers who were just completing their patrol? Or anyone else in fact, police or civilian?

At this very moment, all the late turn constables would be heading for the police station to book off duty but that was about quarter of a mile away. They'd be congregating a short distance from the station, waiting in the shadows until it was time to go inside, using shop doorways or sheltering under any kind of temporary cover. It was unlikely they would hear his whistle over such a distance or against the constant rumble of night-time traffic and other sounds of a town at leisure.

Stead might hear it, that was feasible – he was probably the nearest. His route from No 6 beat would take him down Fern Lane which was only a hundred yards or so from the eastern boundary of the park . . . and so Simpson blew and blew. And waited and waited. But no one came. It seemed ages and ages but probably it was only minutes. He checked his watch. Three minutes to ten. Surely there must be someone in the park? Or walking on Park Road? Or any of the surrounding roads? Surely they would hear his frantic whistling because the sound was unmistakeable. Again and again he blew, the shrill blasts almost deafening him; he knew he could not leave this man, yet he must get medical help. It was with some horror that it dawned on him that this was surely the scene of a murder – another reason why he could not leave. Any evidence at a murder scene must be protected and preserved. Nonetheless, he needed a doctor to state categorically that this man was dead or even to pronounce there might still be a spark of life and he knew better than to move the fellow because of those very severe head and facial injuries. There might be other internal damage or wounds to the brain or spine. He daren't even try to move him, not even just a little so that he could place something warm beneath him, such as his own tunic. As Sergeant Simpson blew his whistle until his cheeks hurt, he became increasingly sure this was Edward Albert Swainby, a face from his past but one which was much older than he remembered. If it was Swainby, it was not surprising someone had thrashed him to the point of death but if this did develop into a murder enquiry, then the whole story would surely emerge . . . and Sergeant Simpson did not want that to happen.

He wanted his private life to remain private, but if it was murder, he would not be able to stop the inevitable in-depth enquiries. Trying to put all that kind of thing to the back of his mind, he knelt at the man's side, still blowing his whistle and feeling utterly weary. He began to note a description of the man – his clothing was not distinctive, he was not clad in evening wear or overalls but was dressed like a local man would dress for a leisurely evening out – a blue-grey sports jacket and grey flannels, white shirt and coloured tie . . . blue, yellow, red. And his physical appearance? Aged about fifty, grey hair, heavy build, taller than average . . . not the handsome, dark-haired, slim-built rogue he'd been twenty years ago.

Sergeant Simpson remained on his knees wondering how best to deal with this situation and continued to blow his whistle so long as his breath permitted, and then, with immense relief, he heard someone running towards him. It was the courting couple he'd seen earlier, the girl in the black coat and her young man.

'Thank God!' breathed Sergeant Simpson as they halted a few feet away, faces anxious as they absorbed the scene in the light of the sergeant's torch. 'Look, this man has been attacked, I need help and can't leave him.'

'It looks like Mr Swainby,' said the young man.

'Swainby?' That confirmed it.

'He's come to live near me, we saw him earlier, coming into the park by the bottom gate . . .' said the man, hardly able to take his eyes off the sight.

'*Living* here? Are you sure?' That put a totally different complexion on things; why would Swainby come back to *live* in Hildenley?

'Look,' he quickly gathered his wits. 'Look, can you run to the police station? Urgently. Very urgently. Get them to call a doctor and the ambulance and tell them I need a senior officer here, immediately, and other policemen, as many as can be found. Tell them a man is lying very seriously injured near the museum. Got it?'

'Yes,' said the girl as the young man at her side continued to stare at the still figure.

'I'm Sergeant Simpson, tell them I sent you. It really is most urgent.'

'Yes, yes of course,' the girl's voice was low and frightened. She was a pretty blonde about twenty years old.

'You should just catch the night shift coming on and the late shift going off if you hurry . . . it really is most important and very, very urgent. You'll have to run all the way.'

'Is he dead?' asked the young man, a dark-haired youth about twenty years old who wore a thick white sweater and dark trousers but no hat.

'I'm not sure, we've got to assume he's still alive . . . look, this is desperately urgent, you must hurry . . . now.'

'Come along, Alan,' the girl was tugging at his sleeve. 'Come along . . . .'

'You know where the police station is?' asked Sergeant Simpson.

'Yes,' said the girl. 'Come along, Alan, I'm going now, we have to go now.'

'I need your names,' said Sergeant Simpson, almost as an afterthought.

'Alan Wetherill, this is Shirley, my fiancée . . .'

Even as they called their names and before he could ask for any addresses, they were running down the path which sloped towards the bottom of the park and the south gate. He didn't want to stop them to ask for more details, not in a case like this. Their mission was vital, every second mattered. If they ran all the way, they could be at the police station within a couple of minutes and that could be crucial if this man was alive. The office duty constable would record their names and addresses, take a statement and decide upon whatever action was necessary. All Sergeant Simpson could do now was wait.

Again, he felt for a pulse, there was none; he listened again for signs of breathing and there was none. From his kneeling position, he shone his torch across the surrounding area but saw nothing suspicious, no weapon, no lurking attacker. And no sign of life as his light touched those eyes.

The fact that this was almost certainly Edward Albert Swainby threatened to destroy all that Simpson had worked for; it could destroy his happiness if the story was resurrected. He shuddered at the thought and wondered what on earth he could or should do about it, then immediately felt overwhelmingly tired. He slumped onto his haunches and rocked on his heels, resting as best he could under the circumstances.

So what had Swainby been doing over the past twenty years or so? Where had he been? And why come back here? Even in Hildenley, as Sergeant Simpson knew, there were plenty of people with personal reasons for wanting him dead . . . .

But murder was murder, whatever the reputation and status of the victim. Sergeant Simpson, knowing his immediate actions were vital, continued to squat on his heels to rest a little whilst he swept the beam of his torch around the shelter and the bench, then across the lawns and the rockery spread before him. What was he seeking? A suspect lurking in the darkness? A killer revisiting the scene and watching events from a hiding place in the shadows? The murder weapon? Other evidence left behind unwittingly? There was lots of debris in the shelter, waste paper mainly, dropped by people who'd been eating fish and chips, potato crisps, sweets and chocolate. The seat was made of thick wooden beams with concrete uprights, three of them, one at each end and one in the middle. Had he smashed his face on one of those? There was no sign of blood but he daren't sit on the bench, it might bear some evidence. The wood was painted green, also without any sign of blood. There was no blood on the sides of the shelter either. No broken glass. The bench would hold four people, he thought, five at a pinch, while the shelter was constructed of glass reinforced with wire netting except for the lower portions which were of brick. It surrounded the bench on three sides and had a sloping roof, also of reinforced glass which sloped to the rear. There was no sign of damage to the shelter, no sign of the attack taking place in here, he thought. The front opened across the downward sloping parkland with its lawns and special rockery.

Then he saw something glistening in the beam of his light. It was on the grass about fifteen feet away to his right, to the west. He rose rather stiffly and went towards it.

What he found shocked him to the core. Had he been foolish enough to drop this, here of all places? He stared this piece of evidence then quickly picked it up and pushed it into his pocket, hoping no one had seen him. There was nothing else of evidential value at the scene and he felt tempted to search the victim's pockets to establish or confirm his identity, but decided he should leave that to the investigating team. There was little doubt the man's identity would be confirmed as Edward Albert Swainby and it was too late to do anything else about that.

The attention paid to preserving the scene of a murder in 1960 was by no means as thorough as the situation in the early years of the twenty first century. At that time, it was not unusual for the first police officers at the scene to wander about, leaving footprints and fibres as they did what they thought best in the circumstances. The truth was that they were usually unwittingly destroying evidence and generally making the work of the CID and forensic scientists more difficult. And so Sergeant Simpson, torch in hand, wandered around the shelter, its bench and nearest section of lawn doing what he thought was immediately necessary, flashing his torch along the ground, seeking a discarded murder weapon or some more evidence or even a suspect hiding somewhere. Tired though he was, he felt he should be doing something positive as he awaited the arrival of some assistance.

Later, he could write an account of those first few minutes in his pocket book and would have to record that he had done all that was possible by way of searching for the assailant or the weapon, A quick check of the immediate surrounds was sensible and necessary for a positive report. But his efforts revealed nothing.

An immediate appraisal of the scene suggested the suspect had fled, taking the murder weapon with him; there were no discernible footprints on the grassed areas however, or in the bare earth of the flower patches, and nothing to show the killer's route of escape. As he waited, it seemed another long period of useless inactivity had passed but in reality it was only a few minutes before sounds of running feet heralded the arrival of assistance.

The first to appear was PC Harry Stead, having been retained on duty. He was a senior constable with some twenty-three years' service, a level-headed sort of man who had not passed any promotion exams but who had a weakness for women. For all his dallying, much of it done when on duty beyond the knowledge of his supervisors, he was a very good police offi-cer. Panting with the exertion of running from the police station, he gasped, 'Doctor Buchanan's on his way, Sarge, that young couple caught me just before I went in to book off. I asked them to go to the nick and be sure to ask for reinforcements . . . so what have we here? Oh my God . . . .'

He shone his torch on the body but did not venture closer than five yards.

'He's had one hell of a battering and I think it might be Edward Albert Swainby.' Sergeant Simpson spoke quietly and moved away just in case the man was alive and could hear their conversation. 'That young couple thought they recognized him, or at least the man did. It certainly looks like him, I must admit, even though it's been twenty years since he lived here and since I set eyes on him. That young man's name is Wetherill by the way, Alan Wetherill; we need to talk to him and his girlfriend about seeing this man earlier. They could be the last to see him alive.'

'He's dead, is he?'

'I'm sure he is,' whispered Sergeant Simpson.

'This is all we need!'

'I don't think that young couple were responsible, Harry, but they are material witnesses, it's vital we talk to them.'

'They'll have taken their details at the nick, I sent them in to raise the alarm.' Stead paused to take several deep breaths, then said, 'If Swainby left town all that time ago, why come back? Someone's really had it in for him.'

'Maybe he was up to his old tricks.'

'He was the rapist, wasn't he? It was before I was posted here but I've heard the name, they still talk about him in the pubs around town. There's a tale of him trying it on with a butcher's wife and getting chased out of town with a meat cleaver!'

'That's him, that's Swainby, he took off to Garmingham so far as I remember,' said Sergeant Simpson, wondering if that's all the town remem-bered about Ted Swainby. People had long memories, especially in small towns. Simpson knew he was not going to enjoy this enquiry even if it was his first case of murder; it could throw up too much dirt from the past.

'It looks as if he's got what he deserves this time! Are you sure he's dead, Sarge?'

'As sure as I can be. There's no pulse, no breathing, no sign of life in his eyes. The signs are all there, I'm sure he's gone.'

'You obviously got here very early, so did you see his attacker?'

'I saw a young chap running out of the park as I was heading this way but there's nothing to link him to this, not that I'm aware of. No sign of the weapon either.'

'Looks like murder then? With a possible suspect?'

'What else?' said Sergeant Simpson.

'Does that mean calling in the Yard or do we do it ourselves?'

'If I know the chief constable, he'll want us to sort this one out ourselves, the days of this Force calling in Scotland Yard are over. But it's out of our hands . . . ah, voices . . . .'

Within minutes, the scene was alive with police officers and Sergeant Simpson saw the lights of one or two cars beyond the trees as they pulled up outside the East Gate. These men comprised the remainder of Sergeant Simpson's late shift, all four of them plus the office duty constable, all of whom should have gone off duty at ten o'clock; there was also the oncoming night shift of six constables who were reporting for duty at ten. In addition, a couple of Road Traffic Division drivers had turned up. By chance, they had just arrived in Hildenley for their mid-shift refreshment break and were going to eat their sandwiches in the police station. They were due to go off duty at 2 a.m. but had been directed to the scene with their car. It was equipped with radio, and thus the officers in the park could now liaise with both Hildenley Divisional Police Office as well as the Information Room at Force Headquarters.

The total now present amounted to fourteen constables, two sergeants and one inspector. Each carried a powerful torch and from their midst appeared the officer in charge of Hildenley Division, Superintendent Firth. He was in civilian clothes, having been recalled to duty from his home. He had arrived in his official car too, which was parked near the East Gate and was also fitted with radio. Now there were adequate means of communicating almost directly from the scene.

'Wait there, keep your distance,' Firth ordered the assembled mass, pointing to a patch of grass about twenty-five yards away to the west. 'Wait until I have assessed the situation with Sergeant Simpson. Sergeant?'

Sergeant Simpson saluted his boss even though he was not in uniform and, from a point away from the body, said, 'Sir, I was making my final check of the park and museum whilst en route to the station to book off duty. I'd come from a conference with PC Stead on Six Beat, and I found the victim as you see him now. I examined him and was sure he was dead but we need medical confirmation. When I saw the extent of his injuries, I realized they could not have been caused accidentally and knew there was nothing I could do, this was not a case for first aid. It looks like the work of a maniac with a blunt instrument, and so I blew my whistle to get help and a young couple, who happened to be in the park, heard it and responded. I sent them to the station to get help, to raise some assistance. In fact, they are material witnesses too. They might have been the last to see the deceased alive. They saw him earlier, coming into the park by the bottom gate, that's the south gate, sir.'

'Good, it's important to find such witnesses. So what time did you find this man?' asked Superintendent Firth.

'It would be about 9.55, sir, I can't be more precise.'

'And he was dead then?'

'Almost certaintly, sir, I checked his pulse, breathing and eyes. I've seen dead men before, sir, there was no doubt in my mind.'

'And have you moved the body?'

'No, sir.'

'Any sign of his assailant?'

'None, sir, although I did see a man hurrying from the park about ten minutes earlier, leaving the North Gate around 9.45 p.m. but I didn't recognize him. He hurried away along Park Road, to the west. I lost him in the shadows. At the time, I spoke to Mr Stalker, the solicitor, but he didn't see him either. Of course, he might not be connected in any way with this incident, sir.'

'Description?'

'Very vague, it was dark and he was in the shadows. A young man with dark clothing, hurrying away. That's all I can say.'

That's all he wanted to say, he had to say that because it's what he had conveyed to Mr Stalker before finding the body. A young man in dark clothing was vague enough to fit hundreds of similar young men in Hildenley.

'Well, it's not much and of course at that time you would have no reason to be suspicious of him, but he will have to be traced. That's a job for these constables but first, tell me what else you did at the scene.'

'When I examined the deceased, sir, the body was still warm and the blood was fluid and had not congealed. I think the attack had occurred shortly before my arrival. I made an immediate search for both the culprit and the weapon, but found neither. Apart from the couple who raised the alarm, there were no other witnesses.'

'Well done, you did well. Now, do we know the identity of the victim, Sergeant? You know almost everyone in town, so I'm led to believe.'

'It might be a man called Edward Albert Swainby, sir, who used to live in Hildenley, but who moved away some twenty years ago. I can't confirm his identity, his face is too much of a mess and it is some years since I last saw him. This man is a lot older, fatter and greyer than the Swainby I remember but there is a distinct likeness, and the couple of young witnesses said it was Mr Swainby.'

'You searched his clothing for clues?'

'No, sir. I felt it best not to touch anything but if there's any doubt, his fingerprints should confirm his identity.'

'Fingerprints?'

'If it is Swainby, he's known to the police, he has a record. He's a convicted sexual offender and rapist although he got away with a lot. He was active in the town before you assumed command here, sir, then went to live away, to somewhere near Garmingham, I think, but he may have returned for reasons we must establish.'

'When did he return?'

'I don't know, sir, I wasn't aware of his return until now – if it's him.'

'Is he suspected of being one of our active criminals?'

'Not to my knowledge. We've had no reports of rape or indecent assault during the last few months, and he's not come to our recent notice, sir.'

'But his criminal past must be significant, surely? Maybe this is the outcome of a battle between two local villains? Or a sex victim retaliating? Was he a peeping tom? Someone getting revenge even? Something along those lines? So you didn't search the entire park for the assailant?'

'No, sir, I did the best I could in the circumstances, a brief search of the immediate parkland just in case the attacker was hiding nearby. I didn't wish to leave the body or the scene unattended which meant I couldn't undertake a thorough search.'

'But it was enough to satisfy you that the assailant had fled the scene?'

'Yes, sir, I saw and heard no one here or nearby.'

'And the weapon?'

'I have no idea what it could be, sir, except that it looks as though a blunt instrument of some kind was used. I have found nothing nearby though. The post mortem should provide further clues. A search of the scene and whole park in daylight must be done, sir, that's vital.'

'Indeed, yes, and you need to get your uniform cleaned as soon as you can, Sergeant, it's covered in blood,' observed Firth, screwing his eyes against the poor light. 'Ah, Dr Buchanan's arrived.'

A stocky man in his fifties was easing his way through the silent throng of officers who were awaiting their instructions in the poor light; he wore a long grey macintosh, trilby hat and carried a walking stick as well as a black bag.

'Superintendent?' He ignored the lesser ranks and made straight for the most senior officer.

'Doctor, we've a man who is the victim of a very serious attack about the head and face. He's lying near that park bench. We believe life to be extinct, I should tell you, so this looks like a murder enquiry. If he is dead, the body shouldn't be moved until it has been examined by the forensic service and our own CID. All that will take time. We need to keep the scene as clean as it is now and disturbed as little as possible.'

'I understand. Has the man been moved at all?'

'No,' said Sergeant Simpson. 'He's just as I found him, I didn't move him due to the likelihood of brain or spinal injuries. I felt any attempt at first aid could do more harm than good.'

'Very sensible, Sergeant. And if he is still alive, can he be moved?'

'Of course, his life is of paramount importance. He must get immediate treatment but it must be done with care to preserve the scene.'

The doctor strode forward in the light of many torches to carry out his examination. It didn't take long.

'Superintendent,' he said, when he had finished. 'I can confirm death, time 10.27 p.m. It's not my duty to estimate the time of death but judging by the rather fluid condition of that blood, which is quite sticky now, I'd say he's been dead for less than an hour. I can't be too specific, of course. Certainly, though, it's a very recent death – and a very brutal one.'

'As we thought,' muttered Firth.

'It's not my duty to state the *cause* of death either, Superintendent, that's the job of a pathologist, but I think he's been subjected to a sustained and frenzied attack about the head with some kind of blunt instrument. That's merely an opinion but you might need to consider that as you start your enquiries and search for the weapon. I'd say it is some-thing solid with a sharp corner, a brick perhaps.'

'Thanks, doctor, you'll let me have your report in writing?'

'Tomorrow morning at the latest, Superintendent. Do we know who this is?'

'Not with any degree of certainty but there's a possibility it's a man called Swainby, who is known to some of my officers. Not to me, I might add. One of our first duties is to establish his identity, recent history and movements. Unfortunately, those kind of formalities will have to wait until the scene has been forensically examined. And we must trace any relatives as soon as we can.'

'At least you can send the ambulance away,' said the doctor. 'It's not required now he's dead.'

'You've just confirmed my worst fears,' said Superintendent Firth. 'Now I must set in motion a murder investigation, the first in Hildenley, I believe.'

If this was to be the first murder enquiry in Hildenley, it was also the first to feature directly in Superintendent George Firth's career. Although he was fifty-six years old with thirty years' service, being qualified for retire-ment if he wished, he had spent his entire police career in uniform and intended to remain in harness until his sixtieth birthday, the compulsory retirement age for officers of his rank. He'd won promotion due to his administrative abilities, organizational skills and astute brain rather than a capacity for detecting serious crime. He had never considered himself a detective, he had never served in the CID and had never detected or been part of any investigation into serious crime, especially not murder.

In many ways, he was very suitable to have command of a division like Hildenley, one which embraced this small town and included a large expanse of countryside with many villages and smaller market towns. He had two inspectors, four sergeants and about forty constables under his command at any one time, although there were also two CID members at Hildenley, a detective sergeant and a detective constable. They had not yet arrived at this murder scene – they would be somewhere in town, in the pubs probably, ostensibly carrying out their onerous duties. They would have to be found and brought here. The office night-duty consta-ble would be frantically ringing all the pubs and the solitary club in the hope they could be traced.

In accordance with force standing orders, Superintendent Firth had to call in Detective Superintendent Will Clifton from force headquarters and he would assume command of the investigation. Nonetheless, Firth was in charge until Clifton's arrival – and that could be at least an hour, probably more. Force headquarters was about fifty miles away and Clifton had to be knocked out of bed or otherwise found at home or in town, and then Clifton would have to raise his assistant, a detective sergeant. They'd have to collect their murder bag from the office and drive out to Hildenley. Although it would take some time for those experts to arrive, much could be done in the meantime. Having briefly examined the scene and secured his first situation report, Superintendent Firth was now in a position to address his men and allocate initial basic tasks, one of which was an immediate search for the young man in dark clothing.

Firth had noticed another park bench some distance from the body, called out to everyone 'follow me', then went and stood on the bench to elevate himself above the crowd and make himself visible. He'd also noticed a lamp standard close to the seat – that meant everyone could see him. It was a good start. Leaving Sergeant Simpson and PC Stead to temporarily guard the body and the scene in which it lay, he waited until everyone else had gathered around, then began to issue instructions. After introducing himself and outlining the task ahead, he said:

'Inspector Burn. We must seal off this park. I need a man on each gate to prevent unauthorized entry until further notice. The entire park must be searched immediately for anything which might be evidence, any sign of a person fleeing, anyone hiding and of course, anything which might be the murder weapon. I know it's dark but it must be done with great care and all unauthorized persons must be told to leave immediately and their names and addresses taken as potential witnesses or even suspects. Use as many constables as you think necessary. Anyone behaving suspiciously should be detained and interviewed rigorously but we need to trace anyone who was in the park between nine o'clock and ten o'clock this evening. Don't overlook anything which could have been used as the weapon, a blunt instrument of some kind with a corner, like a stone or a brick. There are plenty of hiding places beneath all these shrubs and border flowers. Now, a very important factor is that Sergeant Simpson saw a man leaving the park about 9.45 p.m. The man was young and in a hurry; he was dressed in dark clothes. He left through the North Gate and headed west. Sergeant Simpson did not recognize him and can provide no further details. That description fits a lot of young men in town, but this one needs to be found. Don't shrink from drafting in extra support if you need it, you can always call assistance from our rural areas or other divisions if necessary. We must also initiate a search of the entire town to trace that suspect, with enquiries at bus stations, the railway station, taxi firms and so forth in case he has left or tries to leave. Road blocks should be established out of town although if he has a car or motor bike, he'll be miles away now. Get those road traffic lads to contact their division to set them up and make sure they check anyone fitting the suspect's description.'

'Very good, sir.'

'You need to swamp the town immediately with bobbies asking questions about people's whereabouts tonight. Did they see two men fighting or arguing – a young one in dark clothing and an older one in sports jacket and flannels? Ask the regulars at the Blue Star night club for signs of men drinking heavily, fighting in the street or whatever. This could have been a pub fight or even a domestic dispute.'

'Yes, sir, I'll get as many men as possible on to those tasks.'

'Also,' continued Firth, 'we need town patrol constables to visit the homes of all officers who were on late turn this evening. Their families need to be told they will be on duty for some considerable time. Assure the families they are working late, they have not been injured on duty, nor are they missing.'

'I'll attend to all that, sir.'

'Good. Now, Sergeant Williams?'

'Sir?' Sergeant Jack Williams was the incoming night duty town sergeant.

'There's a strong possibility that the deceased is Edward Albert Swainby who lived here twenty years ago. We haven't a positive identification yet. Even so, we need to trace any of his relatives and to inform them, as sympathetically as we can, of his death. Swainby is known to the police, he has a record for sexual offences. Sergeant Simpson tells me that the young man who raised the alarm recognized Swainby as a near-neighbour. It seems he may have returned recently to live here. You'll need to find that young man before he goes to bed to learn as much as you can about Swainby, his address and place of work for example.'

'Yes, sir.'

'And don't forget the CID will also want to talk to that man, he's very much a material witness but they might wait until tomorrow. It'll be some time before they arrive and they might have other priorities. You'd better alert that young man to the fact we regard him as a very important witness. And his girlfriend.'

'Very good, sir.'

'Now, the press. Both the discipline code and standing orders lay down the procedure for dealing with journalists and editors. In short, none of you will discuss this case with the press. It is the duty of Detective Superintendent Clifton to prepare a press release if he considers it necessary and it will be circulated by the Information Room at force headquarters. Should any of you receive enquiries from reporters, refer them to the Information Room.

'Pending the arrival of Mr Clifton, I will confirm we are investigating the suspicious death of a man and that a post mortem is being arranged. We need say no more at this stage and indeed, we are not obliged to tell the press anything. We must be sure not to name the victim in the press, Inspector, certainly not until his relatives have been contacted. There's another task for you – to inform the coroner. The CID will attend to the post mortem arrangements, forensic examination of the scene and body, official photographs and so forth but I shall make sure the hospital mortuary is ready to accommodate us, and that a local pathologist is standing by. We shall preserve the scene until the arrival of the CID and the body will not be moved until Detective Superintendent Clifton has authorized it. Now, I will radio headquarters to call out Mr Clifton but there is one final matter, Inspector. The men will need refreshments, especially those whose shift has been extended. Have words with the Royal Hotel, arrange sufficient sandwiches and enough cups and urns of tea. The force will settle the bill and you may use a car to fetch the food when it is ready. There are toilets behind the museum and plenty of park benches for rest periods, all well away from the scene. Make sure the men don't walk across the murder scene to get to the toilets though, make sure they know a safe route and tell them not to cross the area where the body lies.'

'Very good, sir.'

'All right everyone, you may proceed.'

And so Sergeant Simpson and PC Stead were left guarding the body and the scene of the crime as the first stages of the investigation were established. It's odd, thought Sergeant Simpson, becoming involved with a murder enquiry at this late stage of his service. Like all policeman, he'd always wanted to arrest a murderer.

CHAPTER 3

For Sergeant Simpson the wait for the arrival of the experts seemed interminable but there was nothing he could do save stand a few feet from the body with PC Stead nearby to ensure no one trespassed on the murder scene. In the excitement of those earlier moments, he had overlooked his tiredness but this would be temporary; the fatigue would return and he hoped he wouldn't have one of his nose bleeds, not here! He was sufficiently experienced to realize his role was very important – he was a vital witness, the first police officer at the scene and in any case he had found the body. That, of course, made him a prime suspect right from the beginning. The person who finds the body of a murder victim is always a suspect until eliminated. He knew he would be closely questioned about his movements tonight but was confident he could provide satisfactory answers.

During his vigil, Sergeant Simpson watched the controlled activity in the park. Superintendent Firth had gone to make calls from the patrol car as Inspector Burn organized his slow but systematic search for evidence. Constables were now guarding all entrances to the park and those not required for specific duties had been despatched into town to concentrate upon finding or even just identifying the mystery man in dark clothing. Some were given the task of tracing Swainby's relatives because he would have to be formally identified, while others were told to examine his lifestyle now he had returned to Hildenley. Sergeant Williams was in charge of those operations.

From Sergeant Simpson's vantage point, therefore, the world (and certainly the murder investigation) seemed to be continuing without him; one of the things he thought about was that someone had probably told Pamela the reason for his delayed return of duty. He hoped so; he didn't want her worrying unnecessarily.

Standing some distance away, but well clear of the crime scene, was PC Harry Stead; he, like Simpson, had been uncharacteristically silent during those first minutes of their vigil with Simpson wondering who had attacked Swainby – and why. Stead was thinking exactly the same, with each man ransacking his brains for recent indications of Swainby's presence among the townspeople. And then Superintendent Firth returned. In the dim light, Sergeant Simpson recognized his quick walk as he made his way down from the East Gate, stopping *en route* for an update from Inspector Burn on the search and to acquaint Burn with the results of his calls to headquarters. Then he approached Simpson.

'Sergeant,' he said. 'The chief constable has been informed and has ordered a full-scale murder investigation led by Detective Superintendent Clifton. I have spoken to Mr Clifton and he is on his way; he should arrive within the hour.' Firth glanced at his watch. It was now 11.05 p.m. 'Midnight or thereabouts, I'd say. I need you and PC Stead to remain here until he arrives. He will come direct to the scene and will be accompanied by Detective Sergeant Burrows. They're our force in-house murder team, I suppose we could call them. I am sure they will be as efficient as any whizz-kids from New Scotland Yard. Mr Clifton wants you to provide him with as much information as possible; I have relayed this to Inspector Burn too.

'Meanwhile, I shall return to the station as I have things to do there. The forensic lab has been told, by the way. One of their boffins should arrive around midnight too. Mr Clifton requires a base at Hildenley Police Station and so I shall make arrangements for him to use the local CID office.'

'I'll tell him, sir.'

'Thanks, and I trust we have, in the meantime, found our detective sergeant and his side-kick in the local pubs, they are needed here . . . so there we are, Sergeant. It means a long vigil but sandwiches and tea have been arranged. Might I say you look very tired? You've been looking off colour for a while now. Getting enough sleep, are you? I hope you're not burning the candle at both ends, as they say.'

'I'll be fine, sir, I think it's a combination of advancing age and shift duties.'

'Well, don't overdo it. If things get bad, we might have to consider some lighter work for you . . . .'

'I'm not an office man, sir, I prefer this kind of work, I like the variety.'

'I'm sure you do, but we have to be realistic, haven't we? I don't want you knocking yourself up with too heavy a workload, especially now. But there's one blessing – it's not a cold night for the time of year and it is dry. Find somewhere to sit down if you need to. Well, there we are. Maintain protection of the scene and take further instructions from Detective Superintendent Clifton. I will make sure all officers' families have been told of their retention on duty. Now I must be off. Any questions before I go?'

'No, sir, everything seems to have been taken care of.'

'Good, well then, goodnight, and, er, well done, good work, finding that murder victim and getting things underway.'

'Thank you, sir. Goodnight.'

Once more in silence, Sergeant Simpson watched the superintendent have a quick word with PC Stead and then return the way he had come. Moments later, his car engine burst into action as his headlights shone upon the trees at the top of the park. The gears crunched home, the head-lights swept the skyline and then he was gone. Inspector Burn and his men continued their search by torchlight, traffic was moving in town and an owl hooted in one of the parkland trees.

Moments after the Superintendent had departed, Sergeant Simpson became aware of two men approaching and chattering in the darkness. Who'd let them into the park? They were climbing from the south gate but as they approached, their identities were evident – Detective Sergeant Maurice Huntley and his assistant, Detective Constable Jim Thorne. They were panting with the exertion of the climb even though it was not particularly steep and they halted in front of Sergeant Simpson, smelling of beer. Much of the CID's local work was conducted in pubs and the town's solitary club; that's where they had been tonight, gathering infor-mation which might lead to the detection of a few local crimes. For the price of a pint or two, much crime-solving information could be acquired and this pair were hardened drinkers – and surprisingly good detectives.

'Evening, Dick,' said Huntley. 'We've just heard about this. We'd just got back to the nick and came straight here . . . where's the boss?'

'You've just missed him, he went that way,' and Sergeant Simpson indi-cated the East Gate. 'He's gone back to the station. You'll be pleased to know he's going to commandeer your office for the headquarters murder team.'

'Oh, bloody hell, we're going to be homeless! Right, well, he's the boss. So what's to be done?'

'Nothing more until the headquarters team arrive,' said Sergeant Simpson. 'Everything necessary is being done, we're just waiting for them and the boffins. Bobbies are out in town asking around for witnesses and some are searching the park for the weapon and other evidence. Things are nicely under way. Where have you been?'

'Working, what else? So why wasn't I told?'

'Don't ask me, I've been here all the time. Perhaps nobody could find you? I bet you didn't leave the duty bobby with a phone number of any of your pubs! How is anyone supposed to find you when you're out pubbing in town?'

'Right, well, we're here now so we'd better take a decco at the body,' and he stepped forward.

'No you don't,' said Sergeant Simpson. 'It's out of bounds until Clifton gets here.'

'Don't be bloody stupid, Dick! I'm not going to nobble the scene, drop ice-cream all over, crush evidence with my size tens or anything like that. I am a detective, remember!'

'My instructions are not to let anyone onto the scene or near the body, Maurice, and that includes you. If you try to get past me, I shall record the incident and the boss will be informed. Orders are orders. You could be disciplined, I know you don't want that.'

'Fair enough, Dick, it couldn't be much clearer than that, you're only doing your job. So what's the story?'

PC Stead approached at this point and stood in silence as Sergeant Simpson provided yet another account of the entire incident. Huntley listened carefully. It was when Sergeant Simpson suggested the victim was likely to be Edward Albert Swainby, a man known to the police, that Huntley appeared to come alive.

'Swainby? I've heard that name. Why should I know him? He's not one of our local villains.'

'Not any more,' put in Simpson. 'He left about twenty years ago but for some reason, he's come back.'

'He's remembered around town,' PC Stead added. 'He was a sex offender and rapist, Sarge, and there was some kind of incident with a butcher's wife. He got chased out of town by her husband with a meat cleaver.'

'That's it! Yes, I've heard about that. They still remember it in town!

Not surprisingly. It's one of those Hildenley urban legends now! So we think this is the man in question, eh? So why's he come back after all this time? He doesn't sound like the sort of character we want in our peaceful little community.'

'It seems he's come to live here, maybe not permanently,' added Simpson.

'Live here? Why didn't we know about him? Right, that looks like a job for my department, to find out what he's been doing and why he's come back. Is anyone looking into that? Checking his recent history?'

'Jack Williams was asked to allocate a town constable or two. We want to trace relatives to tell them about his death and to formally identify him, and of course, we want to know all his recent movements and contacts.'

'Leave it with us, Dick. Jim and me will get cracking on that right away and I'll talk to Jack Williams about it. You can tell the headquarters lot I'm dealing with that matter when they arrive. Come along, Jim, let's get back to base to see what our old files can tell us about Swainby. That's unless somebody else is already sitting in our office munching our chocolate biscuits.'

The two detectives, having viewed the body from a distance and been given an account of its injuries by Simpson, then hurried away, taking the path back to the South Gate. Then things fell silent once more. Sergeant Simpson was once again alone with Harry Stead and they could talk. They could not hear the men at the far side of the park, so their own voices would probably not be heard by the other constables and certainly not by members of the public walking past. There would not be many such passers-by at this time of night anyway.

'Harry, how much do you know about Swainby?' asked Sergeant Simpson.

'Not a lot, most of my knowledge is second-hand. He was active before I was posted here but by all accounts he should have been castrated at birth,' snapped Stead. 'The man was a danger to all women, old and young, the townspeople keep talking about him. They'll be horrified to know he's come back. It wasn't so much that he assaulted women, or tried to rape them, it was the violence he used when he did. He used to go berserk, so I was told.'

'He's done time, you know,' said Simpson.

'It seems it didn't stop him. So do you think he's resumed his antics here? Has he come back older but not much wiser? I wonder if a woman has dealt with him this time? Or a woman's husband or lover? Could he have attacked somebody coming out of those toilets, somebody who got the better of him? In self defence?'

'Whoever did this must have been carrying a sledge-hammer! I doubt any normal woman would have the strength to use one like this; in fact, I can't imagine a woman killing him like this. This look like a man's work.'

'It's amazing what people can do in a frenzy or fit of violent anger,' acknowledged Harry. 'He's had a very, very severe knock or two this time . . . I agree with you that it looks more like a man getting revenge than a woman defending herself. A bit more severe than that butcher with his cleaver though!'

'I remember him leaving,' said Sergeant Simpson. 'I was excused war service but the police doctor passed me fit so I joined the force during the war. Swainby was never called up either but don't ask me why. I remember that business with the butcher's wife, it never got to court.'

'So where's that butcher now?' asked Harry Stead, wondering if the fellow could be considered a suspect.

'He sold up and went to live in Lincoln, I think. Worth a check though. His name was Ackroyd, Neil Ackroyd. He could be still around. Tell that to the CID when they arrive, you might get a pat on the back for remembering it. They'll want to trace the butcher, just to make sure he didn't come back and do this!'

Then they heard a car pull up at the East Gate, one of the few now passing along Park Road. Accompanied by the constable from the gate, the man who eventually appeared from it was carrying a large torch-like lamp slung across his shoulders on a strap and an equally large and rather solid black suitcase or very large briefcase. Sergeant Simpson went to meet him.

'This is Mr Fisher, Sergeant, from the Forensic Laboratory,' the constable announced. 'Mr Fisher, this is Sergeant Simpson who found the body.'

'Ah, good. All on your own, Sergeant?' he plonked both items on the ground with an evident sigh of relief. Each was quite heavy.

'That's PC Stead over there in the shadows of the shelter, Mr Fisher, he arrived soon after I made the discovery; we're protecting the body and the scene. Inspector Burn is over there in the parkland, seeking evidence with a team of constables, they're at the far side just now.'

'So things are moving?'

'Yes, we've been quite busy and we have officers in the town, searching for a suspect and any witnesses, and also relatives of the deceased. I'm awaiting our Headquarters CID team, that's Detective Superintendent Clifton and Detective Sergeant Burrows. I'm expecting them literally any moment now.'

'Good, well I spoke to Mr Clifton on the phone before I departed. He will be here shortly but I can commence my examination without him. I am a forensic pathologist, not just a scientist. So, Sergeant, can you tell me what happened?'

Once more, Sergeant Simpson found himself telling the story, making sure he included as much detail as possible. Then Mr Fisher, a slim man with a pale face and large horn-rimmed spectacles, lugged his belongings into the shelter and put them on the bench, then asked a few questions such as whether there had been noticeable changes in temperature or any frost or rain, whether the body had been moved and whether it had been covered with a rug or blanket at any stage. Sergeant Simpson knew that murder victims must not be covered with rugs or blankets in case material like fibres or dust contaminated them and he was able answer all the queries with confidence. The scientist then began his initial examination.

The large portable lamp was operated from a huge battery and he placed this on the bench so that it acted as a kind of floodlight. Then he opened his case. It was like an Aladdin's cave, packed with instruments and articles which would help in his careful work. There was everything from thermometers to pieces of chalk by way of a camera, first aid kit, forceps, assorted brown paper bags and more.

It was evident that Mr Fisher wished to be left alone to carry out his work and so the two policemen stood aside to allow him unrestricted access while observing his actions with keen interest. First he stood well back from the body, then walked around it and viewed it from all angles, sometimes crouching to his knees and he consolidated that visual examination by taking a series of flash photographs, some at close range and others at a distance. Then it was time for a closer examination of the body, albeit without undressing it at this stage; that would be done in the mortuary, under laboratory conditions. Without touching the corpse, he peered closely at the head wounds and even produced a Sherlock Holmes type of magnifying glass which he used to good effect for close range examination, aided by the small but powerful hand torch. He looked into the eyes and ears, up the nose and into the partially open mouth. He produced a thermometer and took the body's temperature from several places, both over and under the clothing. Then he spoke to Sergeant Simpson.

'I shall want the whole of the area around this bench, including the cement where this man is lying and the area within the shelter hoovered, Sergeant. I need to collect every bit of debris and dust for examination in the laboratory. I have a small vacuum cleaner in the car; it operates from a battery but I'll wait until your detective superintendent has concluded his examination and I don't want to move the body until Mr Clifton has seen it. I will wait for him before I do anything else. You might like to know that I can confirm this is a murder. He has suffered extremely savage head wounds, Sergeant. With a blunt instrument.

'I'm sure there are particles of earth or stone adhering to those wounds. That suggests a piece of stone, taken from one of these rockeries perhaps? And repeatedly used. There are at least seven wounds. Violent anger, Sergeant, eh? That suggests a sudden fight with the killer picking up a convenient weapon . . . a form of defence even? Was the killer using a stone to defend himself? Or herself perhaps? That could mean the killer had no premeditated intention of killing this man. That makes for some interesting speculation, does it not?'

'So the deceased might have attacked someone and got his come-uppance in return?' suggested PC Stead.

'It's a feasible theory,' smiled Fisher.

'It matches Swainby's MO,' added Stead.

'Now, Mr Fisher,' said Sergeant Simpson. 'Inspector Burn would be interested in what you have to say. He can ask his men to look out for a suitable piece of stone. It will be a great help to know what they're look-ing for.'

'A good idea, Sergeant. It will be heavily bloodstained, they should realize, which narrows the search somewhat, and it has a sharp right angled corner rather like a brick would have. Slightly smaller than a brick, I'd say, and not so deep. A smallish stone easily wielded with one hand. It was repeatedly used, I am sure of that, and used savagely. That corner caused the real damage, those broken bones and compressed fractures combined with heavy bleeding and brain damage. Used with sufficient force on the head it could kill a man almost instantly if he had a weak skull.

'It's possible the first blow knocked the man to the ground, with the additional blows, and perhaps the fatal one, being delivered while the victim was on the ground, perhaps unconscious. The angle of the indentations and wounds suggests that is how the final blows were delivered, although I need to test that theory in the laboratory.'

'It's a good starting point for us,' smiled Simpson. 'Now, Harry,' and Simpson addressed PC Stead, 'go and tell Inspector Burn what's happened and ask him to come and speak to Mr Fisher, will you?'

'Sure, Sarge.'

Moments later, the tall and slender Inspector Ken Burn arrived and shook hands with Fisher. Fisher explained his theory and the inspector listened carefully.

Then he said, 'Right, Mr Fisher. No problem. We'll give all the rockeries and borders an extra search now we've something positive to look for; we'll go over the original ground again too. This is a big help. If the stone was taken from the park, it'll have left a hole of some kind too. We need to find that as well. I'll redirect my officers. You'll want its place of origin marked and a plaster cast taken?'

'Spot on, Inspector! In fact, I'd like two or three casts; it's always useful to have a spare. It should match the stone perfectly, excellent evidence for the court. There'll be one problem, though. Unless the stone is very smooth surfaced, which few are, it won't bear fingerprints. I've never been able to obtain prints from stone. That might present difficulties proving it was the murder weapon, or that the killer actually used it. Even if the blood samples convince a jury it is the murder weapon, they might not believe it was the accused who actually struck the fatal blow. A good defence counsel could cast doubts. That's something to work on, Inspector.'

Sergeant Simpson then addressed Inspector Burn. 'Sir, there is a rockery a few yards below where the body is lying. I spotted it earlier. If what Mr Fisher says is right, the murderer could have picked up a stone from there. It's the nearest rockery, probably the nearest place where there's something suitable.'

'Ah,' said Fisher. 'I have not ventured that far into the parkland, gentlemen. Show me, Sergeant. And come with me, Inspector.'

Taking care not to trample across the scene of the crime, Sergeant Simpson led the two men in a wide circle, Fisher having the foresight to bring his powerful lamp. Soon they were standing at the edge of the rockery with its specialist plants. The entire patch would be some ten yards along by four yards deep, and it was oval shaped; it occupied a place among smooth lawns on a piece of sloping ground, sloping that is, towards the southern boundary of the park. It was a beautiful piece of the garden, noted for its rock plants and always popular with visitors. The higher parts were very close to the edge of the concrete upon which the body lay, but it was not possible to view it in its entirety from that bench. To appreciate it fully, one had to walk down the sloping lawn and view it from below. That is precisely what Mr Fisher did with his powerful torch. With the inspector and sergeant at his side and PC Stead guarding the body and scene of the crime, he walked around the entire edge of the rockery, playing his torch upon its contents and its borders, pausing some-times for a second or longer look and then continuing.

'Ah!' he said suddenly and with some excitement. 'Ah, Inspector. See?'

The light of his torch had found a hole in the ground. A fresh hole. A hole of the kind left by the removal of a stone with a prominent corner, one which had been lifted out very recently. The weather had not had time to affect the ground from which the stone had been lifted.

'That hole must be preserved, Inspector, and at the first opportunity I need a plaster cast or two,' said Mr Fisher. 'Let's hope no rain comes to damage the sides of the hole or wash earth into it . . . this is vital and, if my memory serves me correctly, that indentation in the ground looks very similar to the indentations in the deceased's skull but I need the post mortem to confirm that. I feel a match would be the result, I really do. And, as you can see, there is earth around the edges of that hole, just as there was earth around the edges of the wounds. We need to match those samples of earth too. This is wonderful, a very good start, so, Inspector and Sergeant, all we have to do now is to find the stone which was taken from here and we need to examine this rockery and its approaches with great care in case there is other evidence.'

And it was at this point that PC Harry Stead called to them, 'Mr Fisher, Inspector, Detective Superintendent Clifton has arrived.'

CHAPTER 4

IT would be difficult to ignore Detective Superintendent Wilf Clifton. A large and loud man in every sense of the word at six feet six inches tall, he towered above most other people, police officers included; he had a massive frame to match his height and a voice to match both. His broad shoulders always made his clothing look ill-fitting; his large-check jackets and coats seemed to hang around him like something from a second-hand shop because when they were large enough to accommodate his shoulders and chest, they were invariably too large for the lower half of his body. He had a surprisingly slim waist and small backside with rather long, slender legs, all of which served to make him look top heavy. It never occurred to him that he should have his more formal clothing tailor-made. Consequently all his clothing looked ill-fitting and baggy, which it was.

The result was that, in spite of his impressive bulk, Wilf Clifton never looked smart. Some colleagues joked it was this trait which had prompted his senior officers to transfer him to the CID. He had looked so dreadful in his police uniform that the powers-that-be thought he might not be such a curiosity if he worked in civilian clothes. Some said that as a young constable waving his arms whilst on traffic duty he looked rather like a top-heavy windmill. For all that, he was a good detective who had quickly risen through the ranks to become the officer in charge of the Criminal Investigation Department of the Benningshire County Constabulary. It was a considerable achievement for a man with no formal education.

Forty-eight years old with a shock of unruly black curly hair, a huge handlebar moustache and a flattened nose which was the result of a youthful but short boxing career, he was indeed a formidable fellow. He had won his youth club's middleweight junior boxing championship when he was fifteen but had not continued that career.

It was his proud boast that as the detective superintendent in charge of the CID, he had continued the force's enviable record of having detected every case of murder with most of the perpetrators being hanged, but in addition during his stewardship a high percentage of other serious crimes had also been solved. They included rape, robbery, burglary, embezzlement, sacrilege, arson and grievous bodily harm. A good many minor crimes remained undetected, however, including larceny, false pretences, housebreaking and shopbreaking, and it was a situation to which he frequently referred when speaking to his subordinates during official visits. He told them it was their job to detect those crimes – that was what they were paid for! Nothing less than a 100 per cent detection of *all* crimes was good enough for Wilf Clifton. Most certainly, he had no desire to become the first detective superintendent in the history of his force to have an undetected murder recorded against his name. He wanted to be known as the man who had maintained that enviable record.

It was against this background that Detective Superintendent Clifton arrived in Latima Park with the resolve to add to his murder success rate. He was confident the man responsible would quickly be arrested and arraigned before the Assize Court with a well-presented case against him.

After all, Hildenley was a small, compact town with a population who would surely know almost everyone living there; they'd also be prone to gossip and if the killer was a resident, he would soon be unmasked by a combination of good police work and public co-operation. Clifton knew that by persuading the public to talk about it, his officers would soon be on the trail of the killer. There would be no hiding place in Hildenley.

Inspector Burn, having been alerted by PC Stead, and as the most senior officer present, went to greet Clifton but did not salute him. One did not salute detectives because they were supposed to be anonymous when among other members of the public. Clifton would have difficulty being anonymous anywhere.

'Sir, I'm Inspector Burn,' the tall man introduced himself to the even taller Clifton just as Clifton's assistant, Detective Sergeant Burrows, arrived; clutching a torch, he was a few yards behind his boss, having locked their car and brought their murder bag. It might not be required if the forensic chap had done his job properly. Three other plain clothes officers were also following, these being members of the force photographic department, which in those days also doubled as the scenes of crime department. These officers combined their skills as crime scene specialists and photographers and one of them bore a large camera already fitted with a tripod.

'Right, let's get this show on the road,' boomed Clifton. 'What's the story?'

'Sergeant Simpson found the body, sir . . . .' and the inspector indicated Simpson who stood some distance away with Mr Fisher.

'All right, I'll talk to him. Sergeant Simpson, tell me what happened.'

Sergeant Simpson stepped forward but before he could speak, Clifton observed 'This light isn't very good but that looks like blood on your hands and uniform, Sergeant.'

'Yes, sir, it happened when I knelt down beside the body to check for signs of life. At the time, I didn't realize I was getting myself stained.'

'All right, get your uniform cleaned when you can. So what can you tell me?'

Yet again, Sergeant Simpson found himself explaining the events of this long and extremely tiring evening after which Mr Fisher gave his account, emphasizing his belief that the killer had acted spontaneously. The fact he had happpened to pick up a convenient stone was evidence of that spontaneity.

'But it is murder nonetheless?' said Clifton. 'The first blow might not have killed him, he might even have been knocked down by someone's fist but you suggest there were several blows to the head?'

'Yes, I expect the post mortem to confirm that.'

'Then it's surely murder. Death from one blow might have been in self-defence – it could be manslaughter – but to rain repeated blows on the head of a man who might or might not have been unconscious means I regard that as murder. I'm not going to get involved in the argument that if he was already dead from the first blow, those extra strikes didn't count – I know you can't kill a dead man, but I don't see that as an issue here. When we get the killer, which we will, he'll get sent down for life as he deserves. It's a pity hanging's been abolished for some categories of murder; it stopped a lot of villains from killing. So who is the victim?'

'Sergeant?' Fisher turned to Sergeant Simpson.

'It's possibly a man called Edward Albert Swainby, sir.' Simpson then provided an account of Swainby's known history, stressing that his identity had not yet been confirmed but that the local detectives were trying to trace relatives and examining his recent behaviour.

'Sex offender, eh? A rapist you say? So could he have attacked someone who retaliated with a stone in his hands? Or her hands. A woman, I wonder? Serve him right if that happened. Villains deserve all they get.

Any suspects at this stage?'

'Only the man I saw hurrying from the park, sir; the town is being searched for him and the park has also been searched without result.'

'Good. He sounds as likely as anyone at this early stage, so he's got to be found. Now, witnesses? Do we have anyone who might be a useful witness?'

Sergeant Simpson told Clifton about the young couple in the park, pointing out they were probably the last to see the victim alive and adding that Sergeant Williams was going to interview them tonight. He also mentioned Geoffrey Stalker's presence outside the East Gate at 9.45 p.m. He suggested Stalker might have seen people either leaving the park or walking within it. Simpson said he knew of no other witnesses, then Inspector Burn gave an account of his search of the parkland and how the area had been sealed off until the police decided to re-open it. He added that no other witnesses had been found within the park. Clifton nodded his large head in apparent satisfaction at what had been done, then said, 'Now it's time to view the body.'

With torches playing across the still form, Superintendent Clifton approached from the feet end and stood motionless for several minutes then he slowly walked around the corpse with his eyes taking in every tiny detail. He scrutinized the area around the bench and shelter, had a look at the rockery with its space left by what appeared to be a missing stone and grunted something to himself.

'Right,' he said eventually. 'Photographer. You know what to do. Scene, body, rockery, general area showing parkland if you can, if not we'll have to come back in daylight for that. And we need a plaster cast of that depression left by the stone. You can take his fingerprints when we get him to the morgue.'

Two photographers, each with the rank of detective constable, came forward and under Clifton's instructions began to take a series of black and white photographs with their powerful flash equipment. It would take time to complete their portfolio, not forgetting the required plaster casts. Both the pictures and the casts would serve as aide-memoires to the detectives as they investigated the case and they would also be used at the inquest, the committal proceedings and subsequent trial.

While they were working, Inspector Burn returned to his men who were still searching for the murder weapon and any sign of suspects or witnesses. Sergeant Simpson, PC Stead and Mr Fisher stood to one side as they awaited their next instructions from Clifton. As the photographers busied themselves, the detective superintendent stood with his chin in his right hand, once more quietly observing the scene without saying a word. When eventually the photographers had finished their scene of crime work, Clifton turned to Fisher.

'Do you need to do anything else here, Mr Fisher?'

'No, I've got all I need but I have to view the body in the mortuary, undressed as well as dressed, and I need to be present during the post mortem. I want a closer and more detailed look at those wounds to the head.'

'You're not conducting the PM?' asked Clifton.

'I hadn't intended to. There's no reason why a local pathologist can't perform it, albeit with my forensic input, providing I'm present as an observer. I don't want to suggest the local man is incompetent!'

'Fair enough. The hospital should have been alerted by the local police; they should understand our basic requirements if Superintendent Firth has done his job – which he will have done. He's very capable. Right, gentleman,' he turned to Sergeant Simpson and others waiting in the dim light behind him. 'We can move the body now. We've got a tarpaulin, have we? And the box?'

The tarpaulin was a large green canvas sheet, about the size of the cover of a double bed and it had a stout rope handle at each corner. It was used to convey bodies from scenes such as this. It meant that whatever dropped from the corpse and its clothing during removal could be collected for laboratory analysis if necessary, and the sheet was flexible enough to remain with the corpse during its journey in the box. The box was a temporary coffin fashioned out of stout dark brown plastic; it was coffin shaped with handles at each end and a loose-fitting lid but it was unmarked and could be carried in the rear of a small van or estate car when either full or empty.

It was regularly used for the transportation of bodies on occasions such as this, or in the case of sudden or unexplained deaths when a post mortem was required, or to carry bodies from the scene of traffic accidents. Two scenes of crime officers came forward with the tarpaulin. It was partially rolled into a long tube and they laid it on the ground as close as possible to the left side of the body. Two uniformed officers were asked to ease the body onto its right side whereupon the rolled-up part was pushed towards the body's back. The body was then allowed to return to rest on its back before being hoisted onto its left side. The rolled edge of the tarpaulin was revealed and it was then unrolled, leaving the corpse in the centre. The four policemen each took hold of one of the rope handles and the body was carried towards the open box. It was deposited carefully inside, still on the tarpaulin, ready to be driven to the mortuary. Mr Fisher and Detective Superintendent Clifton then went forward to examine the concrete which had been beneath the body.

Working in the bright light of Fisher's torch, they scrutinized it carefully but apart from a patch of blood where the head had been, there was nothing else. Even so, Fisher said he wanted to hoover up the dust and debris which had been beneath the body and Clifton agreed. He could benefit from such diligence.

'Right,' said Clifton as Fisher was preparing for another hoovering session. 'Off to Hildenley Hospital Mortuary with that chap. They should be expecting us. Sergeant Simpson, you'd better come with us, you'll be needed to identify the body to the pathologist and we might even find the coroner turns up for his statutory peep. You'll have to be there for that too. Now, where's Inspector Burn got to? Is he hiding behind a bush? Inspector!' he bellowed.

'Sir,' came Burn's response from behind a laburnum.

'We're vacating the scene, taking the body off to the morgue. I'm leaving you in charge. When you've completed your search, stand down officers at your discretion but you'll have to make sure there's one on each gate until tomorrow morning. We don't want dog walkers coming to mess things up. We'll have to make a daylight search of the scene, and of course, we're still looking for the murder weapon. That search must continue until we find something. So what time is dawn?'

'Half past seven, sir, quarter to eight, something like that.'

'Right. Concentrate on looking for the murder weapon and when you are satisfied it is not hidden anywhere within the park, stand down your searchers. You can send them to the police station for further orders. We'll have to look elsewhere – and I don't relish the thought of that, I might tell you. Sergeant Simpson?'

'Sir?'

'The man you saw leaving the park. Was he carrying anything?'

'No sir, I'm sure he wasn't, he had his hands up to his head, like this,' and Simpson put his hands up to to his head, one at each side about the level of his ears.

'Like somebody nursing a massive headache?' suggested Clifton.

'I suppose so, yes, sir.'

'So if that was the killer, he must have left the stone in the park, eh?'

'That seems likely, sir.'

'Good, you understand the importance of that, Inspector?' Clifton smiled a hard smile at Burn. 'A fair indication the murder weapon's still in this park.'

'Yes, I understand, sir,' nodded Burn. 'If it's there, we'll find it.'

'You will indeed. I'll suggest to Superintendent Firth that those who are working overtime should go off duty fairly soon, Inspector. Make sure they have a good night's rest, then get them to report back to the police station in the morning, nine o'clock I suggest. It might be necessary to continue that search in daylight or make further enquiries in town. I'll be here all night. I might catnap in one of the cells. But you must make sure the murder scene is protected all night. We're bound to want another look at it in daylight and don't forget they say murderers always return to the scene of their crime! Look out for nosy parkers, take their names.'

'Yes, sir.'

'Right the rest of you. There are official cars outside the top gate and there's a van for the box; those accompanying the body follow me, and that includes Sergeant Simpson, PC Stead and the photographers. We need pictures of those wounds as they are being examined in the morgue and we need the deceased's fingerprints. I'll radio Hindenley Police Station from my car so the office staff know what's going on. Detective Sergeant Burrows, you come with me.'

And quite suddenly, the emphasis changed. The promised refreshments had not yet arrived but should do so very soon – the remaining searchers would enjoy theirs on location but a supply would be taken to the police station.

For Sergeant Simpson, it had been a tiring and traumatic evening but as the pressure lifted, a wave of weariness returned, fortunately without a nose bleed. He felt extremely weak, reminiscent of recent bouts of severe tiredness but couldn't ask to go home, not in these circumstances. He wanted to remain for as long as possible. Tired though he was, he forced himself to continue. With PC Stead, he found himself in the van which was transporting the body to the mortuary. The opportunity to sit down in the passenger seat was most welcome and he tried to relax.

The anonymous blue van was moving steadily through the streets *en route* to the hospital, which stood on an elevated site only a short walk from the police station. No-one would realize what it was carrying but in truth the streets were almost deserted. Anyone still moving around the town was likely to be stopped and questioned about their recent movements – word of intense police interest would already be circulating even if the town was going to sleep. The van moved easily through the town. It climbed the cobbled bank up to the hospital and drove around the back to the mortuary entrance.

'I'll make sure they're ready for us,' said Sergeant Simpson, momentarily refreshed. He walked the few yards from the parked van, rang the bell on the door marked 'Mortuary' and was greeted by a long-faced individual wearing a green gown. This was Tommy, the mortuary attendant who had been recalled to duty following a call from Superintendent Firth. Tommy's job was to prepare the operating theatre and then cut open the body, peel off the skin which covered the head, slice the top off the skull and perform other aspects of that range of preliminaries.

Tommy was a cadaverous character some fifty years of age whose life was spent cutting up dead people, mainly those who had died suddenly or in other circumstances which required a post mortem.

'We're expecting you, Sergeant,' he said with no sign of a smile. 'Dr Metcalfe is here.'

And he stepped back to allow Simpson to show the others the way to the theatre. Simpson had attended many post mortems in this place, some being suicides but the majority being sudden but natural deaths. Tommy waited at the doorway as PC Stead and the van driver, a policeman from the road traffic department, carried the box inside. Detective Superintendent Clifton and Mr Fisher arrived in separate vehicles, and then followed a van containing Detective Sergeant Burrows and the photographers. In addition to photographing the post mortem, they had to take the body's fingerprints; they had made their plaster cast earlier and it was now in their van. Tommy ushered everyone into the operating theatre where the box was placed on the floor next to a plinth adjoining the operating table. Detective Sergeant Burrows removed the lid to reveal the tarpaulin with its interesting contents.

'A suspected murder, is it?' asked Tommy peering into the box. 'It's years since I had one o' them. The last 'un turned out to be natural causes.'

'We don't think this one's died naturally, Tommy,' said Sergeant Simpson who had known Tommy for years.

'I'll get Dr Metcalfe, he's waiting,' offered Tommy, heading for an intercom on the wall above the desk area. He lifted it, pressed a button and said, 'They've arrived, Dr Metcalfe.' When he replaced the handset, he said, 'Right, well, let's have him out and onto the operating table. It is a him, is it?'

'It is, but let's wait until Dr Metcalfe arrives,' boomed Clifton. 'He needs to see everything, including what's dropped onto that tarpaulin.'

'Oh, it's just that I usually cut 'em open ready,' said Tommy.

'Not in the case of a suspected murder,' boomed Clifton. 'There's things to be done before we start the butchering business and I'm in charge of this corpse, Tommy.' He had picked up on the attendant's name. 'I know you want to get home but I want to catch a murderer, so we're taking this one a bit more slowly and with a bit more care than we would for a chap who'd collapsed in the street.'

'Oh, aye, well, just trying to be helpful,' grinned Tommy. 'So who's got himself bumped off, then? Local, is he?'

'We're not sure . . . ah, Dr Metcalfe?' and Clifton had noticed the arrival of a small man with horned glasses and a shock of brown curly hair. In his mid-forties, he was wearing a white overall and as he entered, he placed a green skull cap on his head and it effectively contained his wild hair.

'Yes, I'm Metcalfe,' he said with a soft Scots accent.

'Clifton, CID from Police Headquarters,' and the huge man, who towered above the tiny doctor, bent forward to shake Metcalfe's hand. It was a crushing handshake which made the pathologist wince ever so slightly.

'And this is Mr Fisher from the Home Office Forensic Lab at Harrogate. He needs to be present during this operation, Doctor. He is a forensic pathologist who has been to the scene and he will present his expert opinion to the court when the trial takes place.' As the two medical men shook hands, Clifton provided an account of the discovery of the body, then asked Metcalfe. 'Are you familiar with police requirements at such post mortems?'

'It is my first case of suspected murder,' he admitted. 'But not my first post mortem. I have a wide experience of violent deaths, superintendent, suicides, road traffic accidents, farm and industrial accidents, maritime deaths and so on. I would welcome your suggestions, though, Mr Clifton, and of course any input from Mr Fisher.'

'Good. Well, Mr Fisher will not get in your way, nor will he try to show you how to do your job, but he will give advice, from the forensic viewpoint, that is.'

'Thank you. Now, let's start. I see the body is wrapped in a sheet?'

'We need to collect dust and debris from the body and its clothing,' said Clifton with uncharacteristic patience. 'That's our first job.'

'Ah, well, you do as you must and I shall watch with interest,' smiled Metcalfe. 'As I said, this is my first case of murder. So what is the name of the deceased?'

'We're not certain; he has yet to be formally identified,' said Clifton.

'I see, well, now I will switch on the tape recorder so that my secretary can deal with this when she arrives for work first thing tomorrow – or today I should say.' He pressed a switch on the wall and spoke into it:

'Recording. Time 12.50 a.m. Friday, 28 October 1960. Dr Metcalfe, Pathology Lab speaking. This is a post mortem on a suspected murder victim, name unknown, who was found on Thursday, 27 October in Latima Park, Hildenley. Present are . . . can I have your names, gentlemen?'

As each of those present gave his name, Dr Metcalfe relayed them into his unseen tape recorder while Tommy and PC Stead lifted the body out of its box. Still in the tarpaulin, it was carefully placed on the plinth next to the operating table. The tarpaulin was slowly unwrapped to reveal the dead man and it was spread out across the plinth which was wide enough to accommodate the broad sheet. Then Fisher went forward with Metcalfe in close attendance to watch with intense interest.

'I need to comb his hair so that any dust and debris is collected on the sheet, but clearly that won't be easy due to his injuries. However, there are some undamaged areas of his head containing dirt.' Fisher took control of this part of the proceedings. 'I need the soil or whatever it is from his wounds to compare with any on the murder weapon when we find it. When we've got enough dirt for laboratory analysis, we need to undress him so that anything lodged in his clothes such as folds in the clothing, his pockets, trouser turn-ups, dust, fibres and whatever, falls onto the sheet too. We'll need to retain samples of his blood for future analysis and to ascertain its group. I shall take his clothing – all of it – to my laboratory for a scientific examination but once it has been removed, the detectives here will want to search it for evidence of his identification and to safeguard his personal belongings.'

Metcalfe relayed all this into his tape recorder as the preliminaries got underway. Very little if anything was combed from his head – perhaps a grain or two of earth or dust from where he had been lying and likewise, very little fell from his clothing as it was carefully removed. Shoes, socks, trousers, jacket, shirt, underwear . . . it all came off and most of the items were placed in sample bags which the detectives had brought; these were then labelled by Detective Sergeant Burrows. Last were the jacket and

trousers because their pockets were searched for personal belongings and evidence of identification. A dirty comb, an equally dirty handkerchief and cash were found in his trousers' pockets. The cash amounted to 18s. 4d, in half-crowns, florins, shillings and pennies. These were all placed in bags by Burrows and labelled. The inside jacket pocket revealed a brown leather wallet, fold-over type, containing more money – £11 in £1 notes and £2. 10s. 0d. in ten shilling notes. Inside one of the flaps they found a name and address written with a ball-point pen on the light coloured lining. It said E. A. Swainby with an address, 35, Heldon Road, Cresslington, near Garmingham, in Garminghamshire county.

'Seems it is Swainby,' said Detective Sergeant Burrows upon seeing the wallet.

'Unless this character stole that wallet from Swainby,' added Detective Superintendent Clifton with typical caution. 'But it's a start, a good one. Right, we need urgent enquiries at that Garminghamshire address, Sarge,' he addressed Burrows. 'Ring the local police. Find out who lives at that address, tell them about the death and get somebody to come to have a look at this man. We need a positive identification by someone who knows him well. And if it's family, ask them to be careful how the news is broken to them. If this is Swainby and he's been true to character while living up there, then he might be known to their CID too. Make sure they know who we've got here, and why. They might be able to shed some light on this affair.'

When they were satisfied there were no other items in the clothing, the trousers and jacket were added to those which would be examined forensically by Fisher; once the body was removed, the tarpaulin would carefully folded so that it would contain its tiny pieces of evidence and that also would be taken to the laboratory by Mr Fisher. Now it was the turn of the body. It was lifted from the plinth by Tommy and PC Stead, Stead coping with the feet end and Tommy skilly hoisting the bare shoulders so that the corpse was conveyed swiftly to the operating table. There it was first visually examined, measured by Dr Metcalfe, and then hauled onto its left side by Tommy so that the doctor could see the spine and back. He then dictated his findings into his tape recorder.

'The deceased is an adult male about fifty years of age, five feet ten inches tall of average weight. He has thinning hair, going grey and somewhat unkempt, balding at the temples and crown. Rigor mortis has not set in which suggests that death occurred recently, probably within the last six hours. The body is well nourished but not very clean. The feet are dirty around the ankles and between the toes, the hands are rough like those of a labourer and the ends of the fingernails are black beneath but neatly cut. There are signs of tide marks around the neck. There are no tattoos or operation scars on the body; he is not wearing spectacles and all his teeth, some of which are decayed, are natural. He is not wearing a wedding ring but has a watch showing the current time. A visual examination of the body shows no external wounds with the exception of the head and face; the head has been viciously attacked with a blunt instrument causing what appear to be depressed fractures to the skull, with suspected damage to the brain. The left cheek bone is also fractured from what appears to be the same cause.'

Clifton interrupted. 'Have we that plaster cast, Sergeant?'

Burrows said, 'Yes, sir, it's been done.'

'Then fetch it now.'

A photographer said, 'I'll get it, sir, it's in our van.'

'Do that, and fetch your fingerprinting kit, we'll do that while we're here.'

One of the scenes of crime detectives left the operating theatre and the post mortem was halted temporarily as he went outside to his van. Moments later, he returned with one of the hardened casts which looked like a lump of icing from a birthday cake, albeit with bits of earth clinging to it. They had been transferred from the rockery and comparison could be made between those and the pieces which had been adhering to the skull. He was also carrying the fingerprinting set – roller, ink and pads.

'Well done that man,' beamed Clifton taking the cast and staring at it. 'So now we know the shape of the missing stone, eh? Or one end of it, or one of its corners. Mr Fisher, I think you need to see this before we go any further.'

'We need to compare it with the skull's damage, preferably with the skin and hair in place, yes. . .' and Fisher took the heavy cast, bore it over to the body and took a long time comparing it with the indentations on the skull while explaining to Metcalfe the salient points. It was purely a visual examination but it seemed to satisfy Fisher. 'See this, Mr Clifton?' he invited Clifton to take a closer look.

'That must be the last strike he made,' Clifton looked at a particularly clear hole which was the reverse image of the cast. 'It's not been damaged by the others.'

'I agree, and yes, the cast fits perfectly . . . I'm sure that's the shape of your murder weapon, Mr Clifton, I'd stake my reputation on it,' said

Fisher. 'A stone from that rockery. The stone which sat in that hole.'

'All we have to do now is find it,' said Clifton, who made due record of that important finding.

'Right, thanks for all that,' smiled Metcalfe. 'Can we proceed?'

'I think it would be a good idea to take the fingerprints now,' said Clifton. 'Before we start taking this corpse to pieces.'

And so two of the scenes of crime detectives came forward and with practised skill, took prints from the fingers of the corpse. They took both full hands and even made palm prints. Clifton smiled. They were doing a good job.

'Right, Tommy,' said Clifton when those formalities were over. 'Now it's your turn.'

Tommy's awful job was to open the body so that the pathologist could first examine the interior of the skull and all the internal organs such as heart, liver, lungs, kidneys, stomach (and contents), intestines, veins and arteries and any other parts which might be relevant. Tommy approached with what looked like an electric drill and made some holes in the undamaged part of the skull. Then with a small circular saw blade, he sliced through the skin of the skull so that the skin and membrane could be hauled back down over the face like a piece of tight rubber so that the bones of the skull were revealed. Then with a wedge like those used for splitting logs and a mallet, he broke open the skull, splitting with his gloved hands; it sounded just like a coconut being torn apart, but this revealed the brain.

'He's got a very thin skull, gentleman,' said Tommy. 'It's very fragile, cracks like an egg shell.'

The police officers noted that Tommy sliced down the middle of the chest and stomach to peel back the flesh so that the contents were accessible to gloved hands wielding knives or gloved fingers delving into the innards. The remains of Edward Albert Swainby were now ready for further examination.

Due to the important nature of this examination, the post mortem took about an hour and afterwards, both Mr Fisher and Dr Metcalfe agreed that death had been caused by repeated blows to the head with a blunt instrument. The skull, which was abnormally thin, had been fractured in several places, all of which would be detailed in the written report, and there had been severe brain damage.

There were facial injuries too, with a broken left cheek bone, but that would not have caused death. Both confirmed the injuries corresponded to the plaster cast of a missing stone's position on the rockery in Latima Park and thus the missing stone was officially accredited with the status of being the suspected murder weapon. For the record, Sergeant Simpson identified the body as that which he had seen lying in the park but no positive identification was recorded at this stage, nor was his name given. Having done this essential duty, Sergeant Simpson went to sit down to recover, finding a chair in the corner of the theatre. Now he felt utterly drained.

The coroner had not arrived for the post mortem – he may have been away from home when Firth's officers had tried to contact him, but further efforts would be made. There was ample time for him to view the body as the law demanded. The body now had the flesh folded back to its original position and stitched with white string to keep it there; the facial and hair-covered skin had been replaced on the skull and face so that no one could see that it had once been removed. The intestines and contents of the rib cage had been packed into the body cavity beneath the stitched skin and the remains dressed in a white shroud. At a casual glance, it seemed the body had not been interfered with. It was placed in a refrigerated unit until such time as the coroner decided to view it, or until it was needed for the relatives or someone else to view it for identification purposes or for any other legitimate reason.

Detective Superintendent Clifton thanked the pathologist and Mr Fisher and said he would now return to the police station in Hildenley to continue with his investigation.

He suggested that all the police officers present should do likewise and that Mr Fisher was more than welcome to join them if he had any further business to discuss. He declined; he had to get back for an early appointment tomorrow and in any case, he had completed his initial work.

'Sergeant Simpson,' Clifton said as they went out to their cars. 'You look like a corpse yourself. Like death warmed up! Can you bear to hang on just a little longer, you and I need to talk. It's important, otherwise I wouldn't ask. Come with me.'

CHAPTER 5

DETECTIVE Superintendent Clifton knew his way around Hildenley
Police Station. He was a regular visitor in his capacity as head of
Benningshire County CID. The local superintendent was in charge of the
station and he administered police coverage of the town and the
surrounding rural area, collectively known as Hildenley Division. In addition he supervised the two resident Hildenley CID officers so far as their
local duties were concerned. Detective Superintendent Clifton, on the
other hand, had a county-wide responsibility for all aspects of criminal
investigation which meant that he also had jurisdiction over the two
Hildenley detectives. He made supervisory visits to Detective Sergeant
Maurice Huntley and Detective Constable Jim Thorne and could call
upon their services if they were needed for some large enquiry in another
part of the county, such as a murder in distant division. During those
visits, Clifton usually checked their notebooks and records to ensure the
pair were functioning efficiently. He was content with them; they had a
good record of crime detection and were reliable enough to work with
minimum supervision.

Shortly after 2 a.m. that Friday, therefore, Clifton led the way into the
police station followed by his assistant, Detective Sergeant Burrows, with
a very weary Sergeant Simpson struggling to keep pace. The entrance was
a house-sized door on a back street called Kipling Terrace which led off
Keld Rise; that doorway led into a dark and narrow passage-like entrance
with descending steps which in turn led to a hatch in a wooden partition. Behind the partition was the somewhat cramped enquiry office to
which members of the public came with their problems and queries.

This was the busiest place in this dingy and cavernous Victorian red-
brick police station, for it contained the telephone and PBX, the force

radio network, filing cabinets, tall stools standing beneath high desks which faced the hatch and a smaller desk bearing one of the few type-writers in the station. There was a coal fire too; it never went out in winter and warmed many a cold constable on his break during a chilly night patrol. Above the hatch was the legend ENQUIRIES, and, in spite of its small size, the station was open twenty-four hours every day of the year. The public could call or ring at any time. It occupied a sloping site which meant the offices overlooking Kipling Terrace were more elevated than others deep within; its hillside site meant the entire place seemed to be filled with staircases and corridors but with very few windows. When Clifton arrived at the hatchway on his rapid trek to the superintendent's office, the constable on office duty did not recognize him.

'Excuse me . . .' he called after Clifton.

In response, Clifton bellowed, 'CID lad, Clifton's the name. Is Mr Firth in?'

'He asked not to be disturbed . . . er . . . sir . . . .'

'Too bad,' said Clifton, and marched onwards and downwards until he arrived at Firth's door. In deference to his position as officer in charge of this police station, Clifton knocked but did not wait for an answer. He strode straight in while calling out to Sergeant Simpson, 'Wait out there, Sarge. Get yourself a cup of tea, you look as if you could do with one, and have a sit down for a few minutes, that might perk you up a bit. You look knackered. Grab something to eat as well if the grub's arrived. I'll talk to you in a few minutes. And you too, DS Burrows.'

'Sit down, Wilf,' invited George Firth. 'Tea?' He indicated a teapot and its accoutrements on top of the filing cabinet in his office. There were sandwiches too.

'Love one,' said Clifton. 'I'll help myself.'

'It's fresh,' said Firth. 'The food's just arrived. Have a sandwich.'

'Thanks, I will. This is a courtesy call to let you know I've arrived,' Clifton went on, as he busied himself with the teapot. 'Thanks for prepar-ing the way and doing all the back-ground stuff, and for fixing the post mortem. I've just come from the scene; your lads did a good job there, and still are doing so. We've just come from the hospital. The PM's finished but the coroner didn't turn up. He'll come later, I'm sure.'

'He wasn't at home when we called. We'll try again in the morning.'

'Fair enough, we can wait for that,' and Clifton settled himself on the chair beside Firth's desk, sandwich in hand. 'Now, the story so far.

Chummy died from severe head wounds as we thought. Not accidental, not self-inflicted. A stone was used to good effect. So it's murder, George. You've got a very brutal killing on your patch which won't look good on your crime returns so we must catch the villain and get him convicted. Or her. It could be woman, it could be anybody, we mustn't forget that.'

'I'm sure you won't let us down, Wilf,' smiled Firth. 'You'll get him. You've never let one get away yet, have you? So what do you want of me or my men?'

'Total commitment, George, with long hours and no grumbling. I want lots of good fresh ideas for lines of enquiry based on local knowledge. I need some good quality local knowledge, good honest gossip, that sort that women discuss over tea.'

'And men in pubs?'

'And men in pubs,' laughed Clifton. 'On the face of it, it looks like a rapist called Swainby who has tried his hand once too often and somebody's made sure he won't do it again. He might have deserved all he got but it's still murder, George.'

'I'm sure my officers will come up to your demanding standards, Wilf. I've a very good crew and they know the town inside out, and everyone who lives here.'

'I should hope they do, we need to get under the skin of this place. Now, the situation is this.'

Clifton updated Firth whereupon Firth agreed to provide the best uniform back-up that was possible, particularly in helping with enquiries within the town and its environs. He concluded with, ' The killer's obviously got a short fuse, George, and we can't rule out other assaults on women by Swainby. Maybe they didn't report them. Some women don't report that kind of thing due to their sensitivities, they don't want their private lives dragged through the courts or logged in police records. I can't say I blame them, I wouldn't want my wife to go through that sort of thing, but don't forget it could be some local woman's husband taking revenge even if we haven't been made aware of any crime. Or Swainby could have been stopped in his tracks while actually attacking someone.'

'Whatever the motive, there's no doubt this will stir up a good deal of muck in town,' said Firth. 'I'll make sure my teams tap into all the gossip.'

'That's where we'll find the answer! Now, the forensic wizard has taken the dead man's clothes to the lab to analyse fibres and dust or whatever he does, so as there's not a lot we can do at the scene until daylight I'll get myself established here.'

'We've an office you can use. It's our detective sergeant's, he shares it with his DC.'

'Sounds all right by me but I'll need more than one office. If we don't trace that suspect tonight, I'll be calling in extra detectives from around the force area, twenty or thirty of them first thing in the morning, so I'll need somewhere to brief them and somewhere for them to have their breaks and refreshments.'

'Will they be staying in Hildenley overnight?' asked Firth.

'No, I'll make sure they're all drawn from stations within travelling distance, that'll keep expenses down. It's really a question of accommodating them here for briefings and rest periods, and having somewhere to compile their reports.'

'There's the muster room, Wilf, that will hold forty if they don't sit down; then there's the billiard room, it'll take a couple of dozen or so standing round the table. Or, if you're really pushed for space I could get permission to use the Church Hall just along the street. They've some of those stacking chairs we could borrow as well. And talking of briefings, I think the town constables need to be more fully briefed if they're to do a proper job. It's not fair for them to work with only half a story.'

'I couldn't agree more, George. Call them in when it's convenient and I'll talk to them. I'll make sure I have regular conferences to keep them informed.'

'Those on night shift are due in around now for their normal refreshment breaks but as you know, they don't all come in together.'

'On this occasion, I think a few streets empty of coppers can be considered necessary, if only for a few minutes, George. At this time of night, the public isn't going to launch a crime wave so call them in, give them all a cup of tea and to hell with the expense. I'll talk to them in the muster room; let me know when they're all here. Now, I'll go and get settled into my new office. Do Huntley and Thorne know I'm their uninvited guest?'

'They do, Wilf. They didn't object.'

'It doesn't matter if they did, does it, George?'

'You're the boss! They can work in the billiard room or even temporarily in my secretary's office; she won't be in until nine in the morning. It's got a phone with internal and outside lines.'

'Right, and looking further ahead, I'll need as many typists as we can rustle up, George, with somewhere for them to operate. From six this morning, they'll be typing statements by the score, several carbon copies of each, all through the enquiry. And if this enquiry becomes a long runner, we'll need a dedicated telephone line or two.'

'I'll see to that.'

'What about the press?'

'I've authorized a statement for release by the information room; I've said we're investigating the suspicious death of a man in Hildenley and that a post mortem is being organized. That's all.'

'Good, there's no need to say anything else. We've no need to tell the press anything we don't want to.'

And so Clifton left Superintendent Firth to his admin duties and called out, 'Sergeant Simpson, DS Burrows? I'll be upstairs in CID. See me there. You've had a bit of a rest, eh, Sergeant Simpson? You can tolerate a few more minutes of me?'

'Yes, sir,' acknowledged Sergeant Simpson who had been resting his legs and sipping a cup of tea in front of the enquiry office fire. With some effort, he drained his cup and followed the big man upstairs, panting with the effort. Burrows had gone ahead and when Simpson arrived at the small CID office, Clifton was already quizzing the two detectives. He paused when Simpson arrived, looking at him with evident concern.

'You look ill, Sergeant, not tired. Get yourself home as soon as you can, I don't want to be responsible for wearing you out! I can talk to you in the morning but if you're as ill as you look from here, I'd say you need a doctor.'

'I'll see how things go, sir, but I'd rather get as much as possible done tonight, sir, I've never worked on a murder case before. I'd like to see it through.'

'Well, it's up to you. First, though, I need to establish some facts. Sergeant Huntley, can we say our victim is definitely this man Swainby?'

At this point, Detective Sergeant Burrows, in his capacity as personal assistant to Clifton, opened his notebook and prepared to record the essentials of this discussion.

'Almost certainly, sir, short of a formal identification,' nodded Detective Sergeant Huntley, picking up a file from his desk. Clifton hadn't even bothered to find a seat by this stage. 'I've spoken to the young man and woman who were in the park and they are adamant the man they saw was called Swainby. They saw him entering the park, alone, around half past nine, coming in by the South Gate but they didn't see him after-wards. Their description fits the man who's dead, but they never saw him again. They saw no one else in the park, except a policeman doing his rounds, they're absolutely sure about that. It must have been Sergeant Simpson, the stories and timings tally. The young couple were the last to see Swainby alive; Swainby's recently moved into a flat near that young man. He's called Alan Wetherill, I've got his address, he lives in Upperholme Terrace, No. 23, it's a self-contained flat. Swainby was at No. 25a, that's a basement flat.'

'That's a good start, I'll need words with that young man too. Go on, Sergeant.'

'I've been in touch with Garminghamshire County Police but their CID office at Cresslington Sub-Division was closed for the night. I managed to get hold of the duty detective inspector and told him it was urgent. When I explained what had happened, he told me he knows Swainby, sir, and confirmed he'd been living in Cresslington until about six weeks ago. Then he disappeared, did a moonlight flit, sir.'

'And the reason? For the moonlight flit?'

'He's not sure, sir, he'd just come out of prison, though. He'd done a five year stretch for rape and was out on licence. For some reason, he just took off, didn't tell anyone where he was going or why. The fact he's done a runner means he's in breach of the conditions of his licence but that's all; it's not a hanging offence!'

'He's not on any wanted list is he?'

'No, sir, he wasn't circulated as wanted but he was suspected of two rape-linked murders in that area, several years ago. He was interviewed and denied responsibility, but there wasn't enough evidence to nail him. They're pretty sure he was guilty.'

'So he's got what was long due to him! An arm for an arm and all that. Serve him right. What's he been doing since he came back here?'

'We've no idea, sir. If he has been here all that time, he's been lying low. We've had no serious assaults reported and had no idea he was here. Garminghamshire didn't know he'd come either, otherwise we'd have been alerted.'

'We need someone to talk to the relatives and friends of that raped woman, Sergeant, the one he did time for up north, and the friends and relations of those dead women.'

'The local police could do that for us, you think?'

'It would help us if they did. They know their patch and might know if anyone's been waiting to get some kind of revenge; they'll all have to be interviewed and eliminated from this enquiry. Have words with Garminghamshire Police and arrange for someone to interview them.'

'Yes, sir.'

'And don't forget you need to talk to his neighbours here in town, we need to know everything about Swainby, especially during the last six weeks. It means you and your mate have some important leg work to do while I'm using your office. Now, is there a good detective in the Garminghamshire Force who knows Swainby well enough to formally identify him for us?'

'Yes, sir, Detective Inspector Luke Cussons, sir, he's on duty now. He's the one I've been speaking to about this.'

'On duty where?'

'At Cresslington, sir.'

'Right, get hold of him for me, I want words. I'll get him to come and positively identify our victim. We need that done as soon as possible then we can start digging deeper into his past. How long a drive is it from Cresslington, do you think?'

'About an hour, sir. Less if you don't worry about speed limits.'

'Good. Call him for me, and if it means ringing the Garminghamshire chief constable and getting him out of bed to get Cussons down here, I'll do it.'

Minutes later, Clifton was speaking to the Garminghamshire detective.

'Detective Superintendent Clifton from Benningshire,' he introduced himself as he took the phone from Huntley. 'You've been helping my DS Huntley over this man Swainby.'

'Yes, sir. If it is him, I can't say I'm sorry – or surprised. He had it coming to him. He's a brute of the first order, and violent with it. We're sure he got away with lots of rapes and at least two murders of women in our area before he got sent down for that recent rape.'

'It seems you might put some good suspects our way, Inspector, family members and friend of the victims? You'll let us have their names? I'll want them interviewed for elimination; I am hoping your officers will do that for us, with your chief's blessing, of course. And we could use a copy of your file on Swainby, the lot, gossip and speculation, background intelligence and a list of his recent convictions.'

'No problem, sir, I'll arrange those interviews and I can despatch a copy of the file tomorrow, by courier if necessary.'

'I was thinking more along the lines of you driving down here immediately if not sooner, and not only with that file, Inspector. I need someone to positively identify Swainby so we can get this enquiry really
moving at top speed.'

'I can recognize him, sir, I've seen him often enough, and interviewed
him.'

'Then you're just the chap even if his features have been forcibly re-
arranged somewhat. Some of our local officers remember him from a few
years back but can't positively say it's him now. Age has withered him, or
something like that.'

'I'm more than happy to come, sir, I'm glad this villain is out of circu-
lation. You'll have to get permission from my boss if you want me to come
down to you, though, as I'm on duty here.'

'Your immediate boss, or the chief?'

'It'll have to be the chief, sir, if I'm to leave my territory and go to
another force area on duty.'

'Fair enough. I'll ring him and wake him from his slumbers. What's his
phone number?'

And so it was that the chief constable of Garminghamshire was
aroused from his dreams by the loud voice of Wilf Clifton who explained
things in very basic terms. The chief would co-operate with all aspects of
the enquiry and Detective Inspector Cussons could drive down to
Hildenley without delay. Cussons was advised to ask for Detective
Superintendent Clifton upon arrival when he'd be asked to view the
body in the mortuary. The liaison with him was a nice job for Sergeant
Simpson, provided he wasn't asleep on his feet or lying ill somewhere.
That done, Clifton told Huntley and Thorne to compile as much information as possible about Swainby. It should include names of contacts,
details of his work or life, friends, relations, names and addresses of his
victims and any other salient information. His Hildenley address would
have to be searched too. That was already on their list of tasks and so they
had sufficient work to occupy them until dawn.

When Huntley and Thorne left to go about their business, Clifton
said, 'Right, at last I can talk to you, Sergeant Simpson. Sorry to keep you
hanging about but before we start, I suggest you go and see your GP,
whether you're on duty or not. In fact, don't just consider it, do it. And
that's an order. Tomorrow morning.'

'Yes, sir.'

Sergeant Simpson moved onto a chair in front of the desk used by Detective Sergeant Huntley as the huge superintendent tried to accommodate his legs in the fairly small space. DS Burrows with his ever-ready notebook was tucked into a corner on a dining-style chair and the office was cramped because it also housed two desks and a range of four drawer filing cabinets and bookshelves with files all over the floor.

'I'll not keep you long but this is important. I want you to tell me as much as you can about the man you saw leaving the park, the young man in a rush.'

'I only caught a glance of him, sir.'

'But you did see him and that's important. This is a vital piece of information, he could be the killer. Certainly, he must be eliminated from our enquiries and we can't do that unless we find him. I regard it as a priority which is why you're here.'

'At the time I thought it was just a man who was in distress, or in a hurry, I had no reason to suspect him of a crime. I saw him before I found the body.'

'Exactly, so tell me about it, right from the word go. Detective Sergeant Burrows will write it all down, Sergeant. I'm treating this as a witness statement.'

'I understand, sir.'

'Right, off you go.'

'Well, I was standing outside the gate of the park . . .'

'Start before then, Sergeant, tell me the route you took to that gate and which gate it was. I need detail, details of events and details of timings, people you saw, incidents which happened. Take us back until half past nine. Every minute is important, remember, an escaping suspect can run a long way in a short time.'

Sergeant Simpson, feeling considerably more weary than he had even an hour ago, took a deep breath and tried to reconstruct events in his mind.

'I had visited PC Stead at his conference point, sir, West End kiosk. I saw him at half past nine and gave him a chalk. West End is a good part of town, sir, suburban with wealthy residents, a nice area. Quiet, free from trouble-makers. Then I walked along Carrington Street and down Scrivener Street before turning along Park Road.'

'Anyone see you?' asked Clifton as Burrows scribbled these words with commendable speed. Clifton was pacing his questions so that his sergeant missed nothing. They had done this sort of thing together on many occasions.

'Several people, sir, I can't remember precisely who they were but several spoke to me, wished me good night and so forth. I checked a few premises too, they were all secure.'

'So you have no named witnesses as to your movements, except PC Stead at nine thirty?'

'Witnesses, sir?' puzzled Sergeant Simpson.

'You found the body, Sergeant, that makes you a suspect. I need to eliminate you and to do that we need to find that mystery man or someone else who saw you.'

'There was Mr Stalker, at the park gate . . .'

'We'll come to that. I'm still interested in your movements immediately after visiting PC Stead. So where would Stead go after you left him?'

'There was half an hour of his shift left, sir, he said he would make his way back to the police station and include a duty visit to The Black Lion while doing so.'

'Any particular reason for that visit to The Black Lion?'

'We've had complaints about noise at closing time, people singing, car doors banging, that sort of thing. We spoke to the landlord and he promised to get his customers to make less noise. The visit by a uniformed officer was just one means of showing him – and his customers – that we were in the area and meant business.'

'Fair enough. I'll talk to Stead later. So you then came along Park Road? On your way back to the police station? That's not the most direct route, is it?'

'No, sir but I told PC Stead I would check the park for vagrants, people sleeping rough, vandals and so on. I said he could ignore it. There was the museum to check too, the usual security checks of doors and windows, and I said I would do all that on my way back to the station. I just had time before knocking off.'

'Was that your usual routine? Checking the park? Isn't that a constable's job?'

'I'd say it was a policeman's job, sir, constable or sergeant. I usually make a point of walking through the park before ending my shift, and it's a simple job to carry out those kind of routine tasks on the way.'

'Fair enough. So you made a sort of diversion to end your shift with a walk through the park. So how long does it take to walk from West End kiosk to the park?'

'About ten minutes, sir. A little longer if you get stopped on the way. I wasn't really stopped, not for any length of time.'

'So you say. You've no-one to vouch for your movements at that time. So what time did you arrive at the park? And at which entrance?'

'No.1 Gate, sir, sometimes called the East Gate. It's the one you used when you entered the park earlier this evening.' Simpson now found himself perspiring; he did not know whether it was due to his condition or a result of the questioning – did Clifton think he was the killer? The tone of his questions was beginning to make it sound like that.

'Ah, got you. Right. So you were there at what time?'

'Quarter to ten, sir, as near as I can tell, give or take a minute or so either way.'

'Anyone see you there? You mentioned a man?'

'Yes, sir, he's called Geoffrey Stalker, sir, he's a local solicitor. He was walking his dog. He does that trip every evening, sir, around that time. He saw me at the park gate.'

'So you expected to see him? And stop for a chat with you?'

'Yes, he's usually there at that time of night and we always have a brief chat. We did so on that occasion.'

'Good. We'll need to talk to him, he's another potential witness – another suspect even – but he might have seen something else or some-body else. So tell me about your chat with him. Is it relevant to your sighting of the man in a hurry?'

'It is, sir, yes. I saw the mystery man just a few moments before I real-ized Mr Stalker was nearby. I mentioned it to Mr Stalker but he hadn't seen him.'

'He didn't see the mystery man, even though they were fairly close to one another?'

'No, sir.'

'Are you sure you saw him? Was there really such a person?'

'Well, yes, sir, of course there was! I saw him. I've told you that.'

'So you have. Who else saw him, I wonder?'

'Well, I don't know, sir, all I know is that I did.'

'All right. Let's continue. I need to get this sequence of events lodged in my thick skull before we go any further, Sergeant. If the fleeing man was the killer, we need every witness we can get and even if your Mr

Stalker thinks he saw nothing, he might recall something of significance when we talk to him.'

'I'm sure he will be pleased to talk to you, sir, to confirm my presence as I've said.'

'I'll talk to him and get him to think it through, minute by minute, step by step. Off you go. Tell me again, in detail.'

'I'd got to the park gate, sir, the one I mentioned. The street lights were on, there was traffic moving along Park Road including some buses, all with lights on. There's quite a wide length of footpath running beside the park boundary. It was the path I was on, but in shadow close to that boundary. The wall of the park, which was on my left, has trees growing alongside, they're just inside the park boundaries and they cast shadows on the footpath, along the inner edge. They are still in leaf, sir, they'll be shedding them very soon. I was about to turn into the gate when I noticed the male figure leave by the next gate along. No. 2 gate, the North Gate as some call it. It's about a hundred and twenty yards away, although I must admit I have not measured the distance precisely.'

'We can measure that. Leaving in a hurry you said?' Burrows continued to write it all down in longhand as Clifton paused between each question.

'That how it appeared to me, sir. He was rushing with his head down and he had his hands over his ears or very close to them, near his eyes perhaps. Holding his head almost as if it was hurting or he had a violent headache, that sort of action.'

'I get the picture.'

'I've been thinking about it and wondering what he might have been doing, it was similar to a man pulling on a tight-fitting woolly hat with both hands.'

'Were you aware of a cap or a hat?'

'No, sir, but it was dark in the shadows. I didn't see a cap or hat, it was just his action that made me think of one.'

'Right, continue. You thought he might be distressed?'

'That thought did occur to me, sir, distressed or hurt or in some kind of a hurry. That was my immediate reaction.'

'So what did you do?'

'I called out to him. If he was in need of help, I wanted him to know I was there to help if necessary.'

'What did you call out?'

'I'm not sure, sir. Hello probably, or hey. Something like that. I think he heard me and he might even have looked towards me but my shout seemed to make him run faster, as if he wanted to get away from me. He broke into a fast trot, I remember that.'

'Did you try to follow him?'

'No, I had no reason to. He was not behaving suspiciously, I had no cause to think he had offended in any way. In my view he was just someone heading home after an evening out, late home perhaps and in a rush. I flashed my torch after him but it was no good, he was too far away. He vanished out of sight, round the bend.'

'And you are sure he had both hands up to his head?'

'Yes, I could see that clearly in silhouette. There was light behind him, a glow from the street lamps.'

'Which means, if he is our killer, he had already disposed of the stone he'd used as the murder weapon. If he'd been carrying that, you'd have noticed, wouldn't you? It would be quite heavy.'

'I'm sure I would, sir, yes, I would have noticed if he was carrying anything but I can state quite clearly that both his hands were up to his head.'

'Fair enough. Now we need something of a description, Sergeant. Height, age, any noticeable characteristics, clothing and so on.'

'It's not easy, sir, I had him in my sights for only a few seconds, all the time in the shadows or in silhouette but I'd say he was young, probably between twenty and thirty, nearer twenty I'd say because he was tall and slim. Not six foot tall, but probably five foot ten or so. Slender build, agile. And his clothing was all dark, sir. Or it looked dark in the shadows, like the fashionable things young men wear these days. I wasn't aware of a jacket flapping so I wondered if he was wearing a dark sweater and dark trousers. But, to be honest, I can't be sure.'

'That's not very much to go on but it's a start. What did you do next?'

'Well, the man hurried away and disappeared around the bend in the road. Due to the lack of light and the shadows from trees, I wasn't sure where he went. He might have gone back into the park through another gate further on, there is a third gate, the West Gate, or he might have trotted away in the shadows.'

'You said the road curves there?'

'Yes, it curves to the left, he was soon out of my sight, or he might have crossed into one of the houses at the other side of the road. I've given it a lot of thought but I have no idea who it was, and I never saw him again.'

'You said his clothing might be fashionable? Lots of young men wear black here in Hildenley, do they?'

'Yes, I'd say he could be one of a few hundred in town.'

'Do you think he might have been seen by other people?'

'I'm sure he must, sir. I was surprised Mr Stalker hadn't see him. Just after I flashed my torch at the man, I realized someone was walking towards me. That was Mr Stalker walking close to the wall of the park, in the shadows of the trees. He had a dog, a spaniel. I think he passed No. 2 Gate only seconds before the man emerged; the man came out behind Mr Stalker which could explain why he never saw him or realized he was there. When Mr Stalker reached me, I asked if he'd seen the man, but he hadn't; he said he'd been walking in the park at the western end but hadn't seen the man, neither had his dog barked. He told me it barked at unusual noises or if it came across someone unexpectedly.'

'Right, I think I've got the picture.'

'It did occur to me, sir, that if Stalker had been walking around the park, he'd have noticed that young man; they must have both been in the park at the same time. I know it's quite spacious with lots of trees and shrubs, lots of shadows, but there are lights along the pathways and noises carry at night. But he was adamant he hadn't seen the man. I didn't quiz him at length, I had no reason to, so we chatted for a few minutes then he left to go home. That's when I entered the park through No. 1 Gate, the East Gate.'

'So when you called out to the young man, do you think he heard you?'

'I don't know, sir. Certainly, he increased his pace, that was pretty obvious to me, almost as if he wanted to put distance between himself and me, but a bus rumbled past, I remember, going the same way as him. It might have drowned my call.'

'He might not have heard you or seen you, or he might have been hurrying to catch that bus! People on board, were there?'

'I can't be sure, sir, I didn't take much notice of it at the time.'

'Was it a service bus? With a bus stop just ahead somewhere?'

'Possibly, sir, they run along Park Road in both directions, some doing a circuit of the town and others heading into the villages. They finish at midnight, sir, and resume at six thirty next morning. It's the town service.'

'We'll check at the bus station. We'll have words with the driver and conductor to see if they saw anything or picked anyone up along Park Road. They might have seen the suspect or, of course, he might have been hurrying to catch the last bus home. It sounds feasible. If he boarded it, I'm sure the conductor will remember. Did other traffic pass at that time?'

'I'm sure there were cars, sir, but I didn't recognize any of them.'

'We'll ask around. Once word gets about that we're interested in people on the move at that time of night in Park Road, we might get someone coming forward with information or sightings.'

'I hope we can find someone else who saw the young man.'

'So do I, Sergeant. So do I. Right, I think I've got a clear picture of those few minutes – and it would be a very few minutes, would it not?'

'Yes, sir, a very few. I was at that gate for a very short time.'

'So we're not talking of you having a half-hour gossip with your solicitor friend? How many minutes were you there, do you think?'

'It would be a matter of only a minute or so, no more than two. Once I saw the young man had gone and didn't want my help, I went into the park to make my final checks.'

'Right, I must have words with Mr Stalker. Where does he live?'

'I don't know his private address, sir, but his office is in Kempland Chambers, that's in Blendgate.'

'We'll find him. So then you found the body. Tell me what you did immediately before finding it.'

'As I said just now, I like to walk through the park on my way back to the station, even if it is a diversion. I like it especially on late shift. As I do so, I check for people sleeping rough in the shelters or on the seats, vandals lurking about, anyone who might be in need of help or accommodation at night, that sort of thing, and of course, there's the museum too. I always check its doors and windows in case there's been a break in, and the toilets behind it, sir. Ladies and gents.'

'I still maintain that's a constable's job, Sergeant. I'm not sure why you choose to do that chore.'

'I've been doing it for years, sir. It's part of my routine.'

'And you found a body, recently killed, with a mysterious man running away from the scene . . . .'

'I didn't kill him, sir, if that's what you're thinking.'

'I'm not thinking anything, Sergeant, I'm just trying to establish the facts. Go on.'

'Once inside, I began at the western end of the park. The place is a maze of footpaths but I don't need to walk along every one because I can shine my torch across some of the lawns into the shelters or onto the benches.'

'Saves leg work, eh?'

'It removes the need for unnecessary walking about, sir. That way, the whole exercise takes about ten minutes as a rule, and that includes the museum. The only people I saw were a courting couple sitting on a bench. I'm sure they were the couple who came to my aid when I blew my whistle, Alan Wetherill and his girl friend. DS Huntley has their details.'

'I'm going to interview them myself, Sergeant, as witnesses and potential suspects. Now, are you absolutely sure there was no one else in the park?'

'As sure as I can be, sir, unless they were hiding.'

'No mystery man in dark clothing? He hadn't gone back into the park, had he? By another gate?'

'I never saw him again, sir.'

'All right. Go on.'

'As I worked my way through the park, I gravitated towards the museum at the eastern end, checked it and found nothing wrong, and then I found the body, sir.'

'What time would it be then?'

'I'm not sure precisely, sir, probably about five to ten, give or take a minute or two either way.'

'I know you've been through this with me already, but we need more detail this time. He was already dead, you think?'

'I'm sure of it, sir. At first I thought it was a drunk who'd rolled off the bench in the shelter but when I saw all the blood I realized it was something more serious. I checked his pulse, breathing, eyes. I knew he was dead.'

'You knew?'

'Well, with as much certaintly as I could have had. I know I'm not a doctor but I know the signs . . . he was dead, sir.'

'You saw no-one nearby? Hiding? Heard movements? Someone running off? Shouting beforehand?'

'Nothing, sir. I was on my own with the nearest telephone being either at the police station or at West End but as I did not want to leave the body, I blew my whistle. I thought PC Stead might hear it on his way back to the station to book off but he didn't; the courting couple heard it, Wetherill and his girl, and they responded. I sent them for help. I thought I'd been blowing for help for a long time but now I think it was only a matter of a few minutes. They found PC Stead on his way in to book off, sir, he raised the alarm and came immediately.'

'Did you search the body? Touch it? Move it?'

'I touched it, sir, to check the pulse, on the wrist. I leaned across to listen for breathing but didn't move anything, although I did get blood on my hands and tunic, as you can see, and on my trousers' knees where I knelt beside him.'

'Suppose he had been alive, Sergeant, what would you have done then?'

'It's difficult to say, sir, but probably just what I did do. Blow my whistle to get urgent medical help. Attempting first aid to a person with those kind of injuries, or even moving them, is always risky. You can do more harm than good.'

'So you did not attempt first aid, even though help was not readily available?'

'No, sir, as I said, I was certain he was dead but even if he'd been alive, I wouldn't have attempted first aid, not with such serious injuries to his head.'

'Fair enough. Now, can I see your pocket book, Sergeant?'

'It's not made up yet, sir, I haven't had the time.'

'Not made up? This is a murder investigation, Sergeant, and it is vital that every ounce of information is contemporaneously recorded. Show me.'

Sergeant Simpson produced his official pocket book from his tunic and handed over to the detective. He flipped it open to the current page.

'The last entry is the chalk with PC Stead, I see. Nine thirty yesterday evening. Nothing since, Sergeant. It's blank.'

'Well, sir, as I said, I haven't really had the time . . .'

'Then you must make the time, Sergeant. In view of what's happened here tonight, there's an awful lot of material evidence that should have been recorded in your note book, recorded at the time. Every recruit knows he must do that!'

'Yes, sir, of course. I know, it's the sort of thing I keep hammering into my men . . . .'

'You must lead by example, Sergeant. Now, of course, there is extra information which, at the time, might not have appeared relevant, such as the man hurrying from the park, your chat with Mr Stalker, your actions before finding the body and of course, what you did when you found it. Your possible identification of the man based on what you heard. And the post mortem . . . quite a lot of important stuff is missing, Sergeant.'

Clifton paused and stared steadily at Sergeant Simpson who did not know how to respond. He knew this looked suspicious . . . a police officer's diary was vital evidence in any case, large or small, but he knew the implications of not having it up-to-date.

'Sergeant, I'm sure you are aware of the interpretation that might be placed on the absence of such a record, a record which could be doctored to fit circumstances . . . need I say more?'

'I had no intention of doctoring it to fit any circumstances, sir.'

'I will make a note of that,' and Detective Superintendent Clifton then drew a fountain pen from his own pocket and drew a line beneath the entry relating to the chalk with PC. Immediately below the line, he wrote, 'Checked this pocket book 3 a.m. Friday, 28 October. No entries since 9.30 p.m. on the 27th'. And he signed it with his name and rank, then returned it to Simpson.

'Right, Sergeant, that's all for now. I shall be speaking to Mr Stalker in the morning. There's no point in rousing him from his bed. I shall also be speaking to that courting couple.'

'I hope they can provide useful information, sir.'

'For your sake, so do I, Sergeant. As you can see, my suspect list is growing already, eh? All I need now is your fleeing man.'

'Yes sir.'

'I know you're almost on your knees and your face is as white as the proverbial sheet but I know you won't give up so before you do anything else, I suggest you find a quiet corner to make up your pocket book. I shall want to see it again, when it's up to date.'

'Yes, sir, I'll do it immediately.'

'Your experiences are vital to this enquiry, Sergeant, and I know you take such things very seriously. You've just time to do that before our friend from Garminghamshire arrives. Now, before I talk to those incoming constables, I want to see what's been done in town in their efforts to find our suspect mystery man.'

And Sergeant Simpson left the CID office to find somewhere to write up his pocket book. Detective Sergeant Burrows would get the notes of the interview with Clifton typed up tomorrow in the form of a statement when Simpson would be asked to sign it as a true record. Clifton followed Sergeant Simpson downstairs in the hope he would be able to speak to the town duty sergeant; he wanted to know if anyone had interrogated the bus station crews to ascertain whether the suspect man in a hurry had boarded any of the late night buses and if so, where he had alighted or disembarked.

There was a lot to do, decided Detective Superintendent Clifton. No time for sleep. And if Clifton's previous knowledge was any guide, that sergeant didn't look as if he was long for this world. He looked just like an acquaintance of his who later died of leukaemia. But could he have killed Swainby?

He could have, reasoned Clifton. He'd been in the park, he'd had the time, there was a dearth of other suspects, the dodgy question of a fleeing man in black and a curious absence of witnesses to the sergeant's movements at the critical time. But had he a motive? If he had, could he be the killer? Most certainly, it was not impossible.

CHAPTER 6

DETECTIVE Inspector Cussons had not arrived from Garminghamshire by the time the briefing commenced soon after 3 a.m. The assembled policemen were provided with sandwiches and tea while Clifton spoke to them. He told of the fleeing young man, the discovery of the body in the park, the nature of its injuries and a suggestion of the probable weapon. He then gave the name of the victim, stressing there had been no formal identification but asked that, during their patrols, the officers tried to learn as much as possible about Swainby and his activities since returning to Hildenley. Details of his haunts, contacts, friends and daily routine were required. He added that Hildenley CID were also making those specific enquiries but any additional information would be welcomed.

'I realize you can't quiz many people at this time of the morning but stop anyone who's in the streets and interrogate them, especially young men in dark clothing; think them as both potential witnesses and possible suspects. If you find a prime suspect, don't interview him or her in depth, that's my job. Bring them into the police station for me to deal with and don't tell the press! In fact, if you're not satisfied with anyone's response, bring them in. Detectives will be drafted into town later this morning, then I'll arrange house-to-house enquiries, concentrating at first on the area where Swainby lived, the Upperholme Terrace area, and the streets surrounding Latima Park, of course.'

Clifton added that the information he was now providing would be circulated by radio to all police stations within the force area and to neighbouring constabularies with a request that they conduct local enquiries. The men warmed to their task – it was the ambition of most, if not all, police officers to arrest a murderer but because about half had been on duty since 2 p.m. the previous day, Clifton decided they should go home. The night shift could adequately cope for the time being so Clifton told the late turn men to book off duty at 3.30 a.m. and claim the period from 10 p.m. until 3.30 a.m. as overtime. He would ensure they got paid from the fund allocated to this murder enquiry.

Some night shift men were still milling around with their sandwiches and tea when Detective Inspector Cussons arrived from Garminghamshire. He was a slightly built individual with spectacles and thin fair hair, looking more like a bank clerk than a detective. Sergeant Simpson noticed his arrival and went to meet him.

'I'm Sergeant Simpson, sir, Detective Superintendent Clifton wants me to escort you to the mortuary, for the identification.'

'Fine, Sergeant, but first I need the toilet and is that tea and food I can smell?' He had a noticeable Garminghamshire accent.

Twenty-five minutes later, after relieving himself, having a sandwich and cup of tea and a chat with Clifton to whom he presented two copies of his own force's file about Swainby, he answered questions about Swainby, not forgetting the rape for which he had served his recent prison sentence, and the two murders for which he was suspected. Then he left for the hospital with Sergeant Simpson.

They walked the short distance in spite of Simpson's weariness, Cussons saying he wanted to stretch his legs and get some fresh air after the long drive.

'So you found the body, Sarge?' said Cussons as they climbed the hill towards the hospital, all ablaze with lights. 'That makes you prime suspect, doesn't it? They always say the person who reports finding the body does so to cover his crime . . . but well done, it was good police work. And I see your uniform is blood-stained?'

'I haven't a spare here, it's not a problem. It was a shock, believe me, sir. He's had a hammering, his skull was smashed in several places, it was abnormally thin, although I reckon those blows would have smashed a normal skull, even a thick one.' Simpson was finding the climb something of a struggle, he was panting heavily and had to stop occasionally for a rest. 'Sorry about this, sir, I'm out of condition, I've not been well lately. Old age and shift work catching up with me.'

'Driving you too hard are they?' The inspector was patient. 'Don't fret, Sarge, I've all night, this is a new experience for me. A nice trip out instead of supervising my night shift . . .'

'I'm not sure what's matter with me, I've been feeling overtired for a few weeks now, but not as bad as this. Anyway, back to Swainby. He used to live here then disappeared into your part of the country. We've not seen him for twenty years or so, then he suddenly turns up again. It seems he's been behaving though, we've had no reports of attacks on women in recent weeks.'

'That's out of character, sarge, he can't stop himself – unless his time inside has had some impact on him. And, don't forget, he's getting older.'

'Like me, no spring chicken!'

'The fact he's older could have calmed him down. But if this stiff is Swainby, I'm not sorry. There wasn't a shred of decency in him and he never showed any sign of a conscience or sympathy towards his victims. There was a deep anger which he turned into physical violence but like a lot of villains, he could turn on the charm – he conned women into friendship, then attacked them. We've two outstanding murders which are down to him but we can't prove them. If this victim is him, somebody's done a great favour to society and to women in particular.'

'I couldn't agree more, sir . . . .' panted Sergeant Simpson.

After their short climb with frequent stops, they arrived at the reception desk of the hospital. Sergeant Simpson was recognized by the night porter and given the key to the mortuary. There was no one on duty there at this time of morning. Now that the hill climbing was over he did not feel so breathless and let himself in, switched on the lights and led the way towards the bank of giant drawers which comprised the refrigeration unit. Only one was occupied. It was provisionally marked 'Latima Park Body' and Simpson drew it open. The body lay inside, naked and still with the head and face caked in dried blood but everything back in place; Simpson remembered that his tunic was stained with the same blood . . . he'd not had the opportunity to change it yet.

'I'm here to provide continuity of evidence,' said Simpson. 'I can confirm that this is the body I found in Latima Park.'

Cussons took a long look at the body. 'I know the routine, Sergeant, and yes, I can confirm that this is Edward Albert Swainby whose last address in our area was 35, Heldon Road, Cresslington. His personal details, date of birth and so forth are all in the file I've given to your boss.'

And so the formal, short but vital positive identification was quickly made. Sergeant Simpson returned the corpse to the cold storage unit, locked the door of the mortuary, returned the key to reception and walked back to the police station with Cussons. There Simpson took the necessary short written statement which would form part of the growing murder file whereupon Cussons said he must return to his own station without delay. At last, Sergeant Simpson could go home, change out of that blood-stained uniform and take it to the cleaner's.

It was nearly 4 a.m. by the time he collapsed into bed; it had been a long day and he was almost too tired to sleep. He was thankful, however, that he had not suffered any nose bleeds during his long shift.

When Pamela Simpson came downstairs, she found a note on the kitchen table. It said, 'If I'm not up by eight, give me a knock, I have to return to duty at 8.30. Dick. xxx'

It was about ten to eight and she could hear him in the bathroom, so she put a pan on the stove to boil some water for his egg and switched on the kettle. She placed a couple of Weetabix in a bowl and placed it on the table beside the milk and sugar. He would be about ten minutes, she knew.

When he arrived, he was dressed in a clean police issue shirt and clean uniform trousers while carrying a fresh tunic over his arm; he hung this over the back of a chair, kissed his wife as he wished her good morning, then sat down for his breakfast.

'God, you look dreadful, Dick, you're as white as a sheet. Is your tiredness worse? And have you had any more nose-bleeds?'

'No nose-bleeds but I was nearly on my knees last night. I couldn't get away, it was nearly four when I turned in. It was a long day, Pam, a very long day.'

'I never heard you come in,' she smiled her appreciation for his kindness in not disturbing her. 'But Dick, seriously, you look terrible, are you fit to go in today?'

'I have to, it's important . . . .' he began.

She interrupted. 'Well I don't think you should, I think you should go and see Dr Ewart, you can't keep avoiding the doctor. You'll have to tell him about those nose-bleeds and feverishness. And that tiredness is far worse than it was. I'd say you were seriously anaemic. I mean it – go and see him, he can give you something for it.'

'I'll do my best while I'm in town today.'

'Good, I'll hold you to that promise! So what time did you say you got in?' Pamela was a stout woman in her early forties. With short dark hair, she had a round and pretty face which always seemed to be smiling but since reaching her thirties, she had broadened out until she was now quite plump. Her ample figure was hidden beneath the large flowered apron which protected her dress as she stood beside the stove, waiting to make the tea and for the water to boil in the egg pan.

'Four o'clockish,' he repeated.

'So why did you have to work so late?' she was quite accustomed to her husband coming home at all sorts of odd hours; that was one of the penalties of being a policeman's wife.

'I found a body in the park,' he told her, trying to break the news gently. 'A man, he'd been murdered, we've a big murder enquiry under-way, the CID are in charge but everyone's needed to help with enquiries in town.'

'A murder?' she turned, the surprise evident on her face. 'A murder? In Hildenley? So who is it? Anyone we know?'

'Prepare to be shocked, it's dreadful news for us, Pam . . . .'

'Oh dear . . .' she put a hand to her mouth. 'Oh dear, it *is* someone we know, is it?'

'Ted Swainby,' he spoke quietly.

Pamela put both hands up to the side of her face, not knowing how to respond and so he got up and went across to her, taking her in his arms.

'Ted Swainby,' she muttered his name. 'God, this is dreadful. But how? Who did it, Dick? Do they know?'

'No, they've launched a hunt for the killer, detectives are being drafted in. It's a case of every man being needed. That's why I have to go in to work, I must. He's been living in Garminghamshire but he came back, five or six weeks ago we think, but we had no idea he'd come back until this happened. God knows why he'd want to come back to Hildenley.'

'Oh, Dick, I don't know what to say, what to do . . . .'

'Don't say anything or do anything, keep everything to yourself for now,' he kissed her forehead. 'It will be all over the papers once the press hear about it, but I thought you should know so we can be prepared. Leave things with me for the time being, I want to know everything that's going on, you can see why I need to go in to work. I can't ignore this, I just can't, I need to know what's going on.'

'So how . . . I mean, how did he die?'

'He was attacked about the head with some sort of blunt instrument, a piece of stone we think. It was very savage, he was dead when I found him, he was near the museum in the park.'

'How awful . . . and you finding him as well . . . .'

'That makes me a suspect. I got a right grilling from the detective superintendent, I'm sure he thinks I did it.'

'You? Not you! You couldn't, could you? Not even if it was Ted Swainby?'

'No, but things will look bad if they discover the connection . . . .'

'Oh my God, this is dreadful, Dick, dreadful . . . what are you going to do?'

'Carry on as normally as I can. We're trying to find out what he's been doing since he returned to Hildenley. He must have been behaving himself otherwise we'd have known he was here. I must admit I didn't recognize him straight away, he's aged a lot.'

'So someone's followed him, you think? To get revenge?'

'That's the most likely answer.'

'I don't know what to say, Dick, really I don't . . .' and as she absorbed the news, both the egg pan and the kettle began to boil, the kettle whistling. Almost automatically, she prepared to make the tea and removed the egg from the pan, placing it in an egg cup before passing it to her husband. He took it and sat down again to begin with the cereal.

'You're not eating?' he put to her, not feeling hungry himself.

'I was going to have mine when you'd gone, but I don't think I can face food now . . . so what happens next, Dick? The funeral, I mean, that sort of thing.'

'I doubt if there'll be a funeral until the case is closed. They like to preserve murder victims' bodies in case the defence raises questions about the cause of death. Sometimes they want to carry out their own additional post mortem, just to make sure the prosecution isn't telling lies.'

'That's awful, keeping people like that . . . like pieces of meat . . . .'

'It's necessary at times, believe me, and we do tend to hang onto murder victims' bodies for as long as possible. There'll be an inquest, of course, but that will be some time in the future.'

'What about his family? Has he anyone?'

'Not to our knowledge but that's something else we're checking.'

'There's Ian, he should have been told right at the start . . . .'

'I'm not sure that would have been wise, Pam.'

'Well, Ted is Ian's natural father, there's no escaping that.'

'Yes but Ian doesn't know that . . . .'

'I know and you know, we shouldn't keep things from Ian, we should have told him years ago . . . .'

'Yes, but we didn't and so as far as Ian's concerned, I'm his father. I've no intention of telling him now, none at all. It would destroy him to know his natural father's a sex offender and convicted rapist – and worse.'

'Well, I might go to the funeral, someone should.'

'After what he did to you?'

'He did father my child, Dick, there's no escaping that, no matter how Ian was conceived, and no matter what Ted's done before or since.'

'We're trying to trace relatives or friends. Garminghamshire police are helping. If he's got family in Garminghamshire they might want him to be buried there, not in Hindenley. I don't think you've any responsibility for him, Pam, none whatever.'

'Have you told the police about him and me?'

'No, I can't see that it's relevant, it was a long time ago and it's a personal matter; besides, he never went to trial over it.'

'Well, you should think about it, you've always told Ian and me to be open and honest where police matters are concerned. Now, after all this time, I've got to get used to the idea he's dead, murdered . . . in spite of it happening more than twenty years ago, it's still a shock, Dick, a tremendous shock . . . .'

'You never loved him, did you?' he frowned. 'No one could love a man like that, surely?'

'I couldn't, and don't, but, like I said, he is the father of my child, that means something. Ian is part of him after all.'

'But my name is on the birth certificate, don't forget. Ted has nothing to do with Ian, nothing at all. This is between you and me, Pam, no one else. We can't tell Ian now, can we?'

She sighed wearily. 'Yes, you're right. There's no need for our family happiness to be ruined over this, over Ted, over what's happened to him. But it's all so dreadful, Dick, so awful to think about . . . thanks for being so calm and wonderful all these years, it can't have been easy, bringing up another man's child . . .'

'Well, I couldn't have any of my own, so his arrival helped and he's been a good lad. We're a nice family, a happy family. I'll tell him about the murder, probably today. I might see him in town or at work but I won't reveal our secret . . . I mustn't, not now. Especially not now.'

'He'll be coming tonight for his supper. You could tell him then, about you finding Ted, I mean.'

'Yes, it might be sensible to wait until he's finished work but I'm sure he'll get to hear about the murder long before we see him. It'll be all over town this morning, detectives will be asking about his friends and movements. Even though his name will be spread about the town, it will mean nothing to Ian.'

'Did you see him last night?' she asked.

'No, I thought about popping in for a cuppa with him, but it was his evening class night. I'll catch up with his news tonight.'

'We need to discuss his twenty-first birthday, Dick. I know it's a few months away but if he's going to have a big party, we need to start thinking about it.'

'The last time I mentioned it, he said he didn't want a fuss, but, yes, we can talk about it tonight. It'll take my mind off other things!'

At that point, Pam came across to the table and kissed Dick on the lips.

'Thanks for being a wonderful father,' she sniffed. 'You really have been wonderful, no one could have asked for more . . . now eat your breakfast if you insist on going to work, and don't be late. And go to see the doctor! If you don't, I'll call him in!'

'I will, I promise. And one other thing. My other uniform's blood-stained, it needs cleaning. Will you be in town today?'

'Ted's blood you mean?' and she shuddered. 'How did that happen? How did you get his blood on your uniform?' Her eyes showed more than a hint of suspicion; he didn't miss it. There were questions on her face, questions she dare not ask.

'I found him like I said, there was blood all over, I couldn't help getting my clothes stained. It got all over when I was trying to help him . . . .'

'You tried to help him?' Pamela took a deep breath and turned away from her husband as she tried to gather her thoughts. 'I'm surprised you did that . . . because it was Ted. I thought you hated him . . . but can't you throw the uniform away and get a replacement? You've plenty of spares . . . .' And she shuddered again.

'I can't throw it away, it's police property. I've hung it in the garage, I'll deal with it later. Not today.'

'If it was up to me, I'd get rid of it. A murdered man's blood! You can't seriously think the force would want you to wear it even if it was cleaned properly?'

'Police forces don't use much imagination when it comes to that sort of thing.' He tried to be lighthearted about it. 'It's police property, it's dirty and so it needs cleaning, that's their logic but I'll ask.'

'And don't forget the doctor . . . .' she called as he hurried to the hatrack for his uniform cap.

Later that Friday morning, the old-fashioned police station with its dark passages, numerous staircases and high windows, was bursting at the seams. It was full of policemen, many in uniform and lots in civilian clothes. Their personnel carriers, cars and bicycles filled the side streets and Detective Superintendent Clifton had arranged for urns of tea to be placed in the muster room, bearing in mind some had travelled a considerable distance. He had also organized lunch – a local café would produce the necessary meals – they could make use of a rear room in the café as a rest room. It was such thoughtful gestures that made Clifton so popular with his subordinates. Loud and noisy though he was, sometimes with a brusque manner and even rude or bullying, he could show surprising signs of kindness which made his subordinates happy to work for him. He always got the best from his staff.

By 8.30, everyone was packed into the muster room and Clifton, in spite of his height, found a chair upon which to stand so that everyone could see him as he made his address. Detective Sergeant Burrows stood at his side, on the floor.

Sergeant Simpson stood next to the large table which occupied the centre of the room – in normal circumstances, this was used by the constables who sat around it and made notes during their pre-shift briefings. Now, he rested his buttocks on the edge as he prepared to listen to Clifton. Simpson knew the big man would have had very little sleep last night yet he seemed as fresh as a daisy, clean shaven with his hair looking well groomed, his shirt collar crisp and his eyes bright with the challenge of this new day.

'Good morning all,' his powerful voice commanded silence as the men faced him. 'My name is Detective Superintendent Clifton from Headquarters CID and the man at my side down here,' and he indicated to his right, 'is my colleague, Detective Sergeant Burrows. We are the force murder team, and, I might add, we are not Scotland Yard. We're much better than them!'

There was a good-humoured roll of laughter which helped to ease the tension as Clifton continued, 'I seem to spend a lot of time talking to groups like you but most of you are new to this – a murder enquiry. You've been drafted in from various parts of the force area so try to get to know one another. I need you to work well together, to work as a team. The uniform men are not only from Hildenley, but from all over this Division; the Hildenley men will, I am sure, be full of local knowledge, they are there to help the CID if required. I don't want anyone's ambition to arrest a murderer to turn this into a one-man race. We work together, all of us. It's a joint effort, as I said, we're a team.'

He paused as if to emphasize that point, then said, 'I have drafted written instructions to all the sergeants in this room, plain clothes or uniformed. They were written in the cool of a new day at five o'clock this morning and have been typed by our super efficient early-bird secretaries. Those orders, which you will collect after this briefing, contain specific written instructions about the role you will each play. So why are we here? We're here to investigate a murder and I can't do that alone. You've all got an important part to play which will become clearer when you start working as a team; each team will consist of one detective sergeant and one detective constable with the uniform branch as back-up and to provide local knowledge. Now, the victim is Edward Albert Swainby, born 30 July 1912 which makes him 48. Swainby was a convicted sex offender – details of his record are on the board over there, make sure you know what sort of person he was, it could be relevant,' and he pointed to the blackboard standing in one corner.

'Take a good look at his mug shots, they were taken while he was in custody but they're not a bad likeness, and while you are making your enquiries about his death, remember we need to know if anyone in town has had contact with him in recent weeks. Did he go into the local pubs and clubs? Was he a sportsman? Did he watch football or cricket? He must have done something with his spare time. He is thought to have lived here for about six weeks in Upperholme Terrace, a basement flat. The address is on the board. His name is not on the electoral register nor in the telephone directory but someone must have come across him. The local CID are checking his links with that address, seeing his landlord or whatever. It's vital we know as much as we can about him during his time in town, both now and in the past. He lived here about twenty years ago, so someone might remember him from that time.'

He told them about the way the body was discovered then went on to describe the man seen by Sergeant Simpson, adding that tracing him was top priority. Had he gone into hiding in town? Was someone sheltering him? Had he taken a taxi out of town last night, or a late bus or train? Or had he found shelter last night in the hope of getting a bus or train out of town this morning? And who was he? Did his description match anyone? Could it be someone still walking round town? Clifton said he would personally interview Geoffrey Stalker, the man who had spoken to Sergeant Simpson moments before the body was discovered, and he would also re-interview Alan Wetherill and his girlfriend, the couple in the park.'

He went on, 'I need not add that if you uncover any other crimes or offences, the murder takes precedence, don't let yourselves be side-tracked. The press have not yet got hold of this but they will; I'm told there is only one resident reporter in town and he's not exactly an action man. Word will be out in town by now so he'll soon find out; if he doesn't, he's not doing his job properly. If you get any enquiries from the press, refer them to the information room. I'll leave press releases there. You know what police regulations say about talking to the press without authority – in other words, don't! Right, it's all down to you now and if there are problems or if you need advice, just ask. I know I am large and frightening but I'm not as fierce as I look. I'd rather you ask than make a balls-up over anything. So, on your way everybody. Out there is a murderer just waiting to be arrested. Sergeant Simpson, good to see you here, I thought you might have reported sick but I'm glad to see you. I have a special task for you. See me when the others have left.'

Clifton believed in setting a fast pace from the start – once the momentum was underway, he could relax and quietly slip away for a few hours' sleep. And so, as the incoming sergeants began to assemble their teams, Clifton caught Simpson's eye.

'This way, Sarge,' he led him up the stairs to the CID office. 'I see you've changed your uniform!'

'I'm not sure it will clean very well. When I saw it in daylight, it looked very deeply soaked.'

'Apply for a replacement but don't destroy it, not yet, we might need that blood analysed. Do me a memo, I'll approve it.'

In the cramped office, Clifton squeezed himself into the space behind the desk as Sergeant Simpson pulled up a chair. 'I'm told by Superintendent Firth that you are the longest serving officer in town?' Clifton began.

'Yes, sir, I came here before the war but the Army wouldn't accept me due to an internal injury in a motor cycle accident. The police surgeon accepted me though.'

'He wouldn't be too happy at the way you look now!'

'I'm fit enough for duty, sir, I want to be part of this.'

'You could have fooled me. Anyway, it's your life, as they say, so let's get down to business. You'll know almost everyone living here? You'll know your way around? You'll be familiar with the underbelly of Hildenley? You'll be aware of all those secrets that people want to keep secret, you'll know who's been knocking off whose wife or husband, which business-men are on the fiddle or about to become bankrupt, you'll know all the petty criminals and what they're up to now, that sort of thing.'

'Yes, sir, I think I know most of that.'

'Good. And I am also told by Mr Firth that you are well liked and trusted by the townspeople?'

This was a marked change from their previous conversation, thought Simpson, so was Clifton being sincere or was he testing him in some obscure way? 'Thank you, sir, I do my best,' was all Sergeant Simpson could think of saying in reply.

'Fine, which is just what I need. I want you, Sergeant, to visit those householders who live close to Latima Park, especially those along Park Road. Lots of those house windows are higher than the park walls and the bordering trees, so I reckon the occupants can see all the comings and goings. I'm sure some do exactly that. I need someone like you who is known to them and whom they trust because I want to know what secrets they might have observed in and around the park, day or night, not just last night but over the past few weeks or months. But especially last night of course. I am sure they'll start gossiping once they know about the murder.'

'It'll certainly start tongues wagging, sir.'

'Exactly, and I want to you tap into the gossip. That's your task, that's why I have selected you for this job.'

'I understand, sir.'

Clifton told Simpson to visit every house overlooking the park and its approaches. If it had been turned into flats, he must visit every flat and talk to the occupants. Clifton suggested the man seen hurrying away last night might live in one of those houses or flats – or he might have taken refuge there, even in a garden shed. He then announced he was going to speak to Geoffrey Stalker, and then Alan Wetherill.

Finally he said, 'One other thing, Sergeant. I was serious about you having a check-up. I'm repeating that because I'm very concerned about you, so I've no objection to you popping in to see a doctor while you're working on these enquiries. You understand what I am saying?'

'Yes, sir.'

And so Sergeant Simpson left the big man's office, put on his cap and strode into town to undertake his special task. And he would see Dr Ewart. Orders were orders – one did not disobey Wilf Clifton! Besides, he'd also promised Pam. Dr Ewart's surgery was on a street near Park Road, only five minutes from the police station, and so Sergeant Simpson decided to check surgery times as he passed. The brass plate told him surgery times were every day except Sunday, from 9 a.m. until 10.30 a.m. and again from 5 p.m. until 6 p.m. When he walked into the waiting room, he noticed one woman waiting; she was reading *Woman's Weekly* as he presented himself to the receptionist. She was a pretty young woman with dark hair and bright red lips. She'd be in her early twenties, he estimated, but didn't know her name.

'Dr Ewart is busy with surgery, Sergeant Simpson,' she smiled, clearly recognizing him. 'Is it important? About the man in the park?'

'It's not about the man in the park,' he laughed. 'But I want to see him, I need his medical opinion, I'll wait my turn.'

'Oh, well, yes, that's no problem, it's quiet this morning. Take a seat, I'll get your file out. When was the last time you were here?'

'Years ago,' he laughed. 'A medical for some life insurance, ten years or whatever.'

'Not exactly one of our best customers then,' she laughed and began to flick through a card index. A man then emerged from the doctor's inner sanctum as the lady, Mrs Vernon, was called in. Simpson was next. The man departed after a brief word with the receptionist who then said, 'I hope you don't mind me asking, Sergeant, but is it true about the man in the park?'

'Is what true about the man in the park?'

'Well, there's a story going about that someone's been murdered in the park, last night it was, but I mean, that sort of thing doesn't happen in Hildenley. It's a very strong rumour, though, I heard it in the newspaper shop before I got to work . . . I hope you don't mind me asking.'

'Not at all,' he said. 'We need people to talk about it, provided they talk to us! But yes, a man was attacked last night in Latima Park and he has died. Lots of policemen will be going around town asking for information, and in fact that's what I shall be doing once Dr Ewart has examined me.'

'Oh how awful . . . how dreadful, Sergeant. Who was it? Can I ask?'

'It's a man called Edward Albert Swainby who has recently come to live here; he came from the Garminghamshire area. We're trying to trace his movements and perhaps find his contacts in Hildenley. We also need to find a motive for his death and obviously we have to trace the person who killed him. Those are our priorities so if you know anything that might help us . . . .'

'Ooh, good heavens no. I don't even live in Hildenley, I live out at Fieldholme, I come in to work by train every morning. This is dreadful though . . . .'

'The name Swainby doesn't mean anything to you then? Was he one of your patients?'

'I don't think so, Sergeant, but I'll check,' and she began to flick furiously through the card index system before shaking her head. 'Sorry, no, he's not one of ours.'

That was one useful official enquiry he had already completed and he made a mental note to jot this down in his notebook; he'd also visit other surgeries to see whether Swainby had registered with a doctor or dentist. Then Mrs Vernon emerged with a smile on her face and the receptionist said, 'Dr Ewart will see you now, Sergeant.'

Dr Ewart, a large man with straw-coloured hair and a bushy moustache, always dressed like a gamekeeper in his tweed jacket, plus fours, long green socks and brogue shoes. He was a man who loved country pursuits, spending most of his free time chasing pheasants and partridges or shooting grouse – and he was a good doctor.

'Sergeant,' he said. 'This is a surprise, it's not often we see you in here. Don't tell me! It's an official enquiry about that chap in the park.'

'No, it's not, Doctor, but whilst I am here, I've asked if he's on your books, and he's not. There has been a murder in town, a man battered to death last night in Latima Park. He's been identified as Edward Albert Swainby lately of Cresslington which is near Garmingham, in Garminghamshire. We think he's been living here about six weeks.'

'Swainby? Can't say I know the name. What was he doing here to go and get himself killed? Murder's not the sort of thing we expect in Hildenley.'

'We don't know. Although he's been living here a few weeks, we haven't come across him. In confidence, he's a convicted rapist who lived here twenty years ago and now he's returned we're looking into the possibility it was some kind of revenge attack.'

'You've arrested someone?'

'Not yet, we've no suspects' names, I must confess.'

'It all takes time, I'm sure. I hope you catch the killer. So if that's not your reason for calling, what can I do for you? I must say you look a little washed out, not the usual robust face I expect to see on you.'

Sergeant Simpson then provided a detailed account of his symptoms, referring to his weariness, nose-bleeds and recurring feverishness. Dr Ewart listened and asked a few questions, then rose from his seat and began to arrange his stethoscope and the apparatus for taking blood pressure.

'No undue strain at work? Not pushing yourself too hard, I hope?'

'No, I never do that!'

'Long periods of shift work with irregular meal-times don't help, you know. You're not as young as you were, you're probably heading for retirement, are you?'

'I can go in eighteen months' time, I'm a long way short of sixty-five though! I can go at fifty-five. In fact, I must retire at fifty-five. I want to reach that point, doctor, I don't want to be forced to retire early due to ill-health.'

'I can understand that but if I were you, I'd retire as soon as possible. There's no shame in taking an ill-health pension, and you'd feel better, I'm sure. No more shifts, regular meals, a more contented and routine life without worries. You've earned that. It's time to reap the benefits of your lifetime's work. But down to business. Take your jacket off and roll up your sleeve. I want to listen to your heart and chest, so you can help by loosening your shirt buttons, and I need to take your blood pressure. Now, any other symptoms?'

'What sort of other symptoms?'

'Bruises? Lumps under the arms? Aches?'

'It's odd that you mention bruises. Yes, I've been noticing some bruises as well . . . .'

'Where?'

'On my arms and legs, as if I'd bumped into something. I thought I was bruising easily, I put it down to getting older.'

'Show me.'

Sergeant Simpson rolled up both his sleeves to show several large bruises. 'I can't remember knocking anything, usually it takes a lot to give me a bruise, but these have just appeared.'

'Recently?'

'In the last week or so, yes. Days even.'

'Anywhere else?'

'My legs are the same. I must have knocked something but wasn't aware of it.'

'Hhm. I don't like the sound of this, Sergeant, I don't like it at all. I'm going to ask for a sample of your blood; it might take a day or two to get a result.'

After testing the sergeant's blood pressure, he pursed his lips and said, 'Your blood pressure is well down and I'd say you were anaemic at the very least. You say you've had nose bleeds? What about lumps? In your flesh? Under the arms for example?'

'I can't say I've noticed any but again, I've not looked.'

'Then let me,' and he removed the blood pressure testing gear.

With the sergeant's shirt buttons open down the front, the doctor pushed his hands inside and began to feel around the area beneath and near the armpits, gently pressing the flesh.

'Well, I can't feel any lumps so that's good news. If you get any, let me know immediately. They can appear quite suddenly.'

'So what is it?'

'My initial assessment is that you are anaemic, Sergeant, seriously anaemic, in which case you need something to put iron into your blood. I'll give you some pills today but other things can help, like green vegetables, Guinness, red meat, liver and so on. We might have to consider a blood transfusion but before I do that I need to send your blood sample away. With the weekend coming up, it might take a few days to get a result, unless I stress it's very urgent.'

'And do you think it's very urgent? I ought to say I had a friend who died from leukaemia. I think my symptoms are very similar.'

'There are several conditions which have almost identical symptoms, Sergeant, but if you are merely anaemic, we can cope with you. First I need to establish whether or not that is your problem, hence the blood test. I will also be checking to see whether there is anything else we should be concerned about. But, and I can't stress this enough, if lumps do develop under your arms, or anywhere else, tell me immediately. And I mean immediately.'

'I understand.'

'Do you feel fit enough for duty? I can write out a sick note if you want.'

'I want to keep working, doctor, it's not every day we get chance to work on a murder enquiry and there is a lot I can do, even if I'm weary most of the time.'

'As you wish, but call me if any lumps do materialize.'

And so it was that Sergeant Simpson, believing he knew his fate even if Dr Ewart would not commit himself, left the surgery to talk to people who lived near the park.

CHAPTER 7

DETECTIVE Superintendent Clifton with Detective Sergeant Burrows at his side lost no time calling on Geoffrey Stalker at his office. They arrived even before Stalker had dealt with his morning mail, had his first cup of tea, read *The Times*, dictated his first letter of the day or welcomed his first client.

'I'm sorry,' said his protective, middle-aged, bespectacled receptionist. 'If you don't have an appointment, I'm afraid he can't see you. Now, there is a gap this afternoon at three . . . perhaps if it's urgent I could make an appointment for then?'

'If that's classed as urgent in your little world, madam, it's not urgent in mine. Urgency in my work is now. Immediately. This minute. And I need to see Mr Stalker urgently. My name is Detective Superintendent Clifton, this is Detective Sergeant Burrows and we are here to talk to Mr Stalker about a murder . . . .'

'Oh, that one . . . oh dear, yes. Mr Stalker did say he'd been near the park last night . . . yes, just a moment please,' and she pressed the inter-com switch on her desk, said that two detectives were in reception and smiled with some relief as her boss agreed to see them. She led the way to a door marked 'Mr Stalker', knocked and opened it to lead them into his office. He was sitting behind a desk piled high with paper and looked more like the busy editor of a newspaper than a solicitor. Clifton was not impressed – he believed in having an empty desk. It was his deep opinion that a man with a desk stacked high with paperwork was not efficient, nor was he particularly busy. The office seemed full of clutter too.

There were heaps of files on the floor, piles of books on most surfaces and ash trays almost everywhere; the place reeked with the scent of stale tobacco. Within moments of entering, Clifton had an uneasy feeling he could not trust this man.

'Can I get you a cup of tea?' Myrtle smiled, her way of apologizing for her lapse in not recognizing the huge man as a police officer.

'Two, one with sugar,' boomed Clifton as he strode in and before the receptionist could announce their names, held out his hand for Stalker to grip. 'Good morning, Mr Stalker. Good of you to see us at such short notice.'

Stalker shook hands, indicated a pair of chairs near his desk and made a weak smile. 'Good morning, gentlemen, er, how can I help you?'

'This is Detective Superintendent Clifton, Mr Stalker, and Detective Sergeant Burrows, it's about that business in the park,' twittered the receptionist.

'Ah!' said Stalker. 'Ah, well, yes, how can I help you? And a cup for me too, Myrtle.'

As Clifton and Burrows settled on their seats, Geoffrey Stalker rose from his chair and walked across to the fireplace where coals were glowing, albeit dimly. Large fires were both too hot and too expensive, but a glow gave a reassuring touch to the cluttered office. A well-built man in his early fifties with balding grey hair, a rosy face and a smart line in inexpensive suits, he rested an elbow on the mantelpiece and adopted what looked like a thoughtful stance with one foot on the fender. Then he took a pipe from his pocket and began to load it with ready-rubbed tobacco from a tin, pressing it deep into the bowl.

In silence, Clifton watched with some interest; clearly this ritual was part of Stalker's means of dealing with a difficult situation. The fellow was obviously a poseur but it gave him time to think before having to provide answers . . . he fumbled in his waistcoat pocket, found a box of matches and proceeded to ignite his pipe amid clouds of sweet smelling smoke. Clifton wondered why this man was having to delay their questions . . . did he have something to hide?

'Sorry, gentlemen,' he smiled through the fog. 'I must have my pipe – rather like Sherlock Holmes? A three pipe problem and all that. Except I just have the one pipe . . . so, the business in the park as Myrtle put it. How can I be of assistance?'

'I believe you were walking your dog near the park last night, Mr Stalker,' began Clifton.

'Yes, I was. I spoke to Sergeant Simpson, I expect he told you.'

'He did, yes. I need to ask you a few questions.'

'Of course, I am well accustomed to dealing with our local police as you can imagine and I know the value of asking the right questions – and getting the right answers.' And he puffed clouds of smoke from his pipe as he tried to coax it into a brighter glow.

'That makes our work that much easier,' Clifton smiled uneasily.

'Before we begin, Superintendent,' Stalker removed the pipe from his mouth and stared into the bowl. 'Can you tell me precisely why you are asking these questions? There are rumours about a murder, you know how these stories spread and gather momentum, so I think it would be helpful if I knew the real situation.'

'I'm coming to that.'

'I'm sure you are, Superintendent. What I need to know is whether it was a natural death, some tramp perhaps, ending his days on a park bench, or was it truly a murder as rumours would suggest? I might add that I heard the rumours this morning on my walk to the office, in the paper-shop.'

'I can confirm it was murder, Mr Stalker. The victim was savagely beaten and has been identified as Edward Albert Swainby, a man forty-eight years old who lived in Upperholme Terrace. He had been living there for about six weeks, having moved here from Garminghamshire. We are in the process of tracing relatives and friends. The killer has not been arrested, Mr Stalker and we are trying to identify and find him, or her, and to trace witnesses, like yourself.'

'Oh, I wouldn't say I was a witness . . . .'

'I would, Mr Stalker. So tell me about this visit to the park last night, then we shall write it all down in the form of a witness statement, some-thing with which I am sure you are familiar, and if you agree to all the contents, I shall ask you to sign it.'

Because Clifton was considering Stalker as a possible suspect, however, he did not elaborate on the precise method of attack, not mentioning it was the head which had suffered such injuries. Sometimes, a suspect would condemn himself by revealing too much knowledge of the means used to carry out the murder . . . .

'Well, there's not a lot I can say, Superintendent,' the pipe was belch-ing forth clouds of smoke now. 'I saw Sergeant Simpson as I was home-ward bound with my dog and we had a chat . . . .'

'Let's go back to the start of that walk, shall we? I like to hear a full story, Mr Stalker, and I think this one begins with you leaving home to walk your dog. Tell me about that, with timings as precise as you are able to give.'

The pipe came out of Stalker's mouth and he stood for a moment in silence, clutching it and staring at it as if for inspiration. Then Myrtle came in with a tray containing a teapot, cups, plates, milk, sugar and sweet biscuits. As everyone waited in silence, she placed the tray on Stalker's desk, moving some of the clutter to one side to make a space, then asked, 'Shall I pour?'

'I'll do it,' said Clifton. 'I am domesticated. Thanks, Myrtle.'

His intervention provided her with a clue that her presence was not required and, true to his word, Clifton poured the tea as Stalker maintained his puffing pose. Clifton even rose from his chair and carried Stalker's cup to him, placing it on the mantelpiece. Stalker smiled and nodded his appreciation; clearly, he was accustomed to being waited upon and, after all, police officers could not match his intellectual abilities.

'So,' said Clifton when Myrtle had left the office. 'Your dog walking last night, Mr Stalker. You were going to tell me all about it.'

'Yes, indeed, Superintendent, not that there is a lot to tell. I left home around nine o'clock as is my practice . . .'

'And home is where?' interrupted Clifton.

'Cherry Tree Avenue, No. 27, a detached, four-bedroomed house. It's near the west end of town.'

'The smart end?' beamed Clifton.

'Some would say so,' acknowledged Stalker with a flicker of pride across his face. 'It is a nice area with nice people.'

'Naturally,' beamed Clifton once more. 'So please continue.'

'Well, we left home . . . .'

'We?' interrupted Clifton.

'Sooty and me, he's my dog, a spaniel, a black one. A cocker spaniel.'

'Ah, of course. Pray continue.'

'We do a regular walk, from home down Scrivener Street and into Park Road, then we go into the park and I let him off the lead for a run, and aim to get home by ten. It's good for Sooty and good for me.'

'Hmm. I see. So last night you did this route?'

'Yes, I did.'

'So where did you encounter Sergeant Simpson?'

'In Park Road, outside the gate of the park.'

'Time?'

'Quarter to ten or thereabouts, I reckon it takes quarter of an hour to get home from the park, counting stops at lamp posts *en route*,' and Stalker laughed at his small joke, one he'd told countless times.

'So which gate are we talking about, Mr Stalker?'

'The most easterly, Superintendent, No. 1 Gate as it is officially known, or East Gate as some call it.'

'That confirms what Sergeant Simpson told me,' Clifton acknowledged. 'So tell me what transpired between you.'

'I was walking towards him, Superintendent, but must admit that, at first, I was unaware of his presence. He was standing in the shadows of the trees. I doubt if I would have seen him if he hadn't flashed his torch and then he spoke to me. He recognized me, we do know one another. Through our work.'

'And it was definitely Sergeant Simpson?'

'Yes it was. He was alone and appeared to be shining his torch beyond me, then he switched it off by which time I was very close to him. I asked if he was working late and he told me he was due to finish at ten, after a walk through the park to check for vandals and vagrants. I remember thinking he had ten or fifteen minutes to get back to the police station.'

'Did Sergeant Simpson say anything else?'

'Yes, he asked if I had seen a man, apparently he had been trying to spotlight a man with his torch. He said it was someone in a hurry or even in distress, and he said he'd tried to attract the man's attention but he'd run off.'

'Where had the man come from? Did Sergeant Simpson give you any idea?'

'He thought he'd come out of the park, by the next gate along, that's towards the west, a hundred yards away or so, I'd say. No.2 Gate in official parlance, or the North Gate as some call it, the one immediately behind me at that time.'

'Did you see this man?'

'I must admit I didn't. I turned to look in the direction Sergeant Simpson was indicating but never saw anyone. It was dark, of course, and there were lots of shadows, but even then I think I would have seen someone moving against the background of the glow from street lights. And Sooty didn't bark either.'

'So you never saw him earlier?'

'No, I did not.'

'So by which gate did you leave the park?' asked Clifton pointedly. The slow use of words told his silent sergeant that this was a key question.

Stalker hesitated just a little too long before saying, 'No. 2 Gate, the North.'

'So if you came out through No. 2 Gate with the man very close behind you, then anyone like me, especially anyone like me perhaps, would think you must have known the man was there. Either you or your dog,' said Clifton. 'Yet you claim you never saw him. Did Sergeant Simpson see you leave by that gate?'

'I doubt it, I would be a few yards along the path heading in his direction by the time he knew I was there, and it was dark, remember, with deep shadows.'

'True,' mused Clifton. 'Now if that was the case, if you were, say, already out of No. 2 Gate and heading east, it is perfectly feasible you would not have known the man had emerged behind you, especially if you went in opposite directions?'

'Yes, yes, that's exactly how I understand it, Superintendent.'

'On the other hand,' said Clifton, 'if you had been in the park with a man so close behind you, with your alert dog at your side, you *would* have become aware of the man, I would suggest.'

'I don't follow, Superintendent,' Stalker was now fidgetting with his pipe which was no longer producing clouds of smoke but which was still glowing.

'There are witnesses, Mr Stalker, who suggest you did not go into the park, and if you did not go in, you could not have emerged, could you?'

'But I explained to Sergeant Simpson that I had been for my walk in the park . . . .'

'You did, you led him to believe you had been in the park, but is it true, Mr Stalker? You were not seen in the park, Swainby was seen entering it but that was some time earlier. I believe he was the only person there except for our witnesses and, eventually, Sergeant Simpson.'

'Does it matter? What matters surely is that I stopped and spoke to Sergeant Simpson at the time and place we both acknowledge.'

'When anyone tells an untruth, however apparently insignificant, during a murder enquiry, Mr Stalker, it is inevitable it throws suspicion upon that person. You can see now why I want to know precisely where you were between nine o'clock and quarter to ten yesterday evening, you and your dog.'

There was a long pause before Stalker said, 'I trust what I say to you will be in the strictest confidence?'

'It will be, unless you are the murderer!'

'I am not the murderer . . . .'

'If you were with someone during those few minutes, that person will be able to provide your alibi, Mr Stalker. Which means I shall want to know her name.'

'Her name?'

'I am assuming you visited a lady friend under the cover of walking your dog, Mr Stalker, it happens. I am not here to condemn you, all I want is the truth.'

'I popped in for a glass of wine, that's all,' he blushed furiously. 'We are not having an affair, I must stress that, we are just good friends.'

'Of course, which means there is no need to be so coy, Mr Stalker. Her name, please?'

'I have no wish to drag the name of a friend into a murder investigation, Superintendent, I cannot see how it can be relevant.'

'Whenever a person's name is mentioned during a murder enquiry, Mr Stalker, we make a point of speaking to that person, both as a means of confirming what the other person has said, and as a way of eliminating suspects. Think of it like this — Sergeant Simpson found that body shortly before ten o'clock. I have a witness who says Swainby was alive at nine-thirty. We know you were talking to Sergeant Simpson at quarter to ten, so where were you between nine-thirty and quarter to ten? You say you were in the park? That puts you in the frame, Mr Stalker, firmly on our list of suspects. Or were you really having wine with a friend? I am sure you can see how important this is, can't you?'

'God, this is awful . . . .' The pipe had now been discarded and was lying unused in an ashtray on the mantelpiece. 'Look, I am no killer . . . God . . . how can these things happen? I was prepared to talk to you as a possible witness and now I find I am under suspicion . . . this is dreadful!'

'You have made yourself a suspect, Mr Stalker, and you will remain so unless you can prove you were not in the park at the material time. If you were visiting a lady friend, I need to know her name so that she can vouch for you. Is this making some kind of sense?'

'My wife must not know.'

'She won't, unless you tell her.'

'All right, the lady's name is Kathleen Gibson, Mrs Kathleen Gibson.'

'And her address?'

'Park View, the big house overlooking the west end of the park. Her husband is away on business; he is one of my clients.'

'Does her property adjoin the park by any chance?'

'As a matter of fact, it does. Well, her garden does to be precise. I did let my dog walk free around her garden . . . it means he was enjoying a walk at the west end of the park, as I said . . . .'

'Ah, naughty of you, Mr Stalker, playing with words to the extent of being misleading, but we shall have to speak to her. I would advise you not to contact her before we do so. We would not want a respected local solicitor accused of interfering with witnesses, would we?'

Clifton also made a mental note to search the garden of Park View – if the murder weapon had not yet been found, it might have been thrown over the boundary fence into that garden. But he would not tell that to Mr Stalker.

'I understand.'

'I am sure she will provide you with the necessary alibi, Mr Stalker. So back to your chat with Sergeant Simpson. I am still anxious to know more about the mystery man who fled from the park. You will understand he is my prime suspect – the circumstances and time of the sighting suggest that. Can I ask you to cast your mind back to those few minutes, to see whether you can recall any sighting of him, the tiniest hint of his presence . . . .'

'I've tried, Superintendent, God knows I've tried. With Sergeant Simpson mentioning it that night, and rumours of the murder this morning, I realized Simpson might have been referring to the killer but, in all honesty, I did not see him nor was I aware of his proximity. I neither saw him nor heard him. Neither did Sooty.'

Clifton was now wondering if Simpson had made up the story about the mystery man. It was odd that no one else had seen him.

'Fair enough. I accept that. Now, one final question – while talking to Sergeant Simpson, you would be fairly close to him?'

'Yes, a yard or so away.'

'And was his uniform bloodstained? Or his hands?'

Stalker thought for a long time, frowning as he tried to recollect those few moments, then shook his head. 'To be honest, I do not know, Superintendent, he was standing in the shadows. And with a dark uniform, I just could not say . . . oh, God, you can't suspect him!'

'We suspect everyone until they are positively eliminated, Mr Stalker, including our own officers. Just as your lady friend can exonerate you, so you might be able to exonerate Sergeant Simpson. Your account agrees with his, except so far as it relates to the running man.'

'I'm sorry I can't say I saw him. I didn't. All I can say is that we talked for a few moments at quarter to ten or thereabouts.'

'I would not wish you to state things which you do not know to be true, Mr Stalker. I shall, of course, be pleased if you do not talk to anyone about the possibility of the sergeant's uniform being bloodstained at the time you met, just as I shall not tell any of your friends about your friendship with Mrs Gibson. I think we understand one another.'

'Yes, I understand, of course. I pride myself on my discretion.'

'Good, then Sergeant Burrows will now take all this down in a written statement, Mr Stalker, and get you to sign it, then I shall call on your Mrs Gibson.'

Park View, the fine home of Roderick and Kathleen Gibson, was an Edwardian house which stood on an elevated site just off Park Road. Substantially built and standing in almost two acres, it had six bedrooms, three bathrooms, a huge lounge, a drawing room, a library, a conservatory, a wine cellar and a kitchen with an Aga. Without doubt, it was one of the most splendid private houses in Hildenley, befitting a man who worked as an internationally renowned financial consultant.

The snag was that Roderick was often away from home which meant Kathleen became bored. She had sometimes thought about taking a job of some sort, just to alleviate the boredom but realized that would become too restrictive. She liked her freedom, she liked to travel where she wanted in her sports car, she liked to go out to lunch with whom she wished and when she wished. And she liked talking to men. Even though Geoffrey Stalker was not the most handsome man in town or the most wealthy, his high opinion of himself amused her even if she had no intention of letting him into her bed. She could string him along, he could visit her with his dog and let it run around her garden, and she could listen to his stories. Geoffrey was a harmless diversion even if he thought he might eventually whisk her away for a wild and romantic weekend at some quiet hotel. When Superintendent Clifton and Sergeant Borrows arrived, therefore, she was eager to hear more stories and immediately offered them tea in the conservatory. They accepted and it arrived within seconds. She must have had the kettle on.

'So Superintendent, what on earth do the police want with me?' she was a plump lady in her early fifties with a head of thick blonde hair beautifully styled, a handsome round face with high cheekbones and deep blue eyes. She'd once been a very beautiful woman, he felt; even now, she was highly attractive. Clifton explained, his news of the murder being the first intimation she had received and there is no doubt it shocked her. But she did confirm that Geoffrey Stalker had called last evening, and he was with her from about nine twenty until about nine forty, enjoying a single glass of wine in the conservatory. There was nothing more than that.

Clifton took a short written statement from her and she signed it.

'Now,' he said. 'Another matter. I believe your garden adjoins Latima Park at its west end?'

'Yes, at the bottom, but there is a high wall between us, and lots of trees and vegetation.'

'We have not found the murder weapon, Mrs Gibson,' said Clifton. 'I would like my detectives to come and search your garden, if you wouldn't mind? The killer could have thrown it over the boundary wall.'

'Yes, of course, please send them along. I shall be at home all day.'

'I will have them there as soon as possible, and thank you,' he smiled, adding, 'But if you find anything that might be the weapon, please don't touch it. Leave it for us to deal with.'

He did not tell her what the weapon might be. Even if she went looking for a knife or a gun, it was likely she would overlook a stone if she conducted her own search. And so they left. Clifton was as sure as he could be that Geoffrey Stalker was not the murderer – it seemed he was not a lady-killer either, whatever his personal opinion of his own powers of seduction.

'Right, Sarge,' said Clifton to Burrows. 'Now it's time for me to talk to that young chap who was in the park last night, Alan Wetherill, and then we'll chat to his girlfriend. Do we know where they work, or will he or she be at home?'

They soon found Alan Wetherill at work.

He was a mechanic in Silvercliff Garage and when Clifton approached his boss, approval was given for him to be interviewed; they could use the spares storeroom. Alan was twenty-one years old, a serious-minded young man who had just completed his apprenticeship and the boss, Jack Silvercliff, said he was a very good workman, trustworthy and reliable. Clifton assured Silvercliff that Alan was not under suspicion for anything;

instead he had become an important witness in the town's first murder hunt.

Wetherill was brought to the office by Silvercliff who left with the words, 'Tell 'em everything you know, lad,' and disappeared, but this time there was no offer of tea and biscuits. The storeroom had a long table in the middle of rows of metal shelves and there were some chairs. Clifton organized three of them in a rough triangle.

'Now, Alan,' he said. 'I am Detective Superintendent Clifton and this is Detective Sergeant Burrows, we're investigating the murder in the park. You have previously spoken to some of my men and made a statement, but I'd like a chat.'

'Yes, I talked to them last night. I told them everything I knew.'

'We appreciate that. My job is to listen to it all again, just to make sure my men got everything from you. So can you can tell me all about what happened last night, then my sergeant here will write it all down and get you to sign the statement. I must also officially eliminate you from suspicion, you see. So, tell me, right from the start, about the events in the park, start at the time you actually went into the park.'

'It was about half past nine,' said Alan.

'You were not alone?'

'Er, no, I was with my girlfriend. Shirley Brown.'

'And where can we find Shirley? She helped as well, so I believe.'

'Yes, she did. She works in Harkers, that's the big shop that sells furniture and household things, ornaments or whatever. It's in Finkle Street.'

'Thanks, we'll find her there. Sorry to interrupt, but I need to get everything sorted out in my mind. So you and Shirley went into the park last night about half past nine?'

'We'd been to the pictures at the Coliseum and it turned out just before half nine, so we decided to go for a walk before I took Shirley home. She lives not far from the top of the park so we went that way, in through the bottom gate. It was a nice night so we sat on a seat for a few minutes and chatted.'

'Was it busy? The park?'

'No, very quiet. Hardly a soul about.'

'I believe you saw Mr Swainby?'

'We did, just before we got into the park. He was walking on the footpath behind us along Portland Road as we came back from the pictures but I don't know if he saw us. Me and Shirl went into the park through the bottom gate and turned towards the end away from the museum, West End they call it. He came in after us but I never saw him again once he'd got through the gate, not until Sergeant Simpson blew his whistle. It's full of paths, though, winding along, zig-zagging and we could easily lose him behind bushes and trees and things, especially in the dark.'

'How did you know it was Mr Swainby?' asked Clifton.

'He came to live near me, in a basement flat. I've often seen him about the place, in the garden, coming and going, and learned he was called Swainby. I think the postman told me. He was looking for the door into the basement flat, he had a football pools coupon for Mr Swainby so I showed him the door, it's at the back.'

'Right, so that Mr Swainby was definitely the person you saw going into the park last night?'

'Yes, it was. I'd know him anywhere.'

'You might like to know we had him officially identified last night, and he is or was, Edward Albert Swainby, previously of Cresslington which is in Garminghamshire. Did you know him very well?'

'No, not really, I might say hello to him, but that's about all.'

'So when you saw him go into in the park, was he with anyone?'

'No, he was all alone but there were people about the streets, mebbe a dozen or more, coming from the picture house. I didn't take much notice of them, I must admit, and we never saw anyone else in the park, except a policeman shining his torch on benches and into shelters and things. That was quite a few minutes after we'd seen Mr Swainby.'

'How many minutes? Any idea?'

'It's hard to say, Mr Clifton, the pictures turned out at half past nine and it was quite a few minutes later when the policeman flashed his torch at us.'

'Did you recognize the policeman?'

'Yes, it was Sergeant Simpson, he didn't come very close to us but was going around the park checking benches and things and when he shone his torch on us it was from quite a long way off. He shouted "Sorry" and went on his way. It would be getting on for ten o'clock by then. Shirl had to be in by quarter past ten, so we couldn't stay too long.'

'Now, Mr Wetherill, this is very important. Did you see anyone else in the park while you were there? Could someone have gone in ahead of you? One of the picture-goers perhaps?'

'No, I never saw anybody. Your detectives have asked me that. There were people leaving the pictures like I said, and walking towards the park, I suppose some could have gone in without us knowing even with just the one gate along there, but it's quite a big place with trees and bushes. But if they did go in, we never saw them. I was busy chatting to Shirl, I wasn't looking far ahead, besides it was dark. I know there's street lights, but they make a lot of shadows among trees.'

'Did you see a man with a little dog?'

'No, definitely not.'

'What about noises? People shouting? Arguing perhaps?'

'We never heard noises, Mr Clifton. It's quite noisy outside the park, you know, with buses passing all the time and cars and things. On that top bit, the sound seems to rise from the town below; it's amazing how noisy it can be sometimes.'

'So, just to recap, when Mr Swainby entered the park, you think he turned towards the museum? And you never saw him alive again?'

'That's right. If he'd come to our side of the park, we'd have seen him when we were on the seat, but we didn't so he must have gone up the other side, up to the toilets or museum. It was only when we went to help Sergeant Simpson we saw him on the ground, very badly hurt. I'd no idea he was dead, though.'

'How did you know it was him?'

'His clothes, I think, he always wore the same things. I'd seen him around his flat dressed like that.'

'Tell me about going to help Sergeant Simpson, Alan.'

'Well, we were just sitting, with me thinking I ought to be getting Shirl home when we heard the police whistle. At first I didn't take much notice, I thought it might be somebody fooling about, kids do that sort of thing, but it went on and on and I said to Shirl it sounded as if a policeman needed help. We'd seen Sergeant Simpson a few minutes before and thought it must be him so we ran towards the sound . . . and there he was, with Mr Swainby.'

'Between leaving your bench and reaching the sergeant, did you see anyone?'

'No, nobody.'

'How about a young man dressed in black? Perhaps in a hurry?'

'No, we never saw anyone. If somebody had attacked Mr Swainby, they could easily have gone out of those top gates without me seeing them. That bit of the park is very well hidden from where I was. Or, I suppose, he could have hidden behind some of those bushes and shrubs, there's enough. We used to play hide and seek in the park as kids, you know. There's plenty of places to hide, you can easily get lost . . . .'

'Tell me, Alan, if Swainby had shouted for help, or if someone had been shouting and screaming and fighting, near where Mr Swainby was found, do you think you would have heard the noise while sitting on that bench of yours?'

'I dunno, Mr Clifton, honest I don't. Me and Shirl talked about that. You'd think at night you'd hear somebody shouting or calling out but sometimes if you hear shouts at night you think it's kids fooling about. And it took a while for us to hear that whistle. I think you'd not hear somebody talking in a normal voice, not over that distance but shouting or screaming, well, yes, I reckon I would have heard it.'

'But you didn't?'

'No. That's what baffled me. How somebody could have attacked Mr Swainby like they did, with all that blood about, without us knowing . . . .'

'It puzzles me too, Alan. Right. So you heard the police whistle and went to help. Then what?'

'Well, Sergeant Simpson told us to run to the police station where we'd catch them changing shifts, so we did. We saw PC Stead walking towards the police station and told him, he ran off to help and told us go into the station to give our names and get more help; we had to tell whoever was on duty to get a doctor, ambulance, more policemen, that sort of thing.'

'You did a good job, a very good job, so thanks for that. If I don't get chance to thank you later, I give you my thanks now. You and Shirley.'

'It was nothing really, but it's really frightening to think somebody can get killed like that, only yards away from where other folks are. We never heard a thing, Mr Clifton, not a thing. Shirl says she'll never go in the park again, not after what happened there.'

'I can't say I blame her, Alan. Now, before we leave you, how well did you know Mr Swainby?'

'As I said, not really well at all, he was just the chap who lived in the basement near my flat.'

'Did he follow you and Shirley to the park, do you think?'

'Well, yes, he was behind us if that's what you mean. Or behind Shirl when we came out of the pictures. I stayed behind to go to the gents and said I'd catch her up, and if I didn't I'd meet her on our usual seat. When

I came out I could see her ahead of me, she was walking towards the park, the South Gate entrance that was, with Mr Swainby walking behind her. I saw him walking behind and must admit I didn't like it, her being alone like that so I ran and passed him, then caught up with her and we walked into the park together.'

'That was probably the best thing you could have done, Alan. Now tell me this, was anyone else following Shirley and Mr Swainby?'

'Well, there was a lot of people about, the pictures had just turned out so there was folks milling about all over, some behind walking my way and some ahead of us, laughing and joking like they do . . . I can't put names to them if that's what you mean. I wasn't really taking much notice of them.'

'You can see the direction of my questioning?' asked Clifton. 'Suppose someone had seen Swainby following Shirley, who was alone at the time, if only for a few minutes. Not knowing you were going to catch up to her. Could someone have been keeping a watchful eye on her, a protective eye perhaps? Someone who knew Swainby?'

'Well, I wouldn't know about that. Whoever it was didn't follow us into the park, only Swainby came into the park behind us, I'd swear to that.'

'Are there other ways into the park from the bottom, the South Gate?'

'There's just the one gate on that bottom side of the park, Mr Clifton.'

'I know, but you said you played there as children; don't children find other ways into parks? Over walls and railings, through neighbouring gardens, that sort of thing?'

'Well, yes, kids do but not last night. I'm sure there was no-one apart from us although, like I said, I suppose somebody could have gone in without us knowing.'

'Right, well, I don't think I need to keep you here any longer, Alan, thanks for talking to us. Now I have to write all this down in long hand – which is why my sergeant has been so quiet, he's been taking notes. You'll need to read through what he has written and then sign it. But you can get back to your work now, I'll see you in a few minutes.'

Half an hour later, they were speaking to Shirley Brown in Harker's Shop and she told the same story as Alan. Like him, she had not noticed a young man dressed in black anywhere in the park.

She'd not been aware of anyone going into the park ahead of them but upon being questioned about those few minutes of walking alone, she had become aware of being followed by the man she now knew as Swainby. She had not been unduly concerned because there were people around, cinema-goers like herself. And when Alan had caught up with her, she had forgotten any momentary fear – but now it had returned.

'This morning, one of the women at work here said Mr Swainby was a rapist, Mr Clifton, that he used to live in Hildenley and had had to leave because a butcher tried to kill him for attacking his wife . . . I mean, he might have attacked me . . . .'

'We didn't tell your Alan about Swainby's past, Shirley,' Clifton acknowledged. 'But yes, he was a known rapist, he has convictions and I have heard the story of the butcher chasing him away from Hildenley.'

'But he never attacked me or Alan, and never said anything to us. If somebody was following him, they must have known who he was . . .' and she shuddered. 'It's dreadful but I never saw anybody looking as if they were watching him.'

'I want you to try and remember who might have followed you out of the cinema, Shirley. It might be someone who recognized Swainby and there might have been a confrontation later in the park. If you can remember any of those people who emerged with you or soon afterwards, give me a call. I'll give you time to think about it, and I'll contact you later. I'll be at Hildenley Police Station if you want to contact me, and if it was really urgent, someone would find me for you. Don't be frightened to get in touch, it could be very important however minor it might be.'

'Yes, thank you. I understand.'

And so they left behind a very frightened but very relieved young woman. But it did seem that Swainby's reputation had lived on in this town in spite of his long absence. It seemed that someone might have realized why he was following the lone Shirley last night, someone who knew Swainby and his past. Out of a town of 25,000 inhabitants, it could be almost anyone. So did Shirley have brothers? Or a father? Or was there another young man who fancied her? That meant further enquiries into the girl's background. And how significant was it that they had not seen the mystery man in black? Could he have gone into the park some distance ahead of the cinema leavers? If so, it was perfectly feasible that the young couple hadn't noticed him. The only person who claimed to have seen him was Sergeant Simpson; he said he'd seen him emerging from the park but his description was too vague to be of any real value.

'Come along, Sarge,' said Clifton to Burrows. 'Let's get back to the nick to see how things are progressing.'

CHAPTER 8

WHILE Clifton and Burrows had been busy with their interviews, Sergeant Simpson was calling at houses along Park Road in his attempt to find anyone who might have noticed relevant events in the park.

The splendid houses formed a long, handsome, graceful and very slightly curved terrace built with white marble-like frontages and blue slate roofs, each property comprising four storeys, a cellar, a front garden and a back yard. Dating from the Edwardian era, they were all light, airy and spacious, the homes of wealthy people of that period and indeed later. With bay windows to the front on the ground floor and balconies on the second, also facing to the front, all the houses faced south with long narrow gardens also sloping to the south, that is, towards Park Road, with hand gates leading onto the road. Although built originally without garages or even coach houses, most now had garages at the rear where they had been constructed in the large yards. A long lane ran behind all the properties and was wide enough to allow access by motor vehicle to each house, and to permit access by vehicles like dustcarts. Even though some of the houses had been neglected over recent years, they were still a splendid sight and made wonderful homes; some, however, had been turned into flats. Due to their elevated site, even the ground floors over-looked Park Road and the park itself; it was true, however, that the ground floor rooms provided little more than the sight of the boundary wall and the trees which grew just inside it, although, in winter when the leaves had fallen, one could occasionally catch sight of the museum, espe-cially when the morning sun touched its eastern wall.

From the upper storeys, however, one could look down into the park, albeit with a limited view due to bordering trees, although the winter, when the trees were bare, afforded more extensive views into the parkland.

Having known these houses for almost all his working life, and also knowing many of the residents, Sergeant Simpson adopted a methodical approach to his task. It was quite simple. He would begin at No. 1 and work his way along to No. 50, ticking off each property after speaking to at least one of the residents and in the case of flats, tick off the number of each flat as he spoke to the occupant. He knew from experience that these houses were home to an interesting variety of people, old and young alike, rich and poor, those in work and those retired, and even one or two mysterious youngsters who rented basement flats, paying their way without any sign of a regular job. He knew that not everyone would be at home this morning but he would return and keeping returning until he had spoken to everyone.

As he went about his important chore, however, it became evident that no one had witnessed anything. Last night, people had been sitting in their lounges or preparing for bed, but none had had reason to look out across the park. In most cases, their curtains had been closed against the night. All made the point that it was dark anyway and therefore impossible to observe events in the park. The only time they might notice something would be if anything happened near one of the park's lamp posts or perhaps beneath a street light in Park Road. As things were, no one had heard any cries or screams, shouts or swearing or indeed any commotion or unusual kind of noise last night. Nor had they seen any young men in black.

With each household giving such unhelpful answers, he moved from house to house in the realization that his efforts were probably going to be fruitless. Nonetheless, all he needed was just one person who had witnessed events between nine-thirty and quarter to ten; just one! So he must persist.

As he struggled along the row, sometimes having to climb dozens of steps up to a top storey flat or attic bed-sit, he becamed increasingly weary and was most relieved when the occasional resident, knowing him well, invited him in to sit down and have a cup of tea. But, he told himself, there was no great panic to get this task completed; it was better to do a thorough job than to rush it and miss someone who might just be able to help with his enquiries. And so he plodded along, noting names and addresses as he went, and recording negative statements the whole time.

If his efforts were unproductive, however, they did alert the residents to the fact there had been a murder only yards from their homes. In most cases, this was their first intimation of the crime. At this early stage, word of it had not yet been published in any newspaper nor mentioned on the news and most of the people still at home had not yet ventured into town to hear the story in the shops and cafes. When they did, he knew it would instil fear into most of them, not only those living along Park Road but throughout the town, especially people living alone. The bonus was that it would also get them talking and gossiping and in that way, clues to the identity of the killer might emerge.

Knowing how the news would eventually spread, and how snippets of valuable information might be forthcoming, Sergeant Simpson made sure to ask the people in Park Road to contact the police station without delay if they did learn something useful. Everyone assured him they would, even if they were not quite sure what sort of information he considered 'useful' except that he was seeking a young man in black.

Sergeant Simpson's morning passed without him gleaning the tiniest piece of valuable information – it almost seemed that life in the park, just across the road from those houses, was of no interest whatsoever to some of the residents. His experience showed it was the younger element, usually those in flats, who seemed distinctly uninterested in the minutiae of life immediately beyond their four walls. It was the more senior people who admitted they spent a lot of time during the daylight hours watching events in the park but it was those same people who shut themselves in at night and did not concern themselves with happenings outside. In the darkness of night, they felt safe behind their curtains, walls and locked doors.

Some of his calls took only seconds; he would knock on a door, a head would appear then look startled to find a policeman outside, but that same head was shaken vigorously once he began to ask questions. Either those people did not know anything or had not seen anything, or they did not want to get involved. Others who knew him or those who were lonely welcomed the opportunity for a chat and so he found himself having to balance out his time. By about twenty minutes to one, however, Sergeant Simpson had visited all the houses even if he had not spoken to all the residents, and it was now almost lunch time.

Like all policemen, he was allowed forty-five minutes for his refreshment break; some officers took this in the station with pack-ups of sandwiches and a flask, but others, like him, preferred to go home. Pamela would have a cooked meal ready and it would also provide a much needed sit down and chance to gather his strength. At one o'clock, therefore, Sergeant Simpson reported back to the police station and told the duty constable he was going for his meal break; he'd return at one forty-five. As he was leaving, Superintendent Clifton spotted him outside the enquiry office.

'Ah, Sergeant Simpson. Anything?'

'Nothing yet, sir, no one saw a thing. Or didn't want to see anything.'

'So what's new? People are like that, don't want to get involved. You asked about the mysterious young man in black, I trust?'

'I did, sir, there's no reports of him being seen.'

'Well, if he exists, someone might have seen him. Going for your break?'

'Yes, sir.'

'Good, you look as though you need it! You'll be back before two?'

'Yes, sir.'

'You've seen your doctor?'

'Yes, sir, he thinks it might be anaemia, he's prescribed some pills and has taken some blood for a test, but didn't sign me off although he might recommend a transfusion.'

'Look, I don't want to put any pressure on you to remain on duty but I've arranged a short conference for everyone involved on the enquiry, just as an update. In the muster room at two. You'll be there?'

'I will, sir.'

'There's not a lot to report,' Clifton opened the conference from his standing position on a chair. 'I don't want to keep you from your enquiries but one important factor is that newshounds are now aware of the murder. So far, I've only spoken to the reporter from the local paper but he'll pass the word around. We can expect telephone calls from all over and if it's going to be a long runner without an arrest, we might get the nationals sending reporters. I've told our local chap, whose name is Laurie Stopford, that we are investigating a suspicious death which occurred in Latima Park last night. I have not released the name of the victim on the grounds that his relatives are unaware of his death but I have said it is a man in his late forties or early fifties who is a resident of Hildenley. His name will have got around town, though, so I'm sure the press will pick it up even if they can't print it. I did say he had been savagely beaten, but did not specify exactly how or where. And that's all. I have left that quote with Information Room in case any other pressmen ring up. Also, I've talked to our witnesses. One is a solicitor called Stalker who spoke to Sergeant Simpson at 9.45 last night. He can be eliminated as a suspect. He has a secret woman friend who can provide an alibi but wasn't much good as a witness. He saw nothing, not even Sergeant Simpson's mystery man or anything else of value to this enquiry. And neither did the young man and woman in the park. I do not regard them as suspects nor was their clothing bloodstained when they raised the alarm with PC Stead. But through talking to them, useful information did come to light; for example, when Swainby entered the park via the South Gate around half past nine, he was alone. And they did not see the mystery young man.'

He told them about the exodus from the Coliseum and how Shirley Brown had been alone for a few minutes as she walked along Portland Road towards the south park entrance at the bottom of the park. Clifton commented on the possibility that Swainby could have followed Shirley with the intention of accosting or even raping her, an action probably prevented by Alan Wetherill when he caught up to her. Even though Alan and Shirley had not noticed anyone else entering the park at that time, the possibility must be explored that there *was* someone else. Was it some-one who had recognized Swainby as he was following the girl? A good citizen keeping watch from a distance, even to the extent of entering the park? Another possibility was that Swainby had disturbed someone about to break into the museum. Or had there been a woman there? Waiting for someone near the museum? Waiting outside the toilets? Or could it have been a female look-out for a break-and-entry merchant? Could Swainby have attacked her only to be severely dealt with by her accomplice? Swainby might have had no idea a man was in the vicinity . . . .

'There are plenty of likely scenarios, gentlemen,' said Clifton. 'What we need now is the name of everyone who attended the cinema last night. It will have its regulars. Get people talking about what they did when they left, who they saw and who they talked to. It's important we trace those who walked towards Latima Park via Portland Road. Did they see Shirley Brown? Or Alan Wetherill? Did they see a man following Shirley? Did they see Swainby? A man walking alone? Did they see the young man in black? Had he been to the cinema? You have Swainby's description so you can relay it to them, and if you do find a likely witness, show them Swainby's photo. If he was not following Shirley, was he following another woman? Did that woman's man get his revenge in the park? Did other people manage to get into the park without Shirley and Alan knowing? Is it a popular short cut from the cinema? Did some other lone young woman use it? Did she unwittingly attract Swainby like a moth going towards a light? And then deal with him?'

He paused to let them digest his suggestions but they provided the ingredients for further enquiries and that was pleasing to all. It gave the officers more reasons to ask questions, and to talk about the murder.

Clifton maintained their interest by saying that the drivers and conduct-ors of all buses operating in town late last night and early this morning had been interviewed along with some of their passengers, but none spot-ted the mystery man or anyone who might be a fleeing killer. He was satisfied the man had not boarded any of the buses going along Park Road after quarter to ten nor indeed any bus operating upon the other routes. He'd not been seen at the railway station either – the last train had left at nine anyway, and the first out of Hildenley this morning was at seven. None of the taxi drivers could help either and road checks had not traced anyone hitch-hiking or suspects racing away in a stolen vehicle.

Clifton could not ignore the fact that the killer could have got clear before the police were able to trace him; a motor bike would carry him a long way in a short time. Was that his mode of escape? So far, there were no such reports. Enquiries at the Blue Star had produced nothing useful. They closed at two, but it had been a quiet night with few customers. CID were tracing members who had left at that time but if they had been in the club at nine forty-five, they couldn't have been in the park. Out of all this, the mystery man remained a mystery.

'So who was he?' asked Clifton. 'We know absolutely nothing else about him. What was he doing in the park? Why wasn't he seen there by the witnesses? Where did he go after leaving in such a hurry? Do we have to round up every young man in Hildenley who wears dark clothing, and ask them to account for their movements? If that becomes necessary, then I'll do it but it would take a long time. But I'd prefer it if you can suggest anyone who fits his description. We are still examining Swainby's past but haven't found any relatives yet. I shall not officially release his name until we do – or until I'm satisfied there are none. And I have initiated enquiries in Lincoln to trace that butcher who reputedly had a go at Swainby with a meat cleaver even if it was a long time ago. Thanks to our enquiries and a very efficient bush telegraph system in Hildenley, news of the murder is spreading like wildfire and it will generate the usual rumours and terror; when you're talking to the public, try to kill any stupid rumours and do your best to prevent unnecessary fears spreading among the populace. The park is still closed to the public, by the way, and so is the museum, and will remain so today at least. We haven't found the murder weapon but we are still searching. So there you are, you're up to date. Back to your enquiries, and thanks for what you've done so far. Remember, listen to gossip, get under the underbelly of life in this town, dig deep, stir up the muck.

Someone will know who did this, and why. And consider this – I think the killer's still in town. If he is, it means we *can* find him. Now, me and Sergeant Burrows had very little sleep last night so we're going to kip down in a couple of cells for an hour or two. We don't want disturbing unless there's some really important news. I'll awake at five thirty and we'll have another update conference at six. Right, back to your duties.'

There was a good deal of muttering and murmuring as the officers in uniform and in the CID, prepared to resume to their enquiries. News of the cinema incident had regenerated some into seeking new areas of enquiry and then Clifton called, 'Sergeant Simpson?'

'Sir?'

'What are your next plans?'

'As I got nothing from the people living to the north of the park, I thought I'd try the houses on the south side, sir, and in view of what you said about the cinema leavers, I think that could beneficial. A lot of them walk home that way and some who live in the high side of town often take a short cut home through the park. Someone living along that road might have seen something.'

'Fine, but you're fit to do that, are you? I can always find you a sitting down job, statement reading, filing or something.'

'Yes, sir, I'll be OK. It won't be too strenuous.'

'Fair enough. Do what you can around those houses, then report back here when you're ready. And don't work till you drop, don't be afraid to give up, Sergeant, there's nothing wrong in doing that that if you're as ill as you look. I don't want to be responsible for making you worse than you are . . . .'

'Understood, sir.'

And so Sergeant Simpson resumed his enquiries.

As Sergeant Simpson was walking along Portland Road which led past the southern boundary of Latima Park, Inspector Burn and his team were concluding yet another thorough search. In daylight, they had literally combed every inch of the parkland, looking beneath shrubs and plants, inside the fish pond, checking every rockery, looking in the dustbins behind the museum and the litter bins around the park, examining the inside of the toilet block, looking along wall tops and in flower beds. Not a square inch of the grounds had been overlooked and even though Burn knew that the best place to conceal a stone was among other stones, the search had proved fruitless. Not only had it failed to trace the murder weapon, it had not yielded any other clue which might lead to the killer, such as footprints in the flower beds, discarded clothing stained with blood or any other piece of evidence.

Burn was in possession of a plaster cast of the stone's shape but so far none had matched the cast nor had they borne bloodstains. He had almost reached the point where he must tell Clifton he considered it a waste of manpower to search any further in the park.

They could now move into neighbouring gardens with fewer officers, for some of his men would be better employed making enquiries in the town, trying to find witnesses or the mystery man. As Inspector Burn pondered his next move, he strolled down to the South Gate, hoping he might find some inspiration, some hint that there was a place he could have overlooked. That's when he saw Sergeant Simpson walking along Portland Road, about to begin his enquiries in the houses opposite the South Gate. The inspector was standing just inside that gate near a small ornamental tree, sneaking a swift cigarette during his few moments of leisure. A uniformed constable, preventing unauthorized access to the park, stood discreetly at a distance.

'Hello, Sarge,' he called, for it was evident the sergeant was deep in thought and might not have seen him. 'How's it going? Anything important turn up at the conference? We couldn't attend – we're far too busy!'

'Oh, hello, sir, didn't see you,' Sergeant Simpson halted and greeted Inspector Burn, then told him what had transpired, emphasizing the exodus from the Coliseum cinema, the fact Swainby might have followed someone along this very route and that the mystery man in black had not been traced.

'It makes sense,' acknowledged Burn. 'I've often thought people could be wandering around the park without others seeing them or knowing they were there. If you're over there to the west, you'd hardly be likely to see someone walking up the paths on the east, especially at night with the trees in leaf. I must say I think that young couple's insistence they were alone in the park has to be taken with the proverbial pinch of salt. We can't lose sight of the fact that even if those people never saw anyone, someone else *could* have been walking around in here. After all, it covers a large area and it was dark. And a man in black could easily merge with the shadows especially if he wanted to be unseen.'

'I agree,' said Sergeant Simpson. 'I've often walked through here at night and been surprised by others already walking around or just sitting quietly on a bench. Trees and shadows at night can hide a lot in spite of the lights.'

'Well, it's empty now, we've still got it closed, the museum too. Which means I can take time off for a crafty drag!' The inspector smiled as he puffed at his cigarette. 'I call it my thinking time if anybody asks what I'm doing! I'd say you were doing a spot of thinking just now, Sarge, it looked as though you were deep in thought. So what's your mission in these parts?'

'Door to door enquiries,' and Simpson waved his hands to indicate the houses at the other side of Portland Road. 'I've done those along Park Road, nobody saw a thing. I'll have to go back sometime though, some of the residents were out.'

'They never do see anything, or if they do they don't appreciate the value of what they see.'

'So you've not found the murder weapon?'

'We've looked at hundreds of bits of stone, Sarge, all shapes and sizes, and none fits the bill. I had no idea there were so many lumps of stone in a park this size, you never notice them when you're just strolling around but just you try finding one particular piece! We've even searched the goldfish pond. Not a sign of it. To be honest, I'm not convinced it's here now. I know you said the mystery man wasn't carrying anything but he might not be the killer; the killer might have taken it with him and got rid of it. It could be miles away, thrown over a hedge somewhere . . . .'

'It all depends how big it was,' said Simpson. 'You can easily carry a small lump, a couple of pounds or so. If a man carried a small piece, he could do so without anyone noticing it. And a small piece can do a lot of damage to someone's skull when wielded by a pair of strong hands, especially if the skull's a very thin one.'

'I realize that, but if you've killed someone with it, you'd still want to get rid of it at the first opportunity.'

'I agree. So have you tried the roof?' asked Sergeant Simpson, a suggestion which only occurred to him at that precise moment.

'Roof? What roof?'

'The roof of the museum, sir. It's flat. Or the toilets' roofs, they're flat as well. Once when I was coming through the park I found a couple of lads, they'd kicked their football and it had gone up there, onto the museum roof. Stuck up there out of sight in the middle of the roof. They thought I was wonderful because I gave one of them a leg up and he scrambled up with a bit of help from me and found it. And he found some discarded beer bottles and a schoolboy's cap as well. All sorts get chucked up onto that roof, sir.'

'But could chummy lob a heavy stone up there?'

'It goes back to what I've just said, it depends on the size and weight of the stone. When you're desperate, you can do all sorts of amazing things. But I don't think the weapon could have been a very large stone. He'd not be able to wield it as a weapon if it was too heavy. I reckon the killer could have thrown it up there in his rush to leave the scene. That roof is not very high and it is certainly very convenient for hiding something, being so close to the murder scene.'

'There'd be no way the killer could have got a helping hand, would there? The parks people don't leave ladders lying about, do they? Or the museum staff?' Inspector Burn was now pondering the very real possibility that the murder weapon could have been tossed onto that low flat roof. He should have searched up there.

'Dustbins, sir, there's a couple of dustbins at the back of the museum. Metal ones with good strong lids. You could stand on one of those and lob a stone onto the roof. Or lob it from ground level if it was fairly small.'

'Would a fleeing murderer make time to do that?' Burn asked.

'Probably not, but you could toss a small stone onto the roof from ground level, I'm sure of that, sir. We could always test it. It's a very low roof as you know. Ten feet or so? They say the museum looks like a shoebox!'

'I know it's a low building, Sarge, but to be honest, I hadn't searched that roof. It never occurred to me chummy might have tossed the stone up there. You'd never think anyone could think of that, let alone actually do it! Not with a lump of stone big enough to crack someone's skull like an egg shell. But I'm making excuses, Sarge, anything is possible. Right, that's my next job! Coming?'

'I can spare a few minutes,' agreed Sergeant Simpson.

'You know the people who live around here,' said the Inspector. 'Who would have a ladder we could borrow?'

'Archie Glenn just over the road, sir. I know him well.'

'Right you go and ask him, and I'll send a couple of my team down to collect it. You don't look well enough to be carrying heavy ladders about the place.'

Five minutes later, a pair of constables arrived at Archie Glenn's spacious house and collected a heavy wooden ladder hanging upon his garage wall. Sergeant Simpson thanked Archie, whom he had known for the past twenty years, and together the constables and Simpson re-entered the park and made their way up the sloping path towards the museum.

Inspector Burn was waiting and reminded them to step away from the place the body had rested.

'Any suggestions, Sarge?' he asked Simpson. 'You've done this before.'

'Not with the luxury of a ladder, sir,' laughed Simpson. 'But looking at the place the body was found and the likely escape route along the paths, I'd say this end, sir, the western end. It's the nearest.'

The twelve foot ladder was easily long enough to permit one of the constables to climb up to roof level and look across the expanse before him and, if necessary, he could then climb higher and step onto the roof. Burn despatched PC Brian Lumley skywards and once he was able to peer across the surface, he stood still and looked at the scene before him.

'There's all sorts up here, sir,' he shouted down to the inspector. 'Half bricks, stones, beer bottles, hats, an old shoe, bits of wood, empty bean tins . . . you name it, folks have thrown it up here. It looks as if they've thrown things up here rather than use the litter bins – in fact, this is one huge rubbish dump!'

'How about our murder weapon then?' returned Burn.

'I'll have to take a closer look, sir. It's hard to recognize anything among all this debris. Would you believe . . . there's quite a lot of stones. That's if the roof will bear my weight.'

'Flat roofs are made to take the weight of men, Lumley, so they can be maintained. So take a look for a bloodstained stone or brick – but if you see what looks like our weapon, don't touch it. Leave it alone, note its position and we'll call in scenes of crime to take charge of it. They'll need to test any bloodstains to see if they match Swainby's and to see if it bears fingerprints.'

Sergeant Simpson knew that a stone of the rough kind in this park would not yield any fingerprints even under the most stringent of laboratory conditions but the one used to kill Swainby could be identified by blood adhering to it. And so PC Lumley, a twelve stone constable some thirty years old clambered onto the roof. He began to walk around with his head down and within a few minutes, he found something.

'Sir, on the northern edge, not far from the gutter. A middle-sized stone, about six or eight inches long, I'd say, four or five inches wide and two or three inches deep. Square at one end . . . and it looks bloodstained. Certainly it's got reddish-brown discolouration at its square end. It's a sort of triangular shape with a blunt end, and sharp corners, not very thick but about the area of a man's open hand. Easy enough to wield single-handedly, I'd say.'

'Right, brilliant!' praised Burn. 'Leave it there . . . hang on up there a while until I get the plaster cast to make a comparison. Don't touch anything but compare the shape of the cast with the shape of the stone . . .' and off he went. Five minutes later, Burn returned with the plaster cast, passed it up to Lumley who, using only his eyes, visually matched the two items.

'It matches, sir, at least it does so far as I can tell with the naked eye.'

'Brilliant . . . absolutely wonderful! Right, Lumley, you found it with a little help from Sergeant Simpson, so you can come down then go and inform Superintendent Clifton. Tell him what it is and where it is and say I suggested we get scenes of crime to come and photograph it without delay, then they can take it away for tests.'

'Sir,' and so Brian Lumley descended the ladder and went about his mission. It would take five minutes or so to reach the police station and in the meantime, Inspector Burn said to Simpson:

'Sarge, the ladder. It could be useful when our experts arrive. Will Mr Glenn let us hang on to it? For a day or two if necessary?'

'I'm sure he'll not object, sir, I'll square it with him.'

'Thanks. It will be safe here, the park will remain closed until we've completed work on this. I'll personally ensure he gets it back. Meanwhile, I can rest my teams but I won't dismiss them until we've confirmed this is what we're looking for. And I will make sure Superintendent Clifton is aware of your part in this.'

'Thanks, sir, it was nothing.'

'It was not nothing, Sergeant! It's saved us hours of further searching and it's located what is surely the murder weapon – that's a major break-through by any standards! We'll remain for a while to guard the scene until the boffins turn up. You did a good job. Thanks again.'

'OK, sir, I'm just pleased we got a result. Well, I don't think I'm needed here now, I'll go and tell Archie Glenn about his ladder then knock on a few more doors.'

The houses were a curious mixture of structures. Fronting the road was a long terrace of beautiful houses very similar to those which over-looked the park to the north – spacious, handsome rooms set in four storeys – but behind the terrace was a seemingly disorganized array of more modern buildings. These were semi-detached and detached houses which had sprung up over the years as parcels of land had become avail-able, and they now spread across the former open space behind the terrace to produce a veritable estate of post war properties. Each house was much smaller than those in the beautiful terrace which in turn meant there were a lot of people for interview by Sergeant Simpson. The prospect of cups of tea and buns, with frequent rests, and the possibility he might uncover some useful information, made him warm to the task. That afternoon, Sergeant Simpson knocked on a lot more doors.

Five minutes after leaving the park, PC Lumley found no one in Hildenley Police Station with whom to share his success.

'They're all out in town,' Jim Stewart, the office duty constable told him. 'Except Superintendent Clifton and Sergeant Burrows, they're having a short nap in the cells.'

'I must talk to Mr Clifton,' said Lumley. 'It's important.'

'I was told not to interrupt him or his sergeant unless it was something very important, like an arrest. They've asked me to wake them at half five.'

'What about Superintendent Firth?'

'Oh, well, yes, he's in his office but the investigation's nothing to do with him, not now Clifton's in charge.'

'I'd better talk to him, Jim. Someone's got to call out scenes of crime and that forensic chap. I can't do it without the authority of a senior officer.'

'Fair enough, go and knock on his door, he won't bite your head off.'

PC Lumley walked down the steps and knocked on the door. 'Come,' shouted a voice from within. PC Lumley entered and came to attention on the rug before the great man's desk but he did not salute as neither was wearing a cap.

'Sir,' he said. 'I've just come from Inspector Burn in the park; we're sure we've found the murder weapon, a piece of stone. He told me to come and arrange for it to be examined by scenes of crime or someone from the forensic lab.'

'It's not me you need to talk to, Lumley. Detective Superintendent Clifton's in charge.'

'Yes, sir, I know but he's asleep in the cells and doesn't want to be disturbed unless we've arrested the murderer. And there's no one else of authority in the station, sir, they're all out in town, making enquiries.'

'Fair enough, so what do you want of me?'

'Just permission to call scenes of crime out, sir, and Mr Fisher from the lab.'

'Well, that's no problem. If this stone is the weapon, it must be examined at the scene. That's vital, so yes, ring them with my authority. I'll make sure Mr Clifton is told when he awakes. So what exactly is this weapon, Lumley?'

'It's a piece of stone thought to have been used to strike the deceased, sir. It was taken from a rockery and found on the roof of the museum. It's possible the killer tossed it up there in the hope it would never be found. Sergeant Simpson suggested it might be on the roof, sir. I went up a ladder at Sergeant Simpson's suggestion.'

'This is very good news. I know Mr Clifton will be delighted. All right, Lumley, go and ring whoever you need to and tell them you have my authority.'

And so Brian Lumley went into the quiet of the muster room to make his calls. The scenes of crime investigators said they would go direct to the museum and should arrive within the hour. They would report to Inspector Burn. When Mr Fisher was contacted, however, he said his presence was not really necessary if the scenes of crime officers attended. They would photograph the stone *in situ*, remove it and later test it for fingerprints.

When that had been done, the stone, duly labelled, would be placed in a scientific box and taken by car to the North Eastern Forensic Science Laboratory in Rutland Drive, Harrogate, where the blood which was apparently staining it could be compared with that of the deceased person, samples of which had already been taken. Mr Fisher said he would later return to Hildenley mortuary to compare the alleged weapon with the fractures in the skull of the deceased and he felt confident they could prove Swainby had been killed with that stone. He passed his congratulations to Inspector Burns and his team. Finding it had given a wonderful boost to the enquiry, a genuine breakthrough.

As PC Lumley returned to his work with Inspector Burn, he knew he had played his part in helping to trace the murderer.

CHAPTER 9

A T six o'clock that Friday evening, after their intensive day's work, detectives and uniformed officers once more assembled in Hildenley Police Station to be updated by Detective Superintendent Clifton. Each of the sergeants and detective sergeants in charge of teams had reported to him prior to his address and he was in a position to relay the information to all. He was a big believer in letting the troops know what was happening even at the end of their working day. The big man had had very few hours' sleep but was sufficiently refreshed to lead the next stage of the investigation even if he now intended to release many of these officers. They could go off duty, have a good rest during the evening and night, and be ready to continue tomorrow; already, many had worked long hours for little return upon their labours.

From his stance on the chair in the muster room, Clifton began.

'First, some very good news,' he beamed upon them with obvious pleasure. 'We have found the murder weapon. Or to be precise, we have found what we believe is the murder weapon; we are awaiting confirmation. It was found in Latima Park this afternoon and is being examined as I speak. For your information only, the weapon was a piece of stone taken from a rockery and hidden on the roof of the museum. That is not for the press or the public. If I find anyone has slipped that gem to the press or into the public domain, I shall jump on the offender from a great height – and I am no lightweight.

'The rest of the news is not bad but not very good. We have not made any real progress in spite of your hard work. We have not found the mystery man and no one has any idea who he might be. We must keep asking and we must keep looking, all of us. We have not produced any more prime suspects and have not found any more material witnesses which means this crime is becoming notorious for its lack of witnesses and, to be honest, its lack of suspects. I have not lost sight of the fact, though, that there might not be much else anyone can tell us. Can we therefore learn from the possibility there may be no more witnesses, no more suspects? Is the solution to this staring us in the face? Have we over-looked the obvious? Have we discovered enough about Swainby's life both here and further afield? Local gossip, which is always a good source, has not produced any gems of real interest either. Another nil return! DS Huntley and DC Thorne are combing Hildenley and district to try and find relations or friends of people who might have been attacked by Swainby when he was living here twenty years ago. I have not called them to this meeting because theirs is a rather specialized line of enquiry which only they can pursue but they have nothing to report at this stage.'

He went on to say that once the scenes of crime team had concluded their examination of the museum roof, he intended to re-open the park, probably this evening in time for the weekend. He would make sure the museum was free to re-open tomorrow morning too. He reminded his officers that tomorrow was Saturday when different people could be expected in town – someone other than office workers and residents. It was market day with stalls selling fruit and vegetables, meat, bric-a-brac, antiques, toys, knitware, cakes, household goods, fish and clothing and so it would mean that the detectives would have more people to question.

The visitors might include people whose son or husband had stayed late in town on Thursday. He wanted the uniform officers, and some of the CID when they returned tomorrow, to examine the possibility that the killer might be someone who came into town regularly from one of the villages, perhaps to work, and who had stayed late last night for some reason. If such a person was in the habit of regularly staying in town after work, meeting friends, working late, going to evening class, the cinema or out for a meal, then his presence on a late bus or even in a taxi would not be considered unusual. It was another line of enquiry, a delicate one because Clifton did not wish to throw suspicion upon innocent people, whatever their motives for working late at the office! There could be people among the incomers who might have known Swainby and his reputation. He asked his officers to use their imaginations as they spread their enquiries.

'Tomorrow is another day,' he told his men. 'All those not working the late shift this evening may go home. Book off at six thirty, claim any extra hours as overtime and I will approve it for payment from my budget.

Later this evening, Sergeant Burrows and I will also go home, leaving the late shift to continue our enquiries. All that can be done at the scene has been done; now it is down to you lads to make the right enquiries, to find witnesses and even the person responsible. We will resume at nine tomorrow morning when you'll be given another run-down of any overnight developments. By then, the park will be open and all life will be returning to normal in Hildenley – except for us. Now, any questions?'

There were none.

He bade them goodbye and called, 'Sergeant? The car. Take me up to the park, I want to see that lump of stone and where it was found, then take me to the mortuary to have another look at the damage it did. Then I can sleep peacefully in my bed tonight.'

And among those who went home, undoubtedly more exhausted than the others, was Sergeant Simpson.

'You look dreadful, Dick!' Pam was clearly shocked by his appearance as he returned home and kissed her. 'You can't go on like this, forcing yourself to continue . . . you did see the doctor, didn't you? You're not just saying you did to keep me quiet?'

'I saw him, honest,' he began to take off his uniform tunic, tie and boots, then slumped into an easy chair in their comfortable lounge and exuded a long, heavy sigh. 'He took a blood sample, he said he thought I was anaemic; it's being sent away for analysis. Because it's a weekend, it could take a few days.'

'Isn't there anything he can do? You look like a ghost, as pale as a sheet and so drawn.'

'He gave me some iron pills and talked of a transfusion . . . it's been a long day, Pam, with no let-up since last night . . . I'm whacked. It was a short night but I didn't sleep after finding Ted. I'll be better after a good night's rest. The doctor said I should drink stout, that puts iron into the blood as well, so he said, as well as stuff like red meat and greens. I hope I'm going to be fit enough for work tomorrow.'

She came closer and put a hand to his forehead. 'I think you should get Dr Ewart to see you again. I'll ring him in the morning before he goes out on his rounds. You're so hot, Dick, you're like an oven . . . .'

'I'll be all right, just let me sit here for a while.'

She looked at him with clear concern then said, 'Supper's in the oven. I wasn't sure what time you'd be coming home so it's a casserole, beef.'

'It will be fine, I can wait, it's just what I need,' he smiled faintly. 'I'll go and get changed, I'll feel better if I get out of this uniform and have a wash.'

She watched him struggle up from the deep chair, moving almost as if he was an old man, and then he made his way across the floor towards the doorway which led to the foot of the stairs. He faltered momentarily and caught hold of the jamb to steady himself, then continued without a word. Pamela was worried – this deterioration was so sudden. Was it something to do with Ted's murder?

To try and forget all that his death could mean to her family, Pamela went into the kitchen to check the progress of the meal; even though Dick ate a cooked but very light meal at lunchtime, he liked another in the evening. Especially on Fridays – perhaps it was a legacy from his younger days when fish-and-chips suppers were the standard diet for Friday nights! Tonight, though, it was beef.

'You know Ian's expected for supper,' she called after him. 'He's not rung to say he can't come, and wasn't he going to buy that car he wanted?'

'Yes, yes, I had remembered. I was going to see him at work but hadn't the time,' he called from the foot of the stairs. 'What time's he expected?'

'Any time now, he always likes a beer before we eat,' she reminded him unnecessarily. 'Look, go and get changed, I'll see to him, I've got some bottles of beer in and some stout as it happens. And later I've got to take Mrs Blenkin's dog for its walk, I promised her. She's gone to see her mother in Middlesbrough and isn't expected back until late. I said I'd take Ben out for a walk to do his jobs about half nine.'

'No problem,' he began to climb the stairs, using the handrail as a form of leverage as he hauled himself up the steps like someone who had aged prematurely. Pam watched from the kitchen doorway; this was no ordinary case of anaemia . . . . Then the door bell rang, the door was opened and a soft and rather light male voice said, 'Hello, it's only me.'

'Come in, Ian,' Pam called. 'I'm in here, in the kitchen. Dad's upstairs getting changed, he won't be a minute. Have you walked over?'

'No, I brought my new car, the one I told you I was getting. Well, it's second-hand but in very good condition.'

'You must show us it after supper, and maybe take us for a spin?'

'Love to, it goes really well, but I've got the hard top on now, it's a bit on the chilly side to go about with no roof on!'

Ian Simpson was a tall, handsome and very slender man of almost twenty-one; at almost six feet in height, he had a shock of thick black hair worn rather longer than was fashionable for men at that time, a thin pale face and rather delicate high cheekbones.

His eyes were dark with black brows above them to give him an almost evil appearance, especially when his face was paler than normal – as it was now. He wore a black sweat shirt with long sleeves, black trousers, black socks and black, soft-soled shoes. Tonight, however, he seemed rather nervous; that he was a nervous individual was never in dispute but he was adept at concealing his true feelings – a lifetime of teasing had ensured that. Tonight, though, he seemed rather more on edge than usual.

'Are you all right, Ian?' asked Pam, handing him a beer, a glass and a bottle opener. 'You look ill, so pale and sickly. Is something wrong?'

'Not really,' he admitted. 'I took the day off, I had a bad stomach this morning, diarrhoea. I daren't go to work, not with that sort of problem. I rang in, they were very understanding. It's cleared up now, I took some brandy and port mixed in equal portions just like granny used to recommend for stomach troubles, and it seemed to work. I can cope with supper tonight, no problem.'

'Your dad's not very well either,' she said. 'He looks dreadful to me, I'm sure it's more than just tiredness.'

'He's usually as fit as a lop! Mind, he has been saying he's been over-tired for some time now. That's not like him. Is it overwork or something?'

'He looks anaemic, he's been to the doctor.'

'Doctor? Dad doesn't usually bother with doctors! So what did the doctor say?'

'He said it was probably anaemia and took a blood sample for tests. He gave dad some iron pills and said he should drink stout! Luckily, I've got some in. He seems to have taken a turn for the worse since that murder in the park.'

'I know,' whispered Ian. 'Wasn't it dreadful! Everybody's talking about it, I heard about it at lunchtime, when I went out for some fresh air . . . is dad involved?'

'He found the body, he's been working on enquiries ever since. I know it's only one full day since it happened but he did work very late last night, and was up early this morning . . . .'

'He found the body?'

'Yes, just before finishing last night. He hasn't said much about it, I suppose he can't, but he did tell me who it was . . . not that the name's been made public yet.'

Ian looked steadily at his mother, those big dark eyes staring out of his stark white face. 'Who was it, mum?'

'A man called Ted Swainby.'

'Wasn't he a friend of yours?' Ian frowned and averted his mother's gaze.

'Why did you ask that?'

'I thought I'd heard his name mentioned at home, a long time ago.'

'I wouldn't call him a friend,' she responded. 'But we knew him, your dad and me, he used to live here, that was twenty years ago then he moved to Cresslington, that's in Garminghamshire. It seems he came back to Hildenley for some reason.'

'Did I meet him?' asked Ian. 'When I was little maybe?'

'I'm not sure, but I doubt it. Look, you have a look at the *Evening Gazette* while I see to the supper and lay the table. There's more beer if you want it and your dad will be down in a few minutes. Then you can show us your car.'

'Is there something in the *Gazette* about the murder?' asked Ian.

'I don't know, I haven't had time to look at it yet; it only came a few minutes ago.'

As Pamela returned to the kitchen to deal with the meal, Ian settled on the settee with the *Evening Gazette* and was soon absorbed with the report of the murder. It had made the front page headline – 'Man Found Dead In Park' – with a brief account of the finding of a male body in Latima Park, Hildenley. The report, couched in terms which left the readers in no doubt that this was a murder enquiry, explained how the body had been found last night by an unnamed policeman. The body was that of a middle-aged local man, continued the report, but his name was being withheld until relatives had been informed. The report added that some forty detectives were engaged on enquiries and a post mortem had been conducted. At this point, concluded the report, no one was in custody for the crime and enquiries were continuing. It was necessarily brief and lacked any depth, probably because the report had to be in very early so that it met the deadline, but in spite of its brevity, it did put the murder into the public's domain. The press had clearly gleaned most of their information from the townspeople rather than depending on brief news releases from the police; they probably knew the dead man's name too but had courteously refrained from printing it.

Ian sat alone and in silence for quite a long time, until his mother called through from the kitchen, 'Ian, are you all right?'

'Sure,' his voice was faint. 'I'm just reading about the murder . . . how awful, that such a thing could happen here. I mean, it's not as if this is New York or the East End of London, is it? This is Hildenley for God's sake . . . .'

As they spoke, they could hear Dick coming down the stairs, very slowly and very carefully, clutching the handrail for support. Ian rose from his chair.

'Dad! Oh, God, you look absolutely dreadful . . . heavens, I've never seen you like this . . . .'

He went to Dick and took his arm, helping him down the final few steps until he was on the floor, but even then Ian retained his hold and led Dick across the hall and into the lounge. He took him to his favourite easy chair and helped him settle down, placing a cushion behind his back to provide more support.

'Dad, this is dreadful, dreadful . . . what did the doctor say?'

Sergeant Simpson explained once again as Ian sat at his side, the lad's face drawn with anxiety, then Ian said, 'So you have to wait for God-knows-how-long before you know what's wrong with you?'

'Dr Ewart will speed my sample through the system if he's concerned,' Dick managed a weak smile. 'If it is anaemia, then we can deal with it, there's tablets, the right food, then a blood transfusion if it gets really bad. I should know more next week, and then I can set about recovering from it. Mum's going to call him in tomorrow for another look at me. Now, how about finding me a stout?'

'Yes, sure,' and Ian went to fetch a bottle which he opened before bringing it to his father, complete with glass. And so, as Pam worked in the kitchen and set the table in the dining room, Dick asked, 'So how was work today?'

'I didn't go in,' Ian said. 'I had a bad stomach, something I ate, but it seems OK now.'

'A good job I didn't try to pop in for a chat, then?' smiled Dick. 'I wanted to have a word but was too busy and last night you'd be at drama class.'

'Yes I was. Mum's told me about the murder. It's in the paper tonight.

He was a friend of yours, wasn't he?'

'The paper doesn't name him, does it?' asked Dick.

'No, Mum told me. It's a Mr Swainby,' she told me.

'It is, but he's no friend of mine. An acquaintance perhaps you could call him, or in my case an unpleasant villain from the past.'

'A revenge attack then, you think?'

'That seems as likely a reason as any other. I'm sure he had enemies, even here, and even after all this time.'

'Look, Dad, you look dreadful and I don't want to trouble you with stories about work, not like this . . . no more murder talk, eh?'

'It's thoughtful of you, yes, I wouldn't want to inadvertently reveal something I'm not supposed to talk about! Let's just say that our enquiries are continuing. Now didn't you tell me you were going to get a car. A sports car, wasn't it?'

'Yes, I got it, it's outside. I came in it tonight.'

'Then you must show it to us. Just give me time to get my strength back then we'll go out for a look. That's what I wanted a chat about, to make sure you got the right insurance – you're a young driver, it's a sports car, you've not many years' driving experience – it all adds to your premium. I wanted to advise you not to go for the cheapest insurance, go for the best.'

'Yes, dad, I know, you told me that when I was thinking of buying it.'

And so, after admiring Ian's car, the family talk got underway as Pamela produced another of her splendid meals which they all enjoyed even if Ian seemed somewhat quiet and incommunicative at times, although he seemed to be making an extra effort to be sociable. Meanwhile, probably thanks to the nourishing meal and his iron pill, Dick summoned sufficient reserves of strength to make Pam and Ian forget his fragile condition. Then as the time ticked away, Pam said, 'I must go and walk Mrs Blenkin's dog, I promised I'd see to him. I'll be no more than half an hour, I'll just take him up the road and back.'

'Well, I must be off soon,' said Ian.

'Stay and talk to your dad, don't go until I return,' she asked in what was almost a plea.

'I wouldn't say no to a trip in your car!' Dick Simpson smiled at his son.

Pam left them, promising to return the moment Ben had done the necessary. Ian handed another bottle of stout to his father but declined another beer because he was driving. Then he sat down, his face almost as pale as his father's; he was showing clear signs of nervousness now that the meal was over and they were alone.

Policeman and ladies' hairdresser. Father and son. Not a father and son by blood though . . . .

'Can I ask you something, Ian?' said Sergeant Simpson after a long and rather embarrassing and telling silence.

'Sure, fire away,' and the lad shrugged his slender shoulders.

'Were you in the park last night? Just before quarter to ten?'

'Why? Are you quizzing me? Am I being questioned about the murder or something?' and there was a flare of temper with more than just a sign of viciousness in his voice which rose in its pitch. Simpson knew he had hit the right spot; in his opinion, Ian's somewhat violent reaction was unexpected but his face revealed everything.

'I thought I saw you,' said Sergeant Simpson. 'Hurrying from one of the top gates.'

'What if I was? It doesn't mean I did anything wrong . . . .'

'No one is suggesting you did, Ian,' there was another long silence between them as Simpson found difficulty in finding the right words. 'Look, if something happened between you and Ted Swainby in the park, then you should tell me, not as a policeman but as your father . . . I want to help you . . . .'

'What makes you think I did something to him?' Ian's voice rose to almost a shriek. 'Why do people always have a go at me, think wrong of me?'

'I found this near his body,' and Sergeant Simpson pulled a Timex watch out of his pocket and showed it to Ian. 'It's yours, the one we gave you on your fourteenth birthday. I found it near Swainby's body in the park last night. It's got your initials on the case and the date of your birthday. There's no doubt it's yours, Ian, I recognize it. I bought it for you, remember? And I see the strap's broken.'

'So I lost it when the strap broke . . . it could have happened any time.'

'I haven't shown this to anyone, Ian, not even your mother. None of the investigating team knows about it either. I could get sacked for removing this from the murder scene, it's material evidence. Now this is just between you and me, you must believe me. If anything happened between you and Ted Swainby, you must tell me, then I can help you to avoid being prosecuted.'

The young man just stared at his father, disbelief on his face. 'Avoid being prosecuted . . . ?'

'Yes, Ian. For murder.' Sergeant Simpson wondered if he was outrageously wrong but decided the only way to solve this matter was to confront it. 'You're thinking – why should I do that? Why should I, a policeman nearing retirement, put my pension in jeopardy by interfering with evidence at the scene of a murder? Why should I risk everything to get you off the hook? Why did I risk all that by preventing your watch from getting logged among the evidence found at the scene? I'll tell you why, Ian – Ted Swainby was a rapist of the very worst kind, a killer too, a violent and vicious man, a danger to all women. Whatever happened to him in that park was probably well deserved and I would not want you to be punished if you did hit him. He would deserve everything that happened to him. He should have been hanged years ago. Men like him don't deserve to live. I hope hanging's never fully abolished. If it *was* you, you did a good job for society but if I am to help you avoid being arrested, I must know the truth, all of it. I will not have you punished for a rat like him!'

Ian paused a long time, then said, 'He said you were his friends, you and mum.'

'He told you? You mean you've talked to him? You know him? How's all this come about?' Sergeant Simpson was shocked by this.

'I've spoken to him.' Ian didn't elaborate; his stance was almost defiant.

'We weren't friends, Ian, you must understand that from the start.'

'He was my father, wasn't he? My natural father,' Ian spat out the words. The shock caused Simpson to catch his breath . . . . How did Ian know all this? What did he know? What had Swainby told him? Simpson paused for a long time, not knowing quite how to react to this sudden and unexpected response and found himself staring hard at the lad in front of him. Ian's eyes were now filling with tears.

'How did you know, Ian?'

'He told me. It's true, isn't it?'

'He told you? When, for God's sake?' cried Sergeant Simpson.

'Four or five weeks ago, he came to live here, he found out where I worked, he waited outside the salon and insisted on talking to me . . . he told me he was my father. I didn't believe him but he kept on and on, harassing me. I think he came to Hildenley to find me, to tell me this because I'm nearly twenty-one. He said that's why he had come, to see me now that I'm nearly a man,' Ian was weeping openly now.

'Did you believe him then?'

'Not for a long time. I wanted nothing to do with him and told him so, but he persisted, he came to the salon night after night and waited outside, in the darkness, waiting to catch me after work and all the time telling me he was my real father. He showed me photos of himself when he was young and it was awful, because in my mirror I could see the likeness . . . . I came to think he might be telling the truth, I didn't want to believe it but he kept on and on . . . .'

'It is true, I can't deny it. We didn't want you to know, you're our son, and always have been, always will be. We kept it a secret because we love you, Ian, we want the best for you.'

And Ian broke down, sobbing and sobbing. Simpson left him alone for a few minutes.

'You've got his temper too!' Simpson tried to inject a lighter tone as Ian sniffed back the tears. 'I remember what you did to that lad who played football with that kitten you brought home . . . .'

'Dad, this is dreadful, you've no idea what this has done to me . . . you've no idea at all . . . why didn't you tell me?'

'Your mum wanted you to know, but I resisted, I was so proud of you, am so proud of you. You are my son, Ian, and I love you, we both love you. We did it to protect you.'

'Dad, I've cried my eyes out this week, last week, the week before . . . alone in my flat . . . I couldn't talk to anyone, not you, not mum, not even Swainby . . . I've tried to hide my feelings, tried to keep it from people at work, tried to carry out my normal life. I'm good at that, acting a part. I can put on a good show, I've been doing that all my life, putting on an act, not being my real self. I have to say I'm good at hiding my feelings, well, almost all of the time . . . but you've no idea what it's been like . . . I didn't go to work today, I couldn't face it . . . I wasn't ill. Maybe you realized that.'

'Ian, we need to talk, and I need to tell you all about this, but not with your mother present. I will tell her you know about your parentage, and I'll tell her how you got to know, but I don't want her to know about your role in the park last night . . . it was you, wasn't it? You hit him?'

'I had to, dad, really I had to . . . I lost my temper . . . .'

'Just like him?'

'Yes, just like him. Like father, like son! I've inherited his temper, I know I have . . . I was so sorry about what I did to that boy who hurt my kitten . . . afterwards, I mean. Not at the time. Like last night . . . at the time it was the only thing I could do, I couldn't stop myself . . . .'

'Right, stop right there. You and I must go for a walk, right now, and level with each other. About everything. And I don't want mum to walk in on this discussion, this is between you and me, man to man, father and son.'

'Yes, I'd like that . . . I need to talk, I really do . . . .'

'Without anyone else knowing what we're going to discuss.'

'You're not fit to go for a walk! Dad, you do look ill, very ill . . . are you sure about this?'

'As sure as I can be about anything!'

'There's my car,' the tears were flowing now but Ian, the considerate Ian, was thinking of the man he'd always called Dad. 'You said you wanted a ride in it. Come on, I'll show you its paces.'

'All right, you take me for a drive. I'll leave a note for mum.'

He scribbled a note saying, 'We've gone for a short drive in Ian's new car, back soon. xx Dick.' He placed it on the kitchen table and put a mug at one corner to hold it secure and to bring it to Pam's attention. Then they went outside to Ian's car.

CHAPTER 10

IAN'S car was an MGA hardtop in royal blue which he had bought from a garage in Hildenley. It had had four previous owners but it was in remarkably good condition with no rust on the bodywork. With two doors and rather cramped space inside, it had sound brakes, good tyres, a new exhaust pipe and an engine which had been well maintained. According to the garage, all its previous owners had lavished care upon it, it had been serviced regularly and it was even fitted with a radio. The hardtop could be removed speedily when required and it was capable of eighty miles an hour in safety, with a hint it might even touch a hundred or more if the conditions were right.

Ian asked Simpson if he would like to drive but Dick declined with thanks, saying he was not really fit enough, he'd had a few drinks and besides, this was Ian's chance to show his father how well he could handle this lively vehicle. Ian said he would take it to the top of Beacon Hill and back again, a round trip of some ten miles which would only take a few minutes. If they wanted to stop for their talk, they could do so on the summit where there were seats, a viewing area and car park. During the trip, however, the noise of the wind whistling past the car's protruding parts was such that no conversation was possible – they could only shout above the hissing noises but in fact, they found they had little to discuss on the journey, other than the car's performance, its acceleration capabilities, its cornering and braking. And then, after an exhilarating drive, they reached the summit where Sergeant Simpson said, 'Pull in here, Ian, we've got the place to ourselves.'

During the summer and on fine Sundays at other times of the year, the summit of Beacon Hill was usually very busy; an ice cream van plied its trade as tourists came to enjoy the expansive views from this high point above the town while at night in the summer, courting couples would seek solitude on this isolated site. But now, in late October, the place was deserted. Ian pulled in and drew to a halt with the bonnet facing the view below; they could enjoy the panorama of Hildenley with its lights and shade forming a beautiful picture.

'I like your car, Ian, I think you've found a little cracker! It's a good choice and you drive it well.'

'I had a good teacher, that's police driving techniques for you!' and Ian actually smiled. 'Thanks for that, dad, teaching me.'

There was a long pause, then Sergeant Simpson said, 'I don't like doing this, Ian, but we've got to talk.'

'I know.'

'I want to stress that there's no way I want you punished for a no-good devil of a man like Swainby. So tell me how he came to find you at the salon, and we'll take things from there.'

'Can I ask you something first, Dad? It's been bothering me ever since he turned up. I mean, how did he come to be my father? I must know, you want to truth from me, now I want it from you. He said he and mum had been friends before she married you and he'd made her pregnant. He said she didn't want to marry him and chose you instead.'

'Half truths, Ian, half truths. He raped your mum, that's the truth, just as he raped or attacked many other women. He always used extreme violence while doing so, he was a bastard of the highest order. He's a convicted rapist, Ian, and a serial sex offender and suspected double murderer. He's recently out of prison. So far I've not mentioned his relationship with your mum to any of our enquiry team. I won't unless I'm forced to but it could emerge during their enquiries. I'll have to deal with that if it arises. Swainby never went for trial for raping mum which means it was easy for him to lie about it. He violently attacked her just before our wedding but she decided not to testify against him – I tried not to influence her decision.'

'Why, if he was such a brute, didn't she make him go to court?'

'It all happened just a few days before our wedding and it wasn't long before she knew she was pregnant, with you. She didn't want her child brought up with the stigma of having a convicted rapist as a father and she didn't want the trauma of a court appearance, having to literally bare her soul in public . . . it was her decision even though he attacked her, beat her and raped her when she was returning from the final fitting of her wedding dress.'

'God, that's awful . . . .'

'She got married with bruises all over but they didn't show up on the wedding photos, make-up can hide a lot.'

'Oh my God . . . poor mum . . . .'

'She was wonderful, Ian, you can be proud of her, she was so strong in the face of what she'd gone through, and she thought it would shame him if she went ahead with the wedding as normal. Her parents were marvellous, they'd told friends and neighbours that Pam had been attacked by a drunk without going into the sordid details. They didn't want to spoil the wedding and risk further trouble by somebody having a go at Swainby. I advised them not to take the law into their own hands. The other thing was that I can't father children, Ian. Everything works as it should except I'm infertile, the result of a motor bike accident. I knew before we married, we both knew but we kept it secret from our families. I think I hoped things might mend but they didn't and so when we talked about getting married, we decided to adopt one or even more children after two or three years of marriage, if none arrived. Then you came along! You were our son . . . suddenly we *were* a family. We loved you and cared for you and brought you up with my name on the birth certificate. A honeymoon baby, that's what everyone called you, our honeymoon baby. We never told a soul about who the real father was, there was no need to. You are my son, Ian, our son and that's all that matters. You can see now why we had no wish to spoil your life with the truth about your parentage. I'm only sorry it had to come out like this.'

Ian sat stunned into silence then reached out and touched his father's hand.

'Thanks . . . thanks . . . I don't know what to say, this is all too much . . .' and he began to cry, letting it all come out as his body began to heave with huge sobs as the emotions and trauma of recent weeks overcame him. Sergeant Simpson let him sob and sob as he opened the car door and stepped into the cool night air.

He left Ian alone for nearly quarter of an hour, sobbing the whole time in the confines of the little car and then the boy emerged and came to his side, putting an arm around Simpson's shoulder as they stood together in silence to gaze across the dark light-dotted landscape below. They could see the town's lights grouped in the far distance as a handful of cars passed by. An owl hooted somewhere in the gloom and then they heard a dog bark in an unseen moorland farm.

'I had no idea who he was when he arrived outside the salon,' Ian said eventually, sniffing back more tears. 'It was a few weeks ago. He just appeared out of the darkness one evening as we were closing. He asked if I was Ian Simpson and said he wanted to speak to me. I don't know how he found out where I worked or who I was, but he knew. He told me his name but said nothing about being my father, not at first, he just said he was a friend of you and mum, but asked me not to tell you he'd come back, not yet. All in good time, was what he said.'

'Did he know where you lived?'

'No, just where I worked, he never came to my flat and I didn't invite him, I was very wary of him. I avoided him at first and hoped he'd eventually leave me alone but when he persisted, I thought I ought to talk to him, just to stop him pestering me. He would turn up each evening at the salon, just as we were closing and try to talk to me. I couldn't get away from him and then, after a few visits, I said I would listen to what he had to say just to get rid of him really, and that's when he told me he was my natural father. I didn't believe him, not at first, but he told me about himself and mum, and then, when I looked at him and saw some photos of him as a younger man, well, there was a definite likeness . . . I didn't know what to do. He was quite charming in a funny sort of way, and very persuasive; he said he just wanted to get to know me, his only relative, his flesh and blood, without you knowing because you might want to stop us meeting. He said he'd come specially to find me and meet me. He said I was his only flesh and blood, he used that term a lot and even bought me some presents, a record for my turntable, a picture to hang in my flat, that sort of thing, although I never took him home and he never tried to follow me. I didn't tell you because I didn't want to upset you and mum and to be honest, I had no idea what to do . . . I think he knew I would tell you if he came over a bit too heavy though, so he kept his distance, well, up to a point.'

'If I'd known he was in town, I'd have advised you not to encourage him, Ian, but truthfully I couldn't prevent you talking to him. It's a free country, as they say.'

'He did get nastier as time went on,' Ian had now stopped sobbing. 'He began to tease me.'

'What about?' even as he asked, Sergeant Simpson knew the answer.

'Well, you know, not having a girl friend, being a ladies' hairdresser, being a sissy as he put it. He said he couldn't believe a son of his had turned out like that and said if I wanted to experience the fun of having a woman, he could fix it for me, he said he was good with women, and could charm them into his bed any time he wanted.'

'Charm is not the word I would use! He used brute force to get what he wanted. So this teasing, was it good-natured or do you think he was being vicious?'

'Oh, I think it was good-natured at first, when he was getting to know me a little better, but I sensed it was turning nastier when he realized I didn't want him around.'

'Did anyone see you together? I'm thinking about the enquiries we're making.'

'You mean they might suspect me?'

'We can't ignore the possibility, Ian. If you were seen together, your description will be circulated and you might be questioned. In fact, a vague description of you is already in the files. I provided a description of a young man fleeing from the park, someone dressed in dark clothes, hurrying away at about quarter to ten last night. I had to give that description to the police because I'd already told Geoffrey Stalker, the solicitor, that I'd seen the figure – not absolutely sure it was you at the time and not knowing about Swainby's death. I can't retract it, not now. I did wonder if it was you, it was like you, the way you ran, your carriage and you always wear black, Ian, sweaters and tight trousers. I thought if it had been you, you'd have come to me when you saw me. Instead, you ran away, that made me think it couldn't be you. Now I know why you ran away. As things transpired, Stalker didn't see you but my description is vague enough not to lead directly to you – but you could be pulled in for questioning, just to eliminate you. In your favour, lots of other young men wear black, they'll be questioned as well, as to their whereabouts on Thursday evening. It was when I found your watch near Swainby that I knew you were the man I'd seen hurrying away.'

'So what can we do? More to the point, what can I do? Adopt a change of clothing? I always wear black, both at work and in my free time!'

'Don't change anything, act normal, do everything as you would normally do it. Any deviation from your routine will attract attention and, in view of our enquiries in town, it will also create suspicion. So, are you prepared to tell me exactly what happened last night? I think you should, I really do want to help you.'

Ian did not answer. He hung his head, not looking at his father. Sergeant Simpson pressed on.

'Remember I'm not a policeman asking you to incriminate yourself, I'm your dad trying to help. As I told you, I don't want you arrested for this, not for a man like Swainby. And if I'm to make sure of that, I must know everything.'

'You'll get yourself into trouble, Dad, doing this sort of thing for me.'

'And in my condition, does that matter? I am seriously ill, Ian, I know that even if the doctor hasn't confirmed it.'

'Seriously ill? I thought anaemia could be cured? With pills and trans-fusions and things.'

'Perhaps it can but I have something much worse that anaemia, Ian, even if my doctor won't say so. It's confession time now for both of us, so that's what I'm doing. It might mean you have to care for your mother . . . not even she has any idea how seriously ill I really am and I have no wish to tell her, not just yet. For your ears only, I'm sure I have leukaemia. I've known for quite a while, I know the signs, a friend once caught it. And if it's confirmed, I won't have long to live, Ian, which in turn means I must get the little matter of Ted Swainby sorted out very soon.'

'I don't think I can take any more of this . . .' and Ian burst into tears once again. 'You mean I've lost my natural dad and now, just as if you're telling me you've got flu, you tell me I might lose the only dad I really love . . . .'

Sergeant Simpson flung his arms around his son and they clung together for a long time, both weeping on that lonely hilltop. After a long time, Sergeant Simpson drew away and said, 'Ian, this is going to be tough, there's no point pretending otherwise. You've got to be stronger than you have ever been before. I know you had a tough life as a child, the teasing about being more like a girl than a boy, and more teasing because you are a policeman's son, but all that will have made you strong enough to cope. The future lies with you, Ian, you and your mother, not with me. My time is nearly over. As I've said, I don't want you locked up for anything you did to Swainby, your mum will need you.'

'You're putting a lot of trust in me,' sniffed Ian. 'I don't think I can cope. I'm not practical like you, I don't have your strength.'

'I think you do, and I know you can cope. You've just got to believe in yourself. So, with no one to overhear what you say, tell me about last night. Right from the start. Every tiny bit.'

After a long pause, Ian said, 'He'd been having a go at me recently, about being too much of a pansy for his liking; he said I should get a job in the steelworks on Teesside or go on board a merchant ship or something like that, not work in a ladies' hairdressers. I told him I was happy doing what I liked. I like artistic things like the ballet and the stage, I told him that.'

'I found that hard to accept at first, I might add! But I would never criticize you for it, it's your life. Go on.'

'He had a real nasty go at me in the park three or four nights ago when I was coming back from Simeon's.'

'Simeon?'

'He's a friend, a good friend, he works in a bakery, he does the cake icing, wedding cakes and birthday cake decorations, that sort of thing.'

'Sorry, go on.'

'Well, I told him I had no intention of giving up my way of life just to please him, and no intention of living a lie. I told Swainby it was my ambition to establish my own chain of salons and said that working here in Hildenley was just the beginning. Then I left him. He shouted something after me, something rude I think, but I ignored him.'

'So that was when?'

'Tuesday, I think. Tuesday night, I had been to Simeon's and left at about half past nine to walk home, I always come from Simeon's via the park. Simeon has to get up early for work, he starts at half past five on a morning.'

'So you walk regularly through the park? When you leave Simeon's place? So where does he live?'

'Behind the Coliseum, he's got a flat.'

'So what happened last night?'

'I went to see Simeon, it's a regular thing for us after drama classes, he comes to my place sometimes and I go to his for a chat and a drink. We're very good friends.'

'And you left when?'

'About half nine, as near as I can tell. The cinema was turning out at the same time. I walked along among several cinema-goers, towards the park, the bottom gate.'

'The South Gate, the one in Portland Road. Right, I can visualize that. Was Swainby there?'

'Yes, he was waiting to speak to me after what had happened on

Tuesday. He knew I went somewhere in that part of town, but when I wear these dark clothes, I can hide in the shadows. I've always managed to dodge him if I thought he was watching where I went. When I left Simeon's, though, he spotted me in the street as I was hurrying towards the park, and started to follow me. I wasn't part of the crowd leaving the Coliseum, I was well ahead of them. I hurried, I didn't want him to catch up to me and besides, I needed the toilet. There are toilets in the park, behind the museum.'

'Did you notice a young woman walking alone? She'd probably be behind you in view of what you've just said.'

'Yes, she was quite a long way behind me. She might not have noticed me so far ahead but I saw her when I turned to see if Swainby was tailing me. By the time I reached the park gate, though, I was still a long way ahead of her but when I looked back again, I saw she had a man with her, a young man. They weren't looking at me as I slipped into the park; with my dark clothes I can soon conceal myself in the shadows.'

'So what did you do in the park?'

'I ran up to those toilets behind the museum, I was bursting. Me and Simeon had had a few beers, it goes right through me in minutes.'

'Did the young couple follow you?'

'No, they went up the western side and by the time I got to the toilets, I couldn't hear them, I saw no one. The park looked deserted.'

'And what time would this be?'

'Half past nine or so, just afterwards maybe. I can't be sure.'

'Ian, I need to sit down, I'm sorry, can we use the car?'

'Sure,' and so they adjourned to the little vehicle, Sergeant Simpson squeezing himself into the passenger seat once again. As he settled in, he issued a long sigh of relief.

'You all right, Dad?' there was concern in Ian's voice.

'As well as I can be. Forget me, it's you we need to worry about. So you went to the toilet behind the museum. For a pee?'

'Yes, I just made it!' and he laughed. 'Another two minutes and I'd have been wetting my pants!'

'Go on, Ian, can you continue? Can you talk about it?'

'I've got to tell somebody or I'll go mad! When I came out, I found Swainby waiting. He was standing close to the museum so I'd have to pass him as I left the toilet, and when I came out he said he wanted a word with me. He was angry, he said he'd been following me and I'd been avoiding him, and he said he didn't like people avoiding him or walking away when he was trying to talk to them, he said he wouldn't take it from anybody, not even his own flesh and blood. He insisted on calling me his own flesh and blood.'

'Was his voice raised?' Sergeant Simpson was thinking of the young couple who, according to their story, had by this time entered the park. They had walked across to a bench at the western edge of the park, some distance away from the museum. Quarter of a mile perhaps? The probability was they would never have heard voices at the other end, certainly not voices which were spoken in low or normal tones. Simpson hadn't been able to hear the policemen talking as they'd searched.

'No, he was speaking very quietly, almost as if he was menacing me. He said all he wanted was to be friends, he wanted to spend time with his own flesh and blood, he wanted me to go away with him for a holiday to celebrate my twenty-first, to be with him on that birthday, to get to know me better, and I kept saying I couldn't, I had you, both of you, and my work . . . and when I walked away from him, he blew up!'

'Blew up?' puzzled Sergeant Simpson.

'Went berzerk,' said Ian. 'Became very very angry and said my work was not the sort for a proper man, he said I was behaving like a big girl and ran after me and got in front while I was trying to get away, then started to poke me in my chest with his finger saying things like "get a proper job, be a man, get a woman, show her what you're made of . . ." and he was swearing all the time . . . and he kept prodding me in the chest and neck saying he didn't like people walking away from him. I was walking backwards by then! Honestly, I thought he'd gone mad, that he'd lost his reason. He was terrifying . . . now I know what those women must have suffered . . . and mum . . . . Then I tripped over something and fell down as I was walking backwards, it was near that seat. He just laughed. He said I couldn't even stand on my own two feet and jumped on top of me, hitting me in the chest, knocking the wind out of me and shouting "now get up you little squirt . . . now throw me off . . . show me what you can do . . . can you fight . . . can you use your fists like a real man . . . I'm older than you but I can show you what real men do to people like you . . . .'

Ian paused in his narrative and Sergeant Simpson did not reply for some minutes.

'Go on, Ian, finish your story,' he said eventually.

'Well, as he was hammering me on my chest and stomach, I felt my hand touch a stone in the rockery. I was lying half on the grass and half on the rockery, the stone was loose and fairly small, so I picked it up with my right hand and swung it at him. I caught him on the head somewhere, it was a real crack . . . it knocked him off me and I scrambled to my feet. But he grabbed my legs, he was hurt but grabbed me . . . I hit him again, on the head and he fell down and . . . well . . . it was like that lad who kicked my cat. I lost my temper . . . I just kept hitting him and he went all quiet. I don't know how many times I hit him, there was no one around . . . then I realized what I'd done. I put the stone down and tried to revive him, but he was still and silent and not breathing, there was a lot of blood about. I think I knew he was dead.'

'You shouldn't have hit him once he was incapacitated,' said Sergeant Simpson. 'You are allowed to use reasonable force to defend yourself, but nothing more. If you stood trial, the jury might find you guilty of manslaughter or even murder. That's why I don't want you to stand trial: So, what happened next?'

'When I realized what I'd done, I just stood there looking down at him. I was covered in blood, I did try to revive him but it didn't work, so I remembered something you'd said years ago about the need for the police to find the weapon in such cases, so I hid the stone I'd used.'

'On the museum roof?' asked Sergeant Simpson.

'Oh, God, you've found it! Will it have my fingerprints on?'

'No, they don't adhere to rough surfaces like stone, that's why I told the police where it might be. Besides, the stones in that rockery have moss on them, I knew they'd never carry fingerprints. I had a good reason for helping the police to find the stone, by the way, which I won't explain now. So what did you do then?'

'I stood for a long time, well it seemed a long time, wondering what I should do, whether I should report it but chickened out. I ran out of the park by one of those top gates, I was crying by then . . . .'

'And holding your head with your hands? I saw you.'

'I remember a policeman shouting something and flashing his torch, I had no idea it was you, but there was no way I was going to stop, not then even if I had known it was you. I was distraught and covered with blood, I had lost my temper again . . . like him, I suppose, like father like son.'

'And you went home, to your flat?'

'Yes and cried myself to sleep, then couldn't face up to going into work next morning. I was in a dreadful state, I nearly came to see you, to see what I should do but didn't want to embarrass you and mum. I didn't know what to do.'

'If you'd killed him with a single blow in those circumstances, you could plead self defence and you might be acquitted or you could be convicted of manslaughter, but to rain repeated blows onto his head, when he was probably unconscious and no threat, would, I am sure, be construed as murder in any court of law. It means, Ian, I don't want you to admit to anything. If the police do quiz you – as they might if they do their job properly – you'll have to tell the truth.'

'How do you mean, tell the truth? I can't tell them the whole truth, can I?'

'Not the entire truth, but a lot of it, those parts which are real and can be checked. If they ask where you were that night, say you went to see Simeon, say you left around nine thirty, say you walked through the park on the way home, but don't mention going to the toilet near the museum. Say you walked up the western side of the park and were in a hurry to get home to go to the toilet . . . don't admit being anywhere near the museum or those toilets. And use real timings.'

'Yes, I understand, yes, I can do that.'

'That will have a ring of honesty and they'll realize you were the mystery man I'd seen. Your story and timing can be checked – and it will be, Simeon will confirm his side of things. Your landlady might have heard you going into your flat. That's another piece of confirmation of your tale. It all adds strength to your story and explains your hurry. It was quarter to ten then, remember that. You were running to go to the toilet and didn't go behind a tree in case someone saw you. The young couple didn't see you – that ties in with their evidence because you were ahead of them as you went into the park. All of that is perfectly logical and can be verified.'

'Yes, I can see that, honest. I can. I can tell that story.'

'That account doesn't point the finger at you as the killer, it puts you in the category of a witness. Say you hurried home to the toilet and once indoors, settled down and went to bed. If they ask, say you saw no one in the park except for that young couple who were some distance behind you. Stick to your timings but make them more approximate – be vague about the precise time you entered the park because it only takes five minutes or so to run through from bottom to top. You might have entered that South Gate at, say twenty to ten or so. Whatever you do, don't volunteer information; try to be as polite and helpful as you can within the parameters I've just given you. Don't tell a lie which can be checked. If in doubt, say nothing. And always come to me if you've problems, but you are on your own now, Ian. Now, your clothes. Were they bloodstained?'

'Yes, they were. And me! I bathed myself umpteen times and I burned all my clothes, everything. Shoes, socks, underpants, the lot.'

'Good God, where?'

'On the moors this lunchtime. I was off work, pretending to be ill but I drove out with a can of paraffin and set fire to the lot, I waited until they were nothing but ashes and scattered them. I wondered if I had left any of my fibres on Swainby's clothes when he jumped on me, so I got rid of the lot.'

'He would have left something on your clothing, so you did a good job there. Did anyone see you burning the stuff? You didn't encounter road blocks?'

'Not the way I went, Dad, I didn't use main roads.'

'Your car's not bloodstained, is it? Or any part of your flat? From the clothes?'

'No, I made sure of that. I had an old wooden box at home, one I bought from a saleroom with some books in. I put the clothes in and burnt it too.'

'Now, I will be at home tomorrow, I'm not going to work, I'm not fit, nor am I likely to be ever again. Come and see me if you wish, but it's important you go about your normal routine, dressed in your normal clothes, and stick to the story I gave you. The only thing that worries me is that someone has seen you talking to Swainby, or seen him hanging about outside your salon, talking to you. Suppose the police question you about him? It does link you to the murder victim. And then me and mum.'

'It's a worry, isn't it and I suppose somebody might have seen us meeting, even if most of the times were in darkness.'

'What matters is that he can still be traced to you; if the CID make the link, you'll be asked if you knew him and what transpired between you.'

'So what do I say?'

'This won't be easy. You could suggest he was showing undue interest in one of the girls working at the salon but I don't think that would be accepted. If the worst comes to the worst, Ian, you'll have to admit he came to see you and claimed he was your father.'

'Do I have to?'

'The truth, Ian, always tell the truth. Well almost all the time! Your story would be that you just did not believe such rubbish, you did not think it worth mentioning to me or mum because you thought he was sick. Just admit he was a pest and that you tried to keep out of his way.'

'But if they work out he really was my father . . . ? Isn't that a motive for wanting rid of him?'

'It might not be, it might be a reason for wanting to know him better! But I think you should say you did not know the truth until after he was dead, you can say I told you then. It will be up to me to handle the rest of the questions. I will confirm you had no idea, your birth certificate bears my name anyway.'

'I don't know if I can handle all this . . . really, I don't.'

'Then say nothing. If in doubt, say nowt! But I think you can handle it. I don't think you'll be in the frame as a suspect, I don't think there's any way they can pin you down to the murder scene, not now you've got your watch back. Admit you ran through the park ahead of that young couple at the actual time you did so, make sure you say you never went near the toilets, you were at the other side, the western side, and emerged at the top. My sighting of you confirms that. In that way, you had no time to kill Ted. They won't find fingerprints on that stone or clothing stained with his blood. In short, there's no firm evidence to link you to his death. It's up to you to tell them a convincing story if they ask − which I am sure they will. In time, they'll regard you as a witness, not a suspect.'

'I'll rehearse it, my drama training will help, but really, dad, I'm terrified, honestly I am . . . I mean, if they start to press me for answers and things, especially something I'm not prepared for, I might go to pieces.'

'Just be natural and stick to your story, that's all I can advise. You're a clever lad, you can do it. Remember that man was a menace to women everywhere, it means you've done a service to the public.'

'I'm worried about all this help you're giving me. Could it mean losing your job if you were found out? Or put in prison?'

'Yes, *if* I was found out, but I won't be. I can take care of myself. Right, I'm just about on my knees, so it's home James and don't spare the horses! Not a word of this to your mother or anyone else. When we get home, we can talk about your twenty-first birthday celebrations. You become an adult then.'

'I don't think I want a party after all this!'

'We can discuss it. Maybe a cosy meal in a nice restaurant as a cele-bration? With Simeon and any of your other friends. Think about it. We'd like to do something for you. Remember things have to look normal – and be normal!'

'I will, and thanks . . . I don't know what to say!'

'Remember, if in doubt, say nowt. If you do say things, make sure they can be proved,' smiled Sergeant Simpson. 'Come along, let's go.'

On the return journey, Sergeant Simpson said he would tell Pamela that Ian now knew the identity of his natural father. Simpson would explain that Swainby had been following Ian around town, trying to get to know him, to persuade him to go away for a holiday or take days out with him, but Ian had resisted all his overtures. The fact that Swainby was Ian's natural father must never reach either the ears of the police or the public domain and so the conspirators drove home with Sergeant Simpson wondering whether Ian could cope with a police interview. He hoped he could; he had only a short time to prepare for the performance of his life.

They drove back in almost complete silence save for the hiss of the wind around the car's bodywork. Simpson hoped no one would discover their family secret – it didn't really constitute a motive for murder and besides, it had happened more than twenty years ago. He dismissed it as not being relevant to the investigation, it was a private family matter. When they returned home, Sergeant Simpson asked, 'Are you coming in for a nightcap, Ian?'

'No, I have to get home. I'm going in to work in the morning, we're open all day Saturday, it's our busiest day. I have to get my life back to normal remember. Besides, I don't think I could face mum just now, knowing what I do. About Swainby, what he did to her. I need time to come to terms with all that. People have always said I was good to my mother, very thoughtful and considerate . . . but you will listen to the doctor, won't you? Accept treatment and so on, whatever it takes? I can't bear the thought of not having you here . . .' and his voice faded into tears.

'You'll have to face mum before too long,' said Sergeant Simpson, trying to be practical about all this.

'I know, but just give me time, let me prepare for that in my own way. I might pop in tomorrow, after work, to see how you are, it gives me time to rehearse! I seem to spend my time rehearsing speeches, putting on an act. But I've been doing it for years.'

'You've had a tough life, Ian, and it's not going to be any easier in the coming months, but you can do it!' smiled Sergeant Simpson, patting him on the shoulder. 'Talk to me anytime you want, I'm always here.'

'Yes, Dad,' he sobbed. 'And thanks. Thanks a million.'

'Well, it's bedtime for me,' and, after handing the watch back to Ian and telling him to get a new strap, they parted, better friends and closer than they had ever been.

When Dick went in, Pam was sitting on the sofa watching the black and white television and said, 'No Ian?'

'He wanted to go straight home, he's at work in the morning.'

'Nice trip?'

'Very,' said Sergeant Simpson sinking into a chair. 'A nice little car, we went up to the top of Beacon Hill. It's spectacular up there at night, the lights of the town are beautiful! But there is something I need to tell you,' and he went over to switch off the television set.

She sat in stunned silence as Sergeant Simpson revealed what had happened to Ian, how he knew the truth about his parentage and of Swainby's attempts to ingratiate himself with Ian.

When he'd finished, she said, 'Dick, it wasn't him, was it? Ian, I mean? Was it him who attacked Ted?'

'Ian? He hasn't got it in him! I think someone with a deep grievance recognized Swainby and took his revenge. He has antagonized lots of people over the years, many in this town. So don't think Ian's responsible – or me! I saw you looking at me recently with an odd glance. But now, this is just between you and me, Pam, this business about Ted being his father, and contacting him in recent weeks. There's no one who can say he isn't mine, my name's on his birth certificate.'

'He came here, Dick, Ted, I mean,' she blurted out. 'He came here wanting to find Ian . . . .'

'Came here? When?' he almost shouted at her.

'A few weeks ago, when he first came back to Hildenley. He found out where I live, that's easy enough, and said he wanted to see Ian.'

'God! You never told me! You kept that quiet! For God's sake why? You should have told me!'

'I didn't think it important at the time, I didn't want to upset you, especially as you weren't too well.'

'So how did he know about Ian? I thought no one knew but us,' snapped Sergeant Simpson. 'Did you tell him?'

'Of course not! I've no idea how he knew.'

'Well he did know, there's no doubt about that, so how did he find out? You should have told me he'd called, Pam, you really should, this could be dreadful.'

And it was with a deep sense of foreboding that Sergeant Simpson realized their family secret was not such a secret after all.

CHAPTER 11

ON Friday night, there were two developments. The retired butcher who had chased Swainby with a meat cleaver had been traced to his home in Lincoln; he had been in his house at the material time and Lincolnshire detectives were satisfied that neither he, nor any of his family, could be linked to the murder in Hildenley. Likewise, relatives of his Garminghamshire victims had also been interviewed and eliminated from the enquiry but, like the butcher, they thought Swainby deserved his treatment, even if it was unlawful. 'An eye for an eye,' they'd all said. This result would serve only to strengthen Clifton's belief that the killer was a local man even though some elements of the press were printing stories that the suspect was being sought in Garminghamshire. Clifton did nothing to correct them.

Meanwhile, Detective Superintendent Clifton was resting at home although his mind remained active, pondering the evidence already collected – not that there was much of real value. To ensure a period of thoughtful quietness, he had left instructions that he must only be disturbed if an arrest was made, or if some other important and dramatic development occurred. He began to ponder upon the lack of positive evidence; no useful information was flowing into the files but the most worrying aspect was that no one, other than the courting couple and Sergeant Simpson – and Swainby – had been observed in the park at the material time. This was aggravated by the fact that no one, other than Simpson, had reported seeing the fleeing mystery man in black. He began to wonder whether there was anything in the sergeant's background that could have sparked off such a fatal confrontation?

Also that Friday evening, the district coroner, Mr Ambrose Carruthers, rang Hildenley Police Station to say he had returned from a business trip and had found the note on his doormat. He said he was now able to

146

formally view the body in the mortuary as a prelude to the eventual inquest. He asked Sergeant Williams, the duty sergeant, to arrange the necessary identifying officer to be in attendance at 8 p.m. As Simpson's condition was known to Williams and to Superintendent Firth, it was agreed that PC Stead, although off duty, could fulfil that role. Stead confirmed that the body was that of Edward Albert Swainby, lately of an address in Garminghamshire and more recently residing at 25a, Upperholme Terrace, Hildenley. The coroner said he would await the full police report into the death before arranging a date for the inquest. That meant another formality had been completed.

Overnight in Hildenley, there was a reduction in the volume of police activity even though both uniformed and plain clothes officers were active. The normal contingent of constables were out and about in town, making enquiries, maintaining observations for the mystery man and generally doing their best to tap into the prevailing gossip and social scenes before Hildenley went to sleep. All young men, and perhaps some who were not so young but who in any case looked remotely like the suspect would continue to be stopped and questioned as to their where-abouts on Thursday night, and all places frequented at night would be visited both by uniformed and plain clothes officers in their efforts to trace and identify the hurrying suspect. This activity would keep the murder fresh in the minds of the night-time socializers and some useful snippets of information could still be forthcoming.

Although Latima Park had been re-opened to the public, Sergeant Williams had instructed a constable to patrol it, at least until 2 a.m. because there was a popular belief that a murderer always returned to the scene of the crime. If anyone did visit the scene, or even show a keen interest, then that person or persons should be interrogated, particularly about their movements on Thursday night. However, the police accepted it was quite feasible that some innocent person would visit the scene – murder always generated a morbid fascination. And so, although the police station appeared to be rather inactive, a good deal of useful supple-mentary work was being undertaken during the night hours.

In the Simpson household, Dick and Pam had a long chat about the awful events which had suddenly enfolded them. Pam repeatedly expressed her deepest regret for not telling her husband about Swainby's visit; it had not seemed important at the time and in her view, it was perfectly reasonable that he might genuinely want to see his natural son as he approached maturity. She had not wanted to upset Dick, never thinking it might become of wider interest to the town's police. But one niggling question remained unanswered – how had Swainby known Ian was his son? Pam had never told him and he had not told her how he'd acquired that knowledge, nor had he been in contact with her since the rape. Dick accepted her assurances that she had never been in touch with Swainby over the years and had not told him about the birth; that made it even more deeply disturbing to realize that Swainby knew their family secret. And if he knew, did anyone else? For Dick Simpson that possibility was profoundly alarming.

Deep into the night, and in spite of Dick's tiredness, they discussed Ian's possible long-term reaction to the shocking and bewildering news that his father was a convicted sex offender, rapist and possible killer, not the much-respected and kindly police officer he'd always known as dad. Pam and Dick agreed they must give him every possible help and support in coping with this dreadful dilemma. Both would show their deepest love as he struggled to come to terms with the devastating news. Pam said he could come and live at home if he wanted – his room was still there and the bed was always made up; his departure for a flat of his own had been Ian's idea, he had not been asked to leave home. He'd felt he was old enough to leave to make his own way in the world . . . and so, long into the night, they talked and talked about Ian and his future. And their own.

During their conversation, however, Dick did not even hint that Ian had followed in the footsteps of his natural father – he did not say he had been particularly violent, so much so that he had killed a man. That was not for Pam's ears – it was not for anyone's ears and it meant Dick was keeping secrets from her although in its way it helped him cope with her modest deception. And so very late into the night, with Dick Simpson feeling feverish and utterly weary, he went to bed but could not sleep. And those swellings under his arms? He found them when he was undressing, and they hadn't been there this morning. Were they real, or was he imagining the worst? They were small but they had appeared quickly or had he missed them earlier? He would show them to the doctor tomorrow. Very soon, the truth about his own sickness must be revealed.

For Pam, unable to sleep, there was a deep niggling and dreadful suspicion, however faint, that either Dick or Ian might somehow be responsible for Swainby's death. Surely they couldn't be working together in this? That blood-stained uniform bothered her . . . was their involvement the reason why Dick was so ill, was it nerves, was it why Ian had taken time off work? She did her best to dismiss any such thoughts from her mind but she did not sleep much that night.

Ian Simpson could not sleep either. He did not try. Alone in his one-room bedsit, he sat with his head in his hands and wept and wept and wept. Only hours ago, his life was improving – he had a good, secure and interesting job, one he liked and at which he was skilled. He had come to terms with his sexuality too, people treated him well now that he was almost an adult and there was none of that childhood teasing and cruelty. He considered himself mature, he had a smart car, a job and a place of his own . . . and then, in a matter of hours, his entire world had crumbled. Not only had he killed a man, he had killed his own father, who was a violent rapist. Ian knew he was the son of a criminal and was himself a murderer now. Like father, like son. But Ian didn't consider himself a bad man who was evil and dangerous . . . he'd always regarded himself as thoroughly decent and very nice. In his misery, he found the whole thing almost unbearable. How could he cope? His brain turned and twisted, he cried and cried and even shouted out on one occasion. Was he going mad? Was it all true? Had he really killed a man? There was always Dad . . . he could talk to Dad . . . by Dad, he meant the man he had known as Dad for all his life. Until now. And his lifetime Dad was ill . . . so ill he was going to die . . . .

In Ian's worst moments and alone in that rather dismal room, he found it useful to have been to drama classes. They had started in Hildenley last winter and the sessions had resumed after the summer break. Classes were on Thursday nights which was how he'd come to meet Simeon; Simeon had ambitions to 'do Shakespeare' he had told Ian. But Ian was not that ambitious – in his view acting was a craft which could be applied to everyday life, a means of taking one out of oneself and thinking oneself into another personality . . . and how! He told himself he must now act out the rest of his life, just as he had been doing recently but with more depth. Tomorrow, Saturday morning, he must go to work, he *must*! He mustn't let this get him down. He must do ordinary things, he must appear normal, he must be confident in his ability to deal with this dreadful trauma and rehearse his speech, or several speeches, to the police if – when – they came to question him.

He must consider everything, absolutely everything, they might possibly ask. And so Ian Simpson cried himself to sleep. Then, of course, he was not acting.

★

Shortly after nine on Saturday morning, Pam rang Dr Ewart's surgery and explained about Dick's deterioration, asking if the doctor would visit him at home. Dr Ewart said he would call immediately after surgery; surgery finished at ten-thirty and he told Pam to expect him around eleven when he had sorted out his paperwork and the last patient had departed. Dick must stay off work, he ordered, and take as much rest as he could, not forgetting his prescribed anaemia pills. Pam listened and assured him Dick would remain in bed.

'How are you this morning?' She was worried about the abnormally pale face of her hitherto very robust husband. He was sitting up but leaning against the headrest on pillows, bare-chested and smiling weakly. She was sure he looked thinner than normal, but that was probably due to his colour or even her imagination. But his cheeks did look hollow and his arms looked thin too, and one had a large bruise above the elbow. She'd never noticed it before.

'A bit groggy,' he said. 'I didn't sleep well, I couldn't, not with all that stuff going on in my head, I kept waking up, I had a nose bleed in the night as well, I didn't make a mess, I got to the bathroom in time. I hope I didn't disturb you.'

'I was awake, I heard you, I thought you were just going to the loo. I couldn't sleep . . .' she said. 'I've rung Dr Ewart, he'll be here about eleven. He said to be sure not to go to work.'

'Thanks, that's an order I can obey without any trouble,' he smiled, adding, 'Has the paper come?' They took the *Yorkshire Post*.

'I'll fetch it up with your breakfast,' she smiled and planted a kiss on his fevered brow. 'The murder's mentioned. I don't know where they get their information from, I've not talked to them. It says they've not arrested anyone yet.'

'Thanks,' he said, sinking into his pillow. Now, for the first time in a murder investigation, he hoped they would never arrest anyone. Pam quietly wondered who they would arrest.

In Hildenley Police Station that morning, things were rather more busy. The detectives and additional uniform staff had all arrived and were in the muster room drinking cups of tea as they awaited Superintendent Clifton's address. They had come from all corners of the force area and all were enthusiastic. They knew there had been no arrest overnight and consequently each man was fired with the desire to be the one who caught the murderer, even though the blackboard in the corner did not name any suspect. The only prime suspect in the frame was still the mystery man who'd been seen hurrying from the park on Thursday night. He had not been traced or named. All the other suspects had been eliminated from the enquiry. The frame, as it was called, was a replica of that which appeared on racecourses to list the runners and their odds. In this case, the only favourite – indeed the only runner – was the anonymous mystery man.

Superintendent Clifton and Sergeant Burrows had arrived shortly after seven that morning to prepare for their day. Clifton had dictated instructions to one of the early-duty secretaries who'd been appointed to work with the murder team. Those instructions would be issued to the sergeants who would be arriving later and they would then ensure their teams worked accordingly. By the time the teams arrived, therefore, Clifton's preparations were complete and he was ready to speak to them from the heights of his chair. Prompt at eight-thirty he mounted the chair in the muster room as Detective Sergeant Burrows called for silence.

'Good morning all,' he boomed when they had settled down. 'It's Saturday morning in Hildenley, it's market day with country people coming into the town to shop, to go to the bank, to do business, to visit the hairdresser or perhaps have lunch. They are people from outside the town, people from the villages, strangers perhaps but a rich source of information for you all. Get among them, talk about the murder, get them talking about it – most of them will know about it by now because it's been in the local papers and on the local BBC news. Ask if they know anyone who came to town on Thursday evening, to the cinema perhaps, or to evening classes, or just to the pub . . . if they provide a name, make sure that name – and every name they mention – is thoroughly investigated and the owners of those names asked to explain their whereabouts on Thursday night. Remember we're looking for witnesses as well as suspects and that includes people going home that Thursday evening after an outing in town. They're the ones who might have seen something or someone of interest to us. So what kind of people might do that?

'It's not just pubbers and clubbers, you must realize; people do other things in the evening, they go to the theatre even if it might only be a play in a church room, they go to evening classes, they go to events like meetings of societies and clubs, choir practices, whist drives and bingo, to talks and restaurants, to see friends, or to let off steam after a family row or just to walk the dog. There's all kinds of reasons for people going out in the evening so when you are working your patch, find out what was happening on it that night, find out who might have been there and go to talk to the organizers, then find out who attended.

'I know our suspect was seen about quarter to ten, but where was he before then? And after then? He must have been somewhere where he would be seen by others; he might even have talked to them. Someone must have seen him – he is not invisible! He can't have suddenly materialized in the park that night: he came from somewhere and went somewhere. So if someone did see him, we want to talk to that person or persons. And it's your job to find them, they're out there somewhere. And we still need sightings of Swainby, not only on Thursday evening but since his arrival in town. What's he been doing, who's he been talking to? Where's he been spending his time? Who are his pals? Whatever he's been doing, someone must have seen him and talked to him. We want to speak to those people.'

The policemen were scribbling notes and so Clifton waited as they digested those opportunities for enquiries, then continued.

'One reason for going out in the evening is to meet other people, legitimately or otherwise,' he reminded them. 'If a person was meeting someone for reasons he or she wishes to keep secret, then we will respect that secrecy. It is not a criminal offence for a married man to commit adultery or to chat to a woman not his wife. But there is a criminal offence that might interest us – remember Swainby was found very close to a public toilet. Is it the haunt of homosexuals? Do they meet there as they do in some cities? Or leave messages for one another?

'Is there such an underlife here in Hildenley? If there is, we need to know about it because we must consider whether Swainby could have propositioned a man – from what I have read in his record, he has never shown that kind of behaviour but there is always a first time. He might have propositioned a man who was using that toilet and paid with his life. So get among the homosexuals of the town, find out where they were on Thursday and remember that our suspect – or even a witnesses or two – might be one of them.'

There was a good deal of bawdy laughter and someone trotted out the old joke when a police lecturer asked, 'What is the definition of gross indecency?' to which a student replied, 'Indecency between a large number of people, 144 I think.'

'All right, all right, there'll be time for joking later,' smiled Clifton. 'Now Sergeant Simpson's reported sick so we'll have to cope without him and his local knowledge. Detective Sergeant Huntley, and DC Thorne, I'd like words with you before you disappear into town. The rest of you can now go about your enquiries and we will have the usual short conference to highlight any developments; it will be after your meal break, two o'clock this afternoon on the dot, in this room.'

He updated them on the result of enquiries in Lincoln and Garminghamshire, and as none of the detectives or uniformed officers had any specific questions, they were dismissed to go about their enquiries. Noisily, they left the room as Clifton led Huntley and Thorne up the stairs to his temporary office; there was no room for them all to sit down so Clifton stood behind the desk.

'I think the pair of you hold the key to this enquiry,' he said quietly. 'You're the local detectives, you know the underbelly of the town but I think the answer to our puzzle lies not so much with the townspeople and with what they saw or did not see, but with Swainby himself. It must do, he must be the key to all this. He has upset someone, he's done something nasty to someone, not for the first time, either here in Hildenley or in Garminghamshire or even in prison. I'm sure this is a revenge attack. It might not be due to a sexual assault on someone's woman, it could be a bad business deal, he could owe money, he could have grassed on someone . . . it could be anything. We need to spread our net wider and think wider than his reputation. So the question you must ask is — does this attack have its roots in some other aspect of Swainby's life here in Hildenley? Past or present? It's your job to find out.

'What I need from you now is some very deep digging into Swainby's past when he previously lived in Hildenley. Twenty years isn't all that long so there must be plenty of people who remember him. I need you to dig out those old files and check for people living here who might still have reason to take their revenge. Get out and about and start digging — and dig deep. Provide me with names and I might decide to interview them with or without you present, or I might let you do the honours but whatever happens you'll get any credit that might flow from all this. And is there anything in Sergeant Simpson's background that might be relevant? I don't want you to air my interest in that side of things, but while you're delving into Swainby's past life, don't ignore Sergeant Simpson. Has he some kind of dark secret which is linked to Swainby? Do you understand what I'm getting at?'

Both men nodded; they were intelligent and could appreciate the direction of Clifton's proposed enquiries. From the file already in their possession they had the names and addresses of Swainby's early victims, they had witnesses statements, they had the names of the police officers who had dealt with his original crimes and they knew who had testified against him in court . . . in short, there were a lot of names to be investigated which suggested a lot of potential witnesses – and a lot of suspects.

Huntley and Thorne warmed to the challenge. Most of the older information in their possession had arisen due to crimes or suspected crimes committed by Swainby, not matters like bad business deals or something like adultery with another man's wife. But every enquiry had to begin somewhere and then grow, like the proverbial acorn growing into a huge oak.

'All I want, gentlemen,' said Clifton, 'is the name of someone, a man or woman, with previous links to Swainby, not necessarily from a criminal point of view, and who cannot provide an alibi for Thursday night between nine-thirty and around quarter to ten. That must narrow things down a bit.'

'We'll get busy right away, sir.'

'Good, and while you're doing that, I'm going to have another look at Latima Park.'

Pamela was not in the room while Doctor Ewart examined Sergeant Simpson. For reasons he did not explain, the doctor said he did not want her present and so, in a predictable way, he listened to the sergeant's chest, took his blood pressure, counted his heartbeats on the pulse in his wrist and even checked his physical reactions by tapping on his knee with the edge of his hand and watching his foot jump into the air. They were all basic tests, but necessary preliminaries to this examination. Although the doctor had asked the same questions only yesterday, he repeated them, asking Simpson about his tiredness and its duration and about any other aches or pains he might be suffering and he quizzed him about the fevers he'd had, the bruises to his body and the nose bleeds. Sergeant Simpson knew his true condition was about to be revealed; he was utterly convinced he was suffering from leukaemia even if he had tried to conceal it, but it had now reached the point where his condition could no longer be concealed. And the events in Latima Park meant he had good reason not to conceal it any longer.

'Those lumps under your arms, Sergeant,' the doctor said in due course. 'They could indicate glandular fever, you know. In a case like this, it's very difficult to diagnose the precise nature of your condition. There *is* anaemia, that is evident and we can deal with that. I'll arrange a blood transfusion as soon as possible but I do need the result of your blood test first. That's vital and that will decide whether I need to refer you to a specialist. I'll chase things up at the hospital.'

'But these lumps under my arms, doctor, they could also mean leukaemia, couldn't they? I had a friend who caught it . . . he had anaemia like me, or what they thought was anaemia until they made more detailed examinations and he developed lumps like these, swellings of his lymph nodes. He was dead within five weeks.'

'Let's not get too worried at this early stage, Sergeant. As I've said, this could be glandular fever but must stress I cannot be certain, I am only a GP, not an expert. In view of this development and the deterioration in your health, I will ring the hospital and get them to treat your blood sample with extreme urgency.'

'So you are not saying I have leukaemia?'

'I am not saying you have and I am not saying you haven't. You *might* have leukaemia, you *might* have glandular fever, you *might* just be anaemic without further complications or you might be suffering from some other condition or amalgamation of conditions . . . and don't forget the sheer stress of your job right now might have contributed. I must wait and see, your blood test will tell us a lot.'

'And in the meantime?'

'You must rest, don't even think of going into work. You must take those pills I prescribed and eat food which will add iron to your body, liver for example, and in the meantime I'll chase up the result of your blood test.'

'And if it does point to leukaemia?'

'You will be admitted to hospital for a sternum marrow puncture which will tell us whether cancer is present in your bone marrow. If it is positive, we will admit you to hospital immediately for a blood transfusion and further tests and any treatment that may be necessary. Sadly as you know, acute leukaemia progresses with extreme rapidity. It is sometimes not diagnosed until far too late and sadly it is often through routine tests for other problems that it is first identified.'

'Like now?' There was no smile on Sergeant Simpson's face.

'Like now, Sergeant. Now, do you want your wife to come in?'

'What am I going to tell her?'

'I'll say I've examined you but at this early stage, I would not wish to state categorically that you have leukaemia. Or that you have not. However, I must be truthful and say it's possible. If it's the acute variety, you must prepare for the worst.'

'I understand. I can wait. Another day or two won't make any difference, so bring Pamela in.'

The detectives investigating the Swainby murder took full advantage of Saturday's influx of extra people. One team of a detective sergeant and detective constable positioned themselves outside Barclays Bank and quizzed everyone going in; others did likewise at the other banks, more operated on the railway station and bus station because lots of people used trains and buses to travel into town. Several patrolled among the car parks or the market stalls quizzing incomers and locals alike, one team decided to visit all the cafés where the incomers had their meals and the pubs also received an influx of police officers who quizzed drinkers. This surge of activity meant the town was enlivened by teams of detectives questioning people as they went about their Saturday routine, but the result was disappointing. No useful information was obtained, no new suspects named and no new witnesses found. This would not worry Detective Superintendent Clifton when the news reached him. In his view, it would serve only to reinforce his view that the killer was someone residing in the town.

He could not avoid the thought it might be someone well-known locally, someone who could almost pass unnoticed among them, someone whose movements would never be suspicious. It was this belief which had prompted him to return to Latima Park. While his men were busy in town, therefore, he walked towards the park, using the route taken by Sergeant Simpson from the West End kiosk. He timed his walk – it took him ten minutes. He walked along Park Road to the first entrance, Gate No. 1, the East Gate. Standing there, he looked around, noting the fact it was now daylight whereas the murder had occurred during the hours of darkness. He could see the impressive row of houses to his right, Nos. 1

to 50, Park Road. From this vantage point, Park Road curved slightly to the left, following the edge of the park which was clearly defined with a wall, rows of trees and the pavement upon which he now stood. Even in daylight he could not look into the park due to the foliage still clinging to the shrubs and trees along the boundary, albeit showing signs of the autumn colours. There was no clear view unless one stepped into the gateway itself. Then a long view down the grassy slopes with the footpaths, flower beds, seats and shelters presented itself.

He could see a solitary constable patrolling inside the park but as he peered ahead towards gate No. 2, he could see that the curve of the road could easily and quickly hide someone hurrying out of gate No. 2 if they turned to their left. Sergeant Simpson's statement that the mystery man had vanished in that direction could be true – the fellow could have easily disappeared, especially in the darkness, not to be seen again if he had kept to that side of the road. So where had he gone from there?

Where could he have gone if he had not caught a bus or been seen by any other witness? Why had no one else seen him? Clifton then entered the park, took a long look at the museum and the place where Swainby's body was found and then strode towards the constable, who recognized him. The constable had approached him and they met only a few yards from the bench beside which the body had been found.

'Good morning, sir,' PC Ingram said.

'Any excitements?' asked Clifton. 'Any sightseers? Murderers returning to the scene?'

'One or two people have walked past the scene, sir, but they didn't stop. I think my presence deterred them. I took a few names and questioned them but couldn't honestly pin any of them down to committing a murder on Thursday night!'

'Good, well the fact you spoke to them will make them talk about it, and that might produce something. One never knows for sure, but gossip is wonderful for generating information, so long as they pass it along to us.'

'I asked them to let the station know if they did hear anything.'

'Good, well I'm just having another look at the scene, just to get it firmly imprinted on my mind. Do you know if those toilets are used by homosexuals for their trysts?'

'Not to my knowledge, sir, in all my time here we've never had any trouble of that sort. Kids don't tend to hang around in the park either or cause trouble, we don't get vandals among the flowers or wrecking the seats. It's probably because there's usually someone else here, dog walking maybe, or just coming for a bit of peace and quiet. The gates are always open, day and night, there's usually somebody moving about the place.'

'I'm heading for No. 2 gate next, that's the way the mystery man left.'

'There's quite a few paths to it, sir, from inside the park. They twist and turn through the lawns and flower beds like spaghetti on a plate.'

'So if the mystery man was the killer and he was heading for No.2 gate, the North Gate, he'd probably go along that path?' and Clifton pointed to one which twisted and turned beneath some ornamental trees. As it progressed, it rose slightly upon its route along the slope and, in daylight, it could be seen from the lower parts of the park. From its route, there was a good view to the south of the park, and of the benches and shelters which occupied other areas. He bade farewell to the policeman and strode along the path, noting the views it both offered and provided, and eventually emerged at gate No. 2. This was now known to be one hundred and fifty-five yards from gate No. 1 – his men had measured the distance – and when he left the park, he could look back to gate No. 1. He knew that in darkness the path was in shadows from the trees and even now, in broad daylight, those same trees gave shelter to anyone walking directly beneath them. Like the supposed mystery man, Clifton turned left and within a matter of half a dozen of his huge strides, he was out of sight from gate No.1; the curvature of the footpath beside the park wall took him beyond the sight of anyone standing at gate No. 1 and in fact he was soon out of sight from gate No. 2 as the curve intensified. And there he stopped to look around.

So if there had been a mystery man, where had he gone from here?

There was another gate further along, gate No. 3, the West Gate, so could he have returned to the park and concealed himself in the shadows or among the trees? But the fact remained there was no report of him being seen in the park, not then, not at any time. As Clifton stood and gazed ahead, he could see the wall of the park turning away to his left and being followed by Park Road until it reached a junction – Park Rise.

Park Rise was a road which came from the south of the park, via a junction with Portland Road, and it climbed past its western boundary beyond the house where the solicitor's fancy woman lived, and then formed another junction with Park Road. Beyond, Park Rise became Latima Road with private houses, hotels, shops and even a garage lining its route. The mystery man might have walked along there . . . or he might not. He knew from reading the statements collected by his teams that all those shops and other premises had been closed, except for the hotels, but no one living or working there had seen the mystery man that night.

But, he knew, if the man was fleeing after committing murder, he would be sure not to let himself be seen by anyone and if he knew the area well, he could quite easily make his way unseen back to his home. He must not let himself be seen by anyone, particularly if he was blood-stained. A murderer who lived in Hildenley and was familiar with its network of streets could quickly hide himself and there was a fair chance he had done that. So the mystery man could be the killer – he had to give Sergeant Simpson some credence because he might be telling the truth.

He would instruct some of his best detectives to swamp this area once more with house-to-house enquiries and he would ask them to check those hotels once more, not just for the names of guests who were resident on Thursday night, but also for members of staff who were, or should have been, on duty. All would be asked to explain their movements at the material time. He felt this had been a useful trip, not that it had presented any fresh ideas or evidence to him but because it served to reinforce his firm belief that the killer lived locally. It was entirely feasible that he had killed Swainby in the park and fled through gate No. 2 for no other reason than that it offered the speediest route either to his home or to some other place of safety.

And that suggested that 'home' was one of those houses standing in that part of town just ahead of him, only a few minutes from the park. Time to get safely home after killing someone. He decided that every house and flat would be visited or re-visited and its occupants invited to explain their whereabouts on Thursday evening. It was all part of the elimination process.

PC Jim Sharpe was one of the uniform constables on duty that Saturday morning. When he was working the town centre beat, he had a nice cup of tea place – policemen on patrol tended to cultivate cup of tea places. These might be shops, hotels, garages, bakeries – anywhere in fact, where a lonely constable could pop in and enjoy a cup of tea behind the scenes as he rested his tired feet. Quite often, they were run by nice young women who fancied the man in uniform, or who were fancied by the man in uniform.

In Jim Sharpe's case, his calling place was the dry cleaner's in Finkle Street. The manageress, a large, blonde and mature lady called Sadie, made no secret of her admiration for men in uniform and so Jim popped in for a cup of tea from time to time when plodding his lonely beat. That Saturday, although the cleaner's was busy, Jim popped in as usual and disappeared into the rear of the shop while Sadie attended to her customers at the counter. In between times, while making him a coffee, she chattered and said she'd been to the cinema on Thursday night but she hadn't been quizzed about it like some other people she knew.

'Well, I saw Ted Swainby, I knew him ages ago and saw he was back in town,' she told Jim. 'He was walking fast along Portland Road, going towards the park. It would be about half past nine, just as the pictures were turning out.'

'We knew about that,' Jim told her. 'There was a girl ahead of him, we know who she was. He could have been tailing her but her boyfriend turned up and nothing happened. They went into the park for a cuddle, we've interviewed them.'

'No,' said Sadie. 'He wasn't following that girl even if she thought he was, I saw the girl. He was following a young man in black and trying to get him to talk to him. Shouting at him at first near the back of the Coliseum and then just following. The young man kept trying to keep well ahead of him, walking very fast but not responding, not talking to Swainby, ignoring him, keeping his distance. He got quite a long way in front of Swainby and that girl. She might not have noticed him because she was chatting to her boyfriend all the time, they only had eyes for each other. Then they all went into the park, the man in black first by a long way, then the young couple who had got together by then, and then Ted Swainby. The couple were gazing into each other's eyes; I don't think they saw the man in black ahead of them, it was dark anyway and there are shadows under the park trees.'

'A young man in black? Are you sure?' asked PC Jim.

'I am sure,' she almost snapped. 'I know him, it was that nice young man who does my hair, he works for Style, the salon in Almond Grove. His name's Ian.'

CHAPTER 12

PC Jim Sharpe, an experienced constable with twelve years' service, told Sadie to keep this to herself for the time being because he wanted to inform the detective superintendent in charge of the enquiry. He recalled Clifton's instructions that he would personally interview any prime suspects.

'He'll come and talk to you about it,' he assured her.

'Oooh!' she didn't know whether to regard this development as frightening or merely important. 'He's not the killer, is he?'

Sharpe smiled and tried to play down this development. 'I doubt it,' he said. 'It's witnesses we're looking for, and we need to trace the last movements of the murder victim. That young man might be able to help us with our enquiries. He could be one of the last to see Swainby alive.'

'Oh, I see,' she said. 'Yes, you do that, Jim, I'll certainly tell him what I saw.'

Six minutes later, Jim Sharpe was entering the police station and was in time to see Clifton approaching after his walk in the park. He waited outside because he wanted to be sure to catch the big man's full attention.

'Sir,' he said. 'I think I've found an important witness, a suspect even.'

'That's the best news I've had all morning!' beamed Clifton. 'And you are?'

'PC Sharpe, sir, one of the local beatmen.'

'All right, PC Sharpe, come up to my office and tell me all about it,' and Clifton led the way into the police station. As he started to climb the stairs, he called to the desk constable, 'Two teas in my office, lad, as soon as you can.'

'Sir,' the desk constable called out to him. 'And Sir, there's a message from scenes of crime.'

'Right – give!' and Clifton paused on the stairs.

'It's about the murder weapon, sir, the stone used to kill Swainby. They've tested it for fingerprints but can't find any. The surface is too rough to take prints, they say. It's being sent off to forensic today, to compare the blood on it with Swainby's.'

'I didn't expect any prints but would expect the blood to match. Make sure a note to that effect goes into the file, will you? Come along, PC Sharpe, tell me your news.'

With Jim Sharpe seated before his desk, Clifton opened a pad of notepaper and after asking the constable a few questions about his career, primarily to put him at his ease, the tea arrived.

'I need tea like a car needs petrol,' grinned Clifton, showing signs of evident happiness. 'Right, PC Sharpe, the floor's yours.'

'I was speaking to the woman in the dry cleaner's in Finkle Street, sir, Green's they call it, and she says she saw Ted Swainby among the crowd who were leaving the cinema on Thursday night. He wasn't following the girl we discussed earlier, sir, she thinks he was following a young man in dark clothing.'

'Does she now?' the interest was evident in Clifton's eyes. 'In dark clothing? Our mystery man, you think?'

'It could be, sir. They went into the park.'

'Who went into the park?' frowned Clifton.

'The young woman who had been to the pictures, sir, with her boyfriend. The young man in dark clothing also went into the park. Not with the couple though. At first, on leaving the cinema, the girl had been walking alone, she was ahead of Swainby then her boyfriend caught up to her and they went into the park together.'

'And the man in black? Where was he then?'

'He was some way ahead of them all, sir, quite a long way in fact and he went into the park too, by the South Gate. The young couple might not have noticed him do that.'

'Right, I understand.'

'Then Sadie . . .'

'Sadie?'

'The woman in the cleaner's, sir. She noticed the girl, as I said, and saw Swainby, she knows him by sight, but said he was not following the girl. He was following the young man in black and trying to engage him in conversation but the young man didn't respond. He kept a long way ahead of Swainby as if he didn't want anything to do with him. When they all went into the park though, they weren't together, not in a group of any sort.'

'Fair enough, I can establish their precise movements when I talk to this Sadie. So does she know the man in black?'

'Yes, sir, she described him as a very nice young man who works in Style, that's a ladies' hairdresser in Almond Grove. His name is Ian.'

'Now this is what I call a breakthrough, PC Sharpe! A name for a suspect, a good suspect too and at last some independent and positive sightings of our mystery man in black. And, it seems, he might have been in the park at the same time as Swainby. I think we might have broken the proverbial ice, thanks to you. If Sadie means what I think she means, he might be homosexual and that makes it even more interesting. Some jiggery-pokery at the toilets near the museum perhaps? And his name is Ian, you say?'

'Yes, sir.'

'Do you happen to know this Ian?' As Clifton asked the question, it appeared to him that Sergeant Simpson was telling the truth. There could have been someone leaving the park at the material time, just as Simpson had explained. But Sharpe's answer changed things yet again.

'Yes, sir, he's Sergeant Simpson's son.'

'Good God . . . are you sure?'

'Yes, sir. I don't know whether Sadie realizes it is Ian Simpson, but I know the lad, he's never been in trouble, he's a decent lad, sir, not the sort who would use violence but he is rather effeminate. He's more into arty crafty things than sport, a very nice boy, like Sadie said.'

'I don't like this, I don't like it at all. So how old is this lad?'

'I'm not sure. In his twenties, I think. Early twenties.'

Then Detective Superintendent Clifton had another flash of inspiration.

'If this was the man seen hurrying from the park by Sergeant Simpson, you'd think he would recognize his own son, wouldn't you?' Clifton wondered if Simpson *had* recognized his son and was now trying to cover up the fact he had been in the park at the material time. He wouldn't have had cause to worry about that aspect of things until he'd discovered the body . . . now this *was* interesting. Most interesting.

'It wouldn't be easy, sir, not in the dark, not if he was trying to conceal himself.'

'So if this lad is not the sort to go around clouting people over the head with lumps of rock, he might be a useful witness. If he was in the park at that time, he could have seen or heard something. Is that what we are saying?'

'That's what I thought, sir. He's probably a good witness.'

'And a bloody good suspect! All right, PC Sharpe, this one's for me. I'll take it from here. I'll talk to him but we need to keep this under wraps for the time being. Not a word to anyone, certainly not to the other constables and definitely not to Sergeant Simpson.'

'I understand, sir. How is he, sir? I hear he's gone off duty sick?'

'He has, he's had the doctor round and he's not a well man, I can tell you that. It looks like anaemia to me, or worse. It could be much worse. Whatever it is, he's too weak to come to work. I have no further news of him, except he's in bed at home.'

'Thank you, sir, he's a nice man, is Sergeant Simpson. One of the best.'

'So I am led to believe, everyone tells me that. All right, PC Sharpe, leave this one with me and I'll go and see this Ian right away. I'll let you know how I get on, and will ensure you get any credit that might arise from this. Now, would you know where Ian lives?'

'No, sir, sorry, I don't know, He doesn't live with his parents, he's got his own flat somewhere in town.'

'The salon where he works, it will be open this morning, won't it? Being a Saturday?'

'Yes, sir. Most of such places are open all day on Saturday, to catch the country people when they come into town.'

'So where is Almond Grove?'

Sharpe explained and the big man thanked him, then Sharpe returned to his beat duties. He would go and tell Sadie what had transpired, and then he might find some other useful snippet of information. There was no doubt the murder enquiry had given him a sense of purpose; it was better than watching out for badly parked cars.

'Where's Detective Sergeant Burrows?' asked Clifton from the office duty constable when he descended from his office.

'He's in the secretary's office, sir, going through the statement files to see if any names are repeated or people need to be interviewed a second time, a sort of cross-referencing and checking exercise, he said.'

'Good, that needs doing but it can wait. Buzz him and tell him to meet me outside, we're going to do some real detective work.'

And so it was that Detective Superintendent Clifton and Detective Sergeant Burrows went to interview Sadie. She repeated what she had told PC Sharpe and couldn't elaborate further, but Clifton knew her sighting was vital. Another breakthrough – and one which suggested Sergeant Simpson had been telling the truth. So now it was the turn of Ian Simpson to be questioned. As a witnesss or suspect? Or joint suspect? The team of detectives decided to walk to Almond Grove. The exercise would be beneficial but they could chat about their tactics whilst absorbing more of the town's atmosphere. It was just after noon when they arrived at Style. Its windows, curtained in a delicate shade of pink, did not allow people to peer inside the premises and view ladies with their heads in driers or their hair in curlers but judging from the smart grey and pink exterior it seemed to be a flourishing and rather smart concern.

'I'm not familiar with these places,' chortled Clifton as he pushed open the door. 'I'm more of a short back and sides man, functional and neat, if you know what I mean, Sergeant.'

'There are some men who frequent these places, sir, to get their hair tinted when it starts to turn grey, not that I would ever do that!'

'I should bloody well hope you wouldn't, Sergeant. I'd be getting very worried about you if you did,' and then they arrived at a reception area. A smart woman in a pink overall bearing the logo 'Style' greeted them.

'Yes, gentleman, how can I help you?'

'Does Ian Simpson work here?'

'He does, yes. Can I give him a message?'

'We'd like to talk to him, I'm Detective Superintendent Clifton and this is Detective Sergeant Burrows.'

'Oh, dear, he's not in any trouble, is he?'

'Not to our knowledge, no, but we think he might be able to help us with our enquiries,' came the bland response.

'The murder you mean?'

'He could be an important witness. Now, if you could tell him we're here, and if it's not too much of an inconvenience, we'd like a word with him.'

'Well, it's a good time now, Superintendent,' said the woman. 'It's his lunch break. He's just finished Mrs Batsford and he'll be upstairs in our staff lounge. You can go up to see him. Shall I call him?'

'No, we'll find our own way, thanks.'

'Through the salon then, and up the stairs at the far end.'

In a haze of perfumed scents, they walked past half a dozen chairs, three of which were occupied by women in various stages of their latest hair-dos, climbed the stairs and found a door marked 'Staff only.' Clifton knocked but did not wait for a reply. He opened the door and noticed Ian Simpson sitting in an armchair with a magazine on his knee. He was alone and had a cup of tea in his hand with a plate of sandwiches on the floor at his side. Struggling to cope with the surprise arrivals without spilling his cup, he rose to his feet, successfully placed the cup on the floor and faced them.

Instinctively, he knew they were detectives and he also knew he must now put on the act for which he had rehearsed so many times.

'Ian Simpson?' asked Clifton as Sergeant Burrows closed the door.

'Yes, that's me,' he replied with just the slightest of lisps. He was a slender young man almost six feet tall, and he looked rather too thin for his height. He had a long narrow face with dark eyes and dark eyebrows, and his cheek bones were rather prominent. Clifton thought he looked like a hungry ballet dancer. He was dressed all in black, including his socks and shoes, and his shop gown was hanging from a coathanger on a stand in the room. As he rose from the chair, there was more than a hint of feminine grace about him.

'I'm Detective Superintendent Clifton and this is Detective Sergeant Burrows, we're investigating the murder of Edward Albert Swainby who died on Thursday and whose body was found in Latima Park, here in Hildenley,' began Clifton in very formal tones.

'Yes, how awful, wasn't it? Here in Hildenley of all places, we don't get that sort of thing in Hildenley, Superintendent. It's been in all the papers and everyone's talking about it, some of my clients are very concerned, I can tell you.'

'Aren't we all,' nodded Clifton.

'Look, why don't you sit down and can I offer you a cup of tea?'

'Thanks we'll sit, but no tea.' Clifton opted for a chair at the table in the corner while his sergeant settled in another of the armchairs, almost opposite Ian and made a great show of opening his notebook and finding a pencil.

'So how can I help you gentlemen?' Ian looked and sounded very calm, eager to assist the police in their enquiries. Underneath, however, his heart was pounding and he wondered how much they knew but he would answer their questions and try to be as helpful as he could. He must put on a good show, perhaps the best show of his fledgling acting career.

'You are Sergeant Simpson's son, I am told,' began Clifton. 'But you don't live at home?'

'Yes, I am, and you are right, I have a flat in town, a small one but very cosy. It's the top flat at number 27, St Hilda's Avenue. More of a bedsit really, but mine. It was my choice to leave home, Superintendent, I wanted to make my own way in the world. I wasn't thrown out, like a lot of youngsters are!'

'It sounds a sensible move, Ian. And how is your father?'

'We're all very worried about him. He's not at all well and when I rang mum this morning, she said the doctor had told dad to stay off work, and he might need a blood transfusion. Anaemia, she thought, although we wonder if it's more than that. Dad thinks it's something much more serious. It worries me, it's most unlike him to be ill, Superintendent, he's always been so fit and strong.'

'Let's hope it can be treated whatever it is. Now, Ian, we're making enquiries around town because we're trying to trace witnesses who might help our investigation.' Clifton now came straight to the point, a tactic which sometimes unsettled interviewees. Without explaining how he had acquired this piece of information, he said, 'I believe you were in Latima Park on Thursday evening?'

It did not appear to faze Ian Simpson. 'Yes I was, well not *in* the park as such, Superintendent, more a case of passing through, hurrying through on my way home.'

'You'd been out for the evening?'

'Yes, I go to drama classes, they're in the Methodist Hall in Wesley Street.'

'What time would that be?'

'They start at seven and finish at nine, I was there all that time.'

'With friends?'

'Yes, and my best friend Simeon was with me. We went back to his place for a drink afterwards.'

'We will need to talk to Simeon, we have to check every story, Ian. Where can we find him?'

'He's got a flat behind the Coliseum Cinema, Wellington Terrace, No. 6. His surname is Hewitson. It's on a name plate on his door but he won't be there now, he works for a bakery in town. Somerville's in Thrush

Road, I think he's due to finish about three this afternoon.'

'All right, we'll catch up with him. So after the drama class, you went to his flat. Times?'

'Well, we left the Hall just after nine and it's about a three or four minute walk to Wellington Terrace. No more. I'd say we got to his place about ten past nine give or take a minute or two.'

'And you went in?'

'I did, he invited me for a quick drink but said it would have to be quick because he had to be up early next morning for work. He starts about four o'clock in the morning, so I had a quick beer, a small bottle it was, and then went home.'

'So what time did you leave Simeon's?'

'Half nine or so, give or take a minute or two either way.'

'And which is your route home?'

'Well, as I said, Simeon is just behind the Coliseum and so I left there and went towards Latima Park, the bottom entrance. I always go home that way from Simeon's. I cut up through the park, it's by far the best way.'

'Were you alone?'

'As alone as a man can be with a cinema audience turning out at the same time! When I left Simeon's, I found myself leading a crowd of people who'd just come out of the pictures, a dozen or two I'd say, they were laughing and talking as people do, and I was a good distance ahead of them. Like leading the Charge of the Light Brigade it was. A lot of them were following in my direction but several turned off before too long, numbers dwindled the further away I got.'

'Did you know any of them?' Clifton asked.

'I didn't look to see, they were all behind me and so I hurried along, not wanting to get overtaken by them. I heard them calling and shouting as people do and some call and shout at me, Superintendent, because they see me as a sissy, so I ignore them ... which is what I did that night. People might not have been shouting at me or calling me, but I wasn't going to respond, so I hurried ahead, wanting to keep out of their way and get straight home.'

'Did anyone catch up to you? To talk? Try to engage you in conversation?'

'No, I made sure they didn't, I kept well ahead, Superintendent, I can walk fast when I have to. I just kept walking very fast, up through the park and out at the top.'

'Was anyone else in the park?'

'A young couple followed me in through the South Gate, I think they'd been to the pictures, I looked back and saw them as I was going up the winding paths, but they didn't follow me. They were quite a way behind me. I think they stayed in the park and sat on a seat but I didn't see anyone else. I hurried out because I needed to go to the toilet, that beer, you know, it goes right through me in minutes.'

'There are public toilets in the park,' said Clifton. 'Near the museum. You could have gone there.'

'Oh, Superintendent, I wouldn't go there . . . not at night . . .' and he shuddered most realistically. 'And I wouldn't pee behind a tree, I might be seen. Besides it's not a very nice thing to do. My flat is very close to the western end of the top of the park so I was home within two or three minutes of leaving the park.'

'So what time were you actually in the park?'

'Well, Superintendent, I left Simeon's just after half past nine so I'd get to the park just before twenty to ten or so. It's a few minutes walk up through the park, so I'd leave about quarter to ten or so. Give or take a minute or two either way.'

'And when you were in the park, were you aware of any noises, unusual noises? Loud voices, a disturbance of any kind? Shouting? Someone running?'

'Nothing, Superintendent, no, nothing at all. But it is a large park, you know, people at one end would probably have no idea what was happening at the other, especially at night. But I went up the end farthest from town, the western end, nearest my flat in fact, but I saw no one, apart from that young couple. I've no idea whether they saw me, I have no idea who they were.'

'Was there a man with a dog in the park?'

'If there was I never saw him, and I never heard any dogs barking like they sometimes do at night.'

'Fair enough. So when you emerged at the top, did you see anyone?'

'My father says he was there about the time I was leaving, but I never saw him. I never saw anyone, but it was dark, you know. Quite dark in spite of street lights.'

'Sergeant Simpson was at the eastern gate at quarter to ten, he told us, as near as dammit. On duty. In uniform.'

'I didn't come out of that gate, I came out of the north one and never saw him, honest. Mind you, if I was hurrying off home for the loo, I'd not be looking around to see who was about and policemen are very hard to see in the dark, those dark uniforms can easily be missed in the shadows. Dad often told me how policemen could hide themselves in the shadows of a town at night by just standing still.'

'Which way do you turn from the top of the park, to reach your flat? You said you often use that route.'

'I do, Superintendent, when I do so, I turn left and go right along Park Road until I get to the junction, then go straight across, through where the shops are. My flat is on the top floor of one of those big houses behind the shops.'

'I was up there only a short while ago, Ian,' said Clifton. 'It's a nice part of town.'

'Very nice indeed, yes, I like it. It suits me, I couldn't do with living in a rough part, or somewhere noisy.'

'A wise choice. Now, remind me, which gate did you leave the park by?'

'The middle one, the second along from either east or west.'

'That's Gate No. 2, sometimes called the North Gate,' said Clifton, mentally noting that this corresponded with Sergeant Simpson's statement. It was now clear in Clifton's mind that this young man was indeed the mystery man who'd been seen by Sergeant Simpson. It also meant the sergeant was telling the truth, so why did he not recognize his own son? Or admit recognizing him? Or if the sergeant had called out to him as he had said, why had the lad not responded? There was something not quite right here and Clifton found both questions highly intriguing. The sergeant had said, however, that traffic was passing and some vehicles, buses especially, can make a lot of noise if they're groaning up a hill – and Park Road was on a slight incline, sloping upwards towards the west. That could explain why the lad had not responded to the sergeant's call but it still didn't fully explain how Sergeant Simpson had failed to recognize his own son. He wondered if they had colluded in some way over Swainby's death.

'Were you wearing a hat of any kind?'

'A hat? Good heavens no, I never wear a hat.'

'A man was seen hurrying from the park via that gate; our witness indicates that the time and place correspond with your account, except that the man had his hands up to his head and face, rather like pulling on a woolly hat.'

'I can't remember doing anything like that, Superintendent, but certainly I was not wearing a hat or cap of any kind.'

'You know why I am asking you all these questions, don't you?' continued Clifton.

'A man was murdered in the park that night, it's all over town. I know you have to ask questions from anyone who might be able to help.'

'We think the crime was committed around the time you would be passing through the park, Ian. The victim might even have been lying dead, or might even have been in the process of being attacked at that very time. The killer might have been hiding in the park, or rushing away. You can see why it is so important for you to tell us if you did see anyone, or hear anything while you were passing through.'

'I realize how important it is, but I didn't hear or see anything or anyone, Superintendent, only that young couple who followed me.'

'We've spoken to them too.'

'I don't know their names, I can't really add anything else.'

'So, let's continue. You went home, you told us. What did you do at home?'

'I got in about ten o'clock, maybe a bit earlier, and made myself a sandwich and a cup of tea. I read for a while, half an hour or so, and then went to bed.'

'Alone?'

'Alone? Good heavens yes, Superintendent.'

'So no one can vouch for that fact?'

'Well, I think my landlady might have heard me, she never misses anything and I know she was in when I got home because I could hear her radio, it was someone talking, not music of any kind, but I don't know which programme it was.'

'We can check. Now, I must ask you this. Do you know the identity of the murdered man?'

'Not until you mentioned his name just now. Dad didn't say, he said the name wasn't being released until his family had been told, and it's not been given in the papers.'

'All right, well I think that's all for now, Ian. Thanks for your time. If we need to check anything further, we'll have to speak to you again.'

'Yes, yes, I understand. I just wish I could be more helpful.'

'Well, if you didn't see or hear anything, there's nothing we can do to change that, Ian. If you do recollect anything you've forgotten or overlooked, don't be afraid to contact us. In the meantime thanks, and give our regards to your father when you see him.'

'Yes, I will be going to see him tonight, we are so worried.'

And so the two detectives left the salon with thanks to the manageress and walked away in silence, intending to return to the police station. They would do so via Latima Park. Then, when they were eventually out of earshot of anyone, Clifton asked, 'Well, Sarge, what did you make of that young man?'

'He's as queer as a nine bob note, sir, there's no doubt about that, but it doesn't make him a killer. And his story sounds feasible, it fits in with what we know to date.'

'He doesn't look strong enough to have dealt with Swainby in the way his injuries indicate,' said Clifton. 'But I could be wrong. Years ago, I knew a male ballet dancer who was as strong as an ox; they reckoned his dancing practice made his muscles as good as, or better than, someone like a long distance racing cyclist.'

'People can gain remarkable strength when they're angry or frightened, sir.'

'I know, and it doesn't take much strength to wield a small stone, and even a small stone can do a lot of damage to a man with a thin skull, as we now know. And as you say, in the hands of a maniac, extra strength can always be found. That attack was almost manic, you know, he struck blow after blow when the first would have felled him at least, except in this case it killed him. The pathologist said he died from the first blow.'

'So the rest wouldn't have any effect, sir? He'd be trying to kill a dead man ... I can see a jury would have a field day with that one, if the defence put it up!'

'Don't start your legal pontificating here, Sergeant,' laughed Clifton. 'In our books this is a cold-blooded murder! It's up to the defence to prove it wasn't.'

'That kind of description, a cold-blooded murderer, doesn't seem to fit that youngster, sir, so would you put him in the frame?'

'Who else is there, Sergeant?'

'It is a puzzle, I agree, sir. We know Swainby was alive about nine-thirty, we know he went into the park because that's where he was found, and we know he was dead by five minutes to ten, give or take a minute or two either way. He died within that short time span so we have to establish just what happened within that twenty minutes or so. It's time enough for murder to be committed.'

'Precisely, Sergeant, and Ian admits he was in the park at that time but not for long. It's odd that no one saw him there but in the darkness with shadows and him in dark clothes, I suppose he'd be almost invisible. Anyway, how long does it take to inflict that kind of damage to a skull? A few blows with a stone. We're talking of seconds here, Sergeant, not minutes or hours. He admits being in the park and I think he had enough time to do it.'

'I'm sure he had, sir. I think Swainby was confronted and died within less than a minute or even less than half a minute. It's frightening that life can be snuffed out in such a short time without a moment's notice.'

'So we agree Ian *could* be responsible? Within the time scale he has given us? His story has a ring of truth, though. He rushed in the South Gate, raced through the park because he was in desperate need of a pee and hurried out of gate No. 2 without seeing or hearing a thing, not even his own father. That sounds perfectly feasible. His mind would be concentrated on getting home as fast as he could.'

'I can understand that, sir. He tells a sound story.'

'He does, so what we must decide, or establish, is whether he's lying and whether he killed Swainby while he was in the park. And if he did, why? What could be his motive?'

'The courting couple were in the park at that time, sir, we can't ignore them. They must have heard or seen something. I think we should talk to them again.'

'They've both been interviewed at length and both claim they didn't see or hear anything. I think they were too wrapped up in each other and I don't regard them as suspects, Sergeant. The first time they knew something was wrong was when they heard the policeman's whistle, but it sounded a long way off, so they said. I believe them: it tallies with what else we've been told. Even if they heard the whistle, they might not have heard the battering – but how much noise does a stone make when used as a hammer on a fellow's skull? Not a lot, I would say. And if Swainby didn't have time to scream or shout out, there'd be very little noise. Like Ian, though, they claim they saw no one. They didn't see Ian, but we know he was there.'

'I agree, sir, I think they are telling the truth; they come over as truthful and honest, with eyes only for each other.'

'A lot of villains seem truthful and honest, Sergeant, and I've known some murderers who seem really nice people! I know the couple were well away from the murder scene, but you'd think they would have noticed something amiss unless they were too wrapped up in each other like a pair of love-sick doves. Having listened to all this and looked around the park, I think it's possible the killing could have occurred without anyone realizing – and that's our problem. We need to think this one through very carefully, Sergeant. We know Swainby was killed after nine-thirty but before nine fifty-five and that means there *was* someone else in the park. That is beyond dispute. The killer was there. Was it Ian? Or his father? Or both? I'm convinced it was not the young couple and the stone hasn't produced any fingerprints. There was nothing else at the scene except the dead body of Edward Swainby, so how can we prove who killed him? And we must *prove* our case.'

'Do we need to search Ian Simpson's flat, sir? If he was the killer, his clothing would be bloodstained, surely? That could provide evidence of his presence at the scene. If you get close enough to wield a stone like that, it's almost inevitable that some blood will splash in your direction and get onto your clothes. But all we need is a single drop.'

'True, but at the moment, I've no grounds for arresting Ian Simpson and no evidence to suggest he is the killer. But we should visit his flat, just as a matter of course, if only to have a look at it. You never know, he might read books about masochistic practices, war books, books about murder and death . . . one's home tells a lot about a person. If we can get more evidence of his guilt, we could search it for other evidence, like his hobbies if they involve violence. We might even find some bloodstained clothing but if his clothing was bloodstained, he'll have got rid of it by now. You can be sure of that.'

'I still think we should search his flat before we finally eliminate him from the enquiry.'

'We'll do that, Sergeant, even if we have to get a warrant. I can see we are thinking in tandem here! Right now, though, I can't do that search without a warrant and getting one takes time. I'm not sure we could get one at short notice, we've no nothing to justify one. I'd rather wait until we have some more positive evidence.'

They walked back to the police station via Latima Park and took another careful look at the layout of the paths, gardens, rockeries and fish-ponds, paying yet another visit to the museum and the bench near which Swainby was found. During that walk, Superintendent Clifton was uncharacteristically quiet but his sergeant did not attempt to interrupt. He knew Clifton needed thinking time, and he knew he was re-appraising the interview with Ian Simpson. They walked back to the police station in silence. The big man was silent because he could not avoid a dreadful thought which continued to nag him. For some time he'd been aware there had been another man in the park at the time of the murder and Ian's account had a ring of truth about it. He readily admitted being there at the material time even if no one else had seen him. But there had been another man. With bloodstained clothing. And with enough time to commit the crime. It was Sergeant Simpson. So was *he* the killer? And was his son involved? Was the sergeant covering up for the son, or vice versa? Could that be feasible? If so, what was their motive? Was the sergeant being over-protective of his effeminate son? Had the sergeant stumbled across something involving Ian and Swainby? Had Swainby done something to the son, not realizing the sergeant was nearby? Had they managed to concoct some kind of cover story?

There was no doubt that since the death of Swainby, the sergeant's behaviour had been decidedly odd, even if he was claiming to be sick. So was he really sick? Or could his physical appearance be due to stress following his involvement in this most serious of crimes? The more Clifton thought about it, the more he realized that father and son could have been jointly involved in Swainby's death, but why? What possible motive could they have? Ian's sexual orientation perhaps?

Those questions would not go away so the blood on the sergeant's uniform might be vital, even if he had explained it. Perhaps he should obtain a search warrant for Ian's flat – and the Simpsons' house? Or might it be prudent to wait until he had more positive evidence rather than basing his suspicions on mere supposition? Or was he being unusually indecisive? He was still deep in thought when he and Burrows returned to the station but Detective Sergeant Huntley was waiting. He was sitting in the office currently being used by the big man, determined not to miss him.

'Sir,' he said, getting to his feet as Clifton and Burrows entered. 'I've got some very sensitive information. It's relative to the murder enquiry, but I think, at this stage, it's for our ears only.'

'About what?' asked Clifton.

'Sergeant Simpson's wife, sir.'

CHAPTER 13

'WHAT about her?'

'She was raped, sir, by Swainby. Years ago. In 1939.'

For what seemed a long time, Superintendent Clifton did not reply even if his brain was rapidly assessing the explosive implications of this news. It reinforced his assessment of the murder and his opinion as to the identity of the guilty party or parties, however unlikely it seemed. Quite suddenly, a motive had now been presented to him. And, of course, Sergeant Simpson had not once referred to this during the investigation. Had he hoped to conceal his wife's links with Swainby?

If so, that had been remarkable naïve. Or criminally culpable.

'Are you sure?' he asked, his big heavy brows creased in concentration. 'I can't remember seeing any mention of it in Swainby's record.'

'Swainby wasn't convicted, sir, the case was thrown out by the examining magistrates at committal proceedings. He got away with it, he was never arraigned, he never stood trial.'

'Far too many guilty people are getting away with crime, Sergeant. English justice is becoming a mockery. Why didn't it go before a jury?'

'The key witness couldn't identify him, sir. They put him up in an identification parade and Pamela Crossley, as she was then, couldn't identify him as the rapist. The other evidence against him was largely circumstantial and he continued to deny the rape, so without a positive ID the defence claimed there was no case to answer. After listening to the evidence, the magistrates agreed.'

'But we got the right man? There was no doubt in our minds?'

'No doubt at all, sir, our lads at the time had witnesses which put him at the scene. The victim's description of his clothing fitted, he beat her and the blood on his clothes was the same group as hers, he had scratches on his face, nail scratches from a woman, he was a known sexual offender even then ... he even admitted being in her house, saying she'd consented. It was all there, sir, a sound case apart from her not picking him out at the ID parade. That created the necessary doubt and he got off with it. At committal proceedings that was, it didn't get to the Assizes.'

'She was single at the time, you say? Not married to Sergeant Simpson?'

'Yes, she was single but this was only days before her wedding, sir, she'd been to visit her dressmaker for a fitting of her wedding dress just in case there were any last minute alterations, three or four days before the wedding that was. The wedding was due to take place here in Hildenley. Swainby followed her home, by all accounts, and attacked her in her home, well, her parents' home to be precise.'

'This all sounds a bit iffy to me, Sergeant. If she described him as her attacker but chickened out at the ID parade, it looks as if she'd changed her mind, or maybe something else had cropped up? Why didn't she make sure he was sent down after what he'd done to her? Do you think she didn't want him convicted? Or was there some other reason for her action? Is there more to all this than we know? I think we need to dig a lot deeper here, Sergeant. I'm beginning to think our worthy Sergeant Simpson is much more devious than we give him credit for. Have we got the original file?'

'Yes, it's here, I dug it out of the attic.' He passed the thick buff folder to Clifton who placed it in his in-tray.

'Great. I'll go through it this afternoon but keep this to yourself for now. I won't mention it at our 2 p.m. conference either and I don't want this spreading to the teams, certainly not to the public. And most certainly not to Sergeant Simpson or that lad of his. Not yet, anyway. How is he, by the way? Any news?'

'Still poorly, so I'm told. Mrs Simpson rang in. The doctor saw him this morning but said he couldn't make any assessment until the results of the blood test come through but signed him off. There was talk of it being glandular fever.'

'That's not very pleasant but it could be worse. It wouldn't surprise me if he's got leukaemia. I know the signs.'

'The medics reckon he's anaemic and will be off work a while.'

'They would say that, wouldn't they? It's all guesswork at this stage; the blood test will get it sorted out. Anyway, tell me more – maybe his illness is fortuitous under the circumstances. We need to keep this development from him until I give the word so it's as well he's out of our way. So how did you come by this gem, Sergeant?' and Clifton now looked much happier than he had at this morning's conference.

'From a contact of mine, sir, a woman who used to work at the hospital, she's retired now. Martha Jenkins. Pamela Crossley was sent there for a check up after the rape. Her doctor, a local GP, wanted a more thorough examination than he could give. A few of the older hospital workers remember the case even if they might not associate Pamela Crossley with Mrs Simpson. Time's a great healer anyway. The press never published anything about it, by the way. They didn't even attend the committal hearing so the case never got into the public domain, apart from some isolated instances of gossip. The public remember the butcher and cleaver yarn!'

'The magistrates could ban the press from some committals in those days, but your Martha woman remembered the rape?'

'Because she looked after Pamela Crossley. And she remembered more, sir.'

'You have been busy, Sergeant!'

'It's my job, sir,' smiled Detective Sergeant Huntley. 'You wanted us to get under the belly of the town, listen to gossip . . . well, I've been doing a bit of that and Martha has lots of memories of that hospital, sir, and the people who went there during her time on the staff. Give her a whisky or two, sir, and it loosens her tongue. She's not the soul of discretion that she might have been in her working days. As she gets older, she tends to reminisce more.'

'A nurse, was she?'

'No, sir, a ward orderly. Took meals in, helped patients out to the toilets or to take a bit of exercise, made beds, did simple dressings to wounds, changed their pyjamas or nightdresses, that sort of thing. Not quite a nurse but with more responsibility than a cleaner.'

'So she would see a lot and know a lot?'

'She did, sir, and now she likes to reminisce about the good old days, so I took her a bottle and she talked to me while she sampled the first few nips.'

'That's what I call good detective work, Sergeant, so you can put that bottle down to expenses. All right, give! What other piece of news did she impart?'

'Sergeant Simpson was a patient there, years ago, before his marriage, sir. She can't remember the date but it was following a serious motor cycle accident. Somewhere in the mid-1930s, he'd be in his teens, she thinks. A lad with his first motor bike. He was very badly injured around the lower half of his body, one of the handlebars entered his lower stomach area and damaged his internal organs. He needed several operations but one thing that was affected was his ability to have children. He was made incapable of fathering a child even if the rest of his tackle was in good working order. His injuries meant he wasn't accepted by the army.'

'But he was fit enough for the police?'

'The police doctor wasn't quite so severe as the military man, so it seems. He reckoned that if Simpson could walk, he could patrol a beat. Simple logic, sir.'

'That figures, but sometimes I think they'll let anybody in our job! I'm waiting for the day they take in one-legged recruits! Well, I think I know what you are going to tell me now, Sergeant. I thought he had a son, that lad called Ian. I've just come from interviewing him.'

'That's what everyone thinks, sir, me too, until now. If what Martha says is right, Ian can't be his son, sir, not his natural son. Martha said when he was born everyone said it was a honeymoon baby, but she knew different. She kept quiet about it, then, so she says. It was more than her job was worth to reveal it.'

'I can see that, yes.'

'But if she knew, sir, then I'm sure others would know as well.'

'Others? Who, exactly?'

'People who'd worked in the hospital, I expect.'

'Seems logical. So it's likely that several people, including your Martha, knew he couldn't father a child because he'd been made infertile?'

'Yes, sir.'

'And Martha, working at the hospital, knew Mrs Simpson, Pamela Crossley as was, had been raped a few days before her wedding?'

'Yes, sir.'

'So she has put two and two together and made four?'

'I think so, sir.'

'So if what she says is right, Sergeant, then Ian Simpson could really be Swainby's child?'

'Yes, sir, that seems very likely. Unless Pamela was very promiscuous and had it off with somebody else just before she got married. Which I doubt.'

'You know her better than me. From what you say, I reckon the rape's the most likely answer but if this is true, why is Martha spilling the beans now?'

'Because of Swainby's murder, sir, it set her thinking and she thought it was something we should know about; she said there was some gossip around town at the time, twenty years ago or more. She's kept quiet about it all these years and thinks most folks will have forgotten about it or never even known.'

'So why tell you all of a sudden?'

'For one thing I was asking her to cast her mind back over Swainby's time here, and secondly, she thought it might have some bearing on the case.'

'She's right about that! So what about Ian himself? Do we know if he is aware of this? Does he know Swainby could be his real father?'

'I don't know for sure, sir, but Martha thinks not. So far as she knows, the Simpsons brought Ian up as their own. He's always been Ian Simpson and they've always been very good parents, loving and caring. He is an only child too. Simpson is infertile, so it would seem, and they never adopted any. People kept quiet about the case, they did in those days, they knew how to keep their mouths shut. There's lots of children living in town whose parents aren't their blood parents, the result of their dads and mums having a bit of nookie on the side. Ian's birth wasn't all that different from that, except his mum had been raped nine months earlier. It seems Ian's not the product of love, sir, he's the product of rape. Not a nice thing for a kid to know about. I'm not surprised everyone's quiet about it – and, of course, it happened a long time ago.'

'Which means, if all this is true and can be verified, Sergeant Simpson would know of Ian's true parentage?'

'Yes, sir.'

'Good God, this gets worse. And so, the next logical question is this – if Simpson knows of Ian's parentage, what about Swainby himself? Did he know?'

'Martha thinks he did, sir. His brother was in hospital at the same time as Sergeant Simpson. A broken leg. According to Martha, they were in the same ward and Swainby's brother knew of Simpson's injuries and the effect they would have on his love-life. They talked about it. Swainby was a regular visitor to his brother.'

'They were local, were they? The Swainby family? At that time?'

'It seems so, sir. The lads had no parents and an aunt brought them up, here in Hildenley. The brothers were very close, so Martha reckons, although Ted's brother wasn't a wrong 'un. He worked for an estate agent, a decent lad, he tried to keep his daft brother on the straight and narrow, so I'm told.'

'She's a fount of information is your Martha!' laughed Clifton. 'We could do with a Martha for every murder investigation. So it's a fair bet Swainby knew of Simpson's infertility before Simpson married Pamela?'

'Yes, sir.'

'So where is that brother now? We need a word with him.'

'He was killed in action, sir, during the war, and the aunt died eight or nine years ago. There's no other Swainby left. Ted was the last, he never married and never produced a family, well not a legitimate one that we know about.'

'Except Ian Simpson, and it seems he's not legitimate. But he could be Swainby's next-of-kin whether he likes it or not, so let me think this one through. If Swainby knew Simpson could never be a father, and then after his rape of her, Mrs Simpson immediately gets pregnant, Swainby would surely realize the child was his? Or at least think it was possible. Right?'

'Right, sir. That's how I see it, sir. He would know – or he'd have a very good idea.'

'So what would he do, Sergeant? Can you see him becoming all paternal and broody about his forthcoming baby?'

'Not him, sir, no. He'd be worried about having to take responsibility for the child and having to pay maintenance if Pamela made application. A domestic court could order him to pay until the child was sixteen or even until twenty-one if he was in full-time education. He'd know the risks, all young men did. And paternity could be proved by blood tests. And she was a policeman's wife . . . he'd not hang about.'

'I agree with you. I can't see a man like Swainby hanging around waiting for a summons to the domestic court if that could be thrown at him.'

'Right, sir. It's enough to scare the pants of any young man, a life-time of paying maintenance. Swainby wouldn't want that, he'd be off like a rocket, running like a hare to get as far away as he could where nobody could trace him. He wasn't to know the Simpsons would treat the child as their own when it was born, and that they'd welcome the lad.'

'Which he did? Swainby. Clear off, I mean.'

'Yes, sir, he went to live at Cresslington in Garminghamshire either because of that or because he was chased off by that butcher with his cleaver. Whatever the reason, the local police were chuffed to bits about it.'

'One less villain to worry about in Hildenley, eh? So why come back after all this time? He's just out of nick on licence. There'll be conditions on his licence but if he really wanted to lose himself, he could have gone anywhere in the world. Why do such a daft thing as come back here?'

'Perhaps he felt safe here now?' suggested Huntley. 'And he might have had friends here, after all this time. People who'd help him get back onto his feet after doing time. Perhaps he thought everyone had forgotten his previous escapades.'

'Could be,' shrugged Clifton.

'There's another possibility, sir,' said Huntley. 'And this one's down to Martha as well, she suggested it.'

'I'm all ears!'

'She reminded me that Ian Simpson must be coming up for his twenty-first birthday, sir, sometime very soon.'

'Are you suggesting that a man like Swainby, a known rapist and villain of the highest order, would come here just because he wants to see the lad who might be his son? The son he's probably never seen? The son he's never cared a jot for? All because he's nearly twenty-one?'

'Swainby had no one, sir, no family, he never married, he had no brothers or sisters alive, no cousins, nothing. Ian was his flesh and blood, his only flesh and blood and with Ian reaching twenty-one, Swainby's responsibility for maintenance would expire; in any case, applications for maintenance had to be made within a year of the child's birth. That burden is now over, he can't be touched for maintenance so perhaps he wanted to come back to find out what sort of child he had fathered? It's not out of the question, for a man with no one else in his very empty life . . . and, sir . . . .'

'I'm listening,' said Clifton as Huntley paused.

'Swainby's just been inside for five years. At his age, he must have been wondering what the future holds. He must have been thinking hard about his life . . . I reckon it's feasible he wanted a chance to look at his child, sir, to see his own flesh and blood . . . his *sole* flesh and blood. The records don't show he fathered any other child. Brooding about that in the nick could have become an obsession once he was out, or it might have been prompted by chats to other family-loving prisoners.'

'It all makes some sort of sense I suppose. I'm sure even rapists and murderers can get emotional and protective when it comes to their own kith and kin. I've no idea whether Swainby would think like that, but he could. I accept that's a possibility. And it might explain his presence in town, it needs to be considered. Nice work, Sergeant. Very nice work. Well done and congratulations. Your local knowledge has proved invaluable, so we must take it from here. Now, gentlemen,' Clifton looked at the two sergeants.

'I know what we've just discussed has been all conjecture and speculation. We don't know whether Swainby really knew he was a father, but it sounds rather good to me. It opens up some very positive lines of enquiry. It means we've got to get this sorted out very soon, and if what you say is true, Sergeant Huntley, then Swainby would surely have made contact with either Mrs Simpson or Ian soon after arriving here. I think he'd do it surreptitiously, so that's our next line of enquiry.'

They nodded in their understanding.

'In the greatest secrecy,' stressed Clifton. 'We need to interview both Ian and his mother, preferably without Sergeant Simpson being aware of our interest.'

'He's bound to find out, sir.'

'Yes he is, so that's why he's last on my list of interviewees. Mrs Simpson first, then another crack at Ian and finally the sergeant, in that order. And I'll conduct the interviews, that's my job.'

'Whatever they say, it puts them all in the frame, doesn't it, sir?' asked Huntley.

'It does indeed, Sergeant. They're all in the frame until they've been eliminated from our enquiries. But, thinking reasonably, can we honestly believe any of our Simpsons would do such a thing? Commit murder?'

'I've known Dick Simpson for years, sir, and I'd say he's not capable of murder, he's just the opposite, a real nice gentle man, a man who puts his family first. He's given Ian a home and I can't see Ian hammering a man like that either . . . not his own father, that's if he knew of the link . . . and Mrs Simpson wouldn't harm a fly . . . .'

'Just like some murderers I've known, Sergeant!' said Clifton, looking at his watch. 'Well, it's lunch time. Get yourselves something to eat, don't breathe a word about this to anyone, and I'll see you both after the two o'clock conference. We'll discuss strategy once we've had time to digest all this.'

★

The two sergeants, thinking it wise not to eat their sandwiches and drink tea with the rest of the murder team in case they let slip something they should not, opted for an outdoor seat on a green which overlooked the hospital. It would be quiet and they'd be away from flapping ears and curious eyes.

Detective Superintendent Clifton also opted to keep away from the others and ordered a cup of tea from the office duty constable, saying he would take it in his office where he was going to have his sandwiches at his desk. He asked not to be disturbed and that no telephone calls be put through. Whatever it was, and however urgent it was, it could wait until two o'clock.

In those precious minutes of seclusion, therefore, he settled down to read the file on the rape of Pamela Crossley. It was the file which contained the evidence which had been presented at the committal proceedings in Hildenley. Held before magistrates, committal proceedings were not trials; their purpose was to assess the evidence in serious criminal cases to determine whether or not a trial should follow at either Quarter Sessions or the Assizes. If they felt there was sufficient evidence, the examining magistrates, as they were known, ordered the case to be heard before a jury at one of those higher courts. If the examining magistrates felt there was insufficient evidence to justify a trial, then no further proceedings were taken and the accused was free to leave the court.

At the time of the rape, Pamela Crossley was a 20-year-old clerk who worked for an architect in Hildenley. A virgin until the rape, she lived at home with her parents at No. 43, Crompton Road, Hildenley. It was a good quality semi-detached house built in the late 1920s and it was owned by her father, Roderick. He was employed by the local bus company as transport manager. The family was well respected in the town, with Mrs Crossley working part-time as a receptionist in the Royal Hotel.

Pamela was their only child and was due to be married at All Saints Church, Hildenley, at 10.30 a.m. on Saturday, 28 May, 1939. Her future husband was Richard Simpson, then a police constable, who hailed from Millingham. He had been a constable in Hildenley since 1937, transferring here from Prestaby.

After work on Thursday, 19 May, 1939, Pamela had arranged to visit her dressmaker for a fitting of her all-white wedding dress. Her mother could not accompany her because she and her father had previously arranged to have a meal with some friends at the friends' home in Hildenley but Pamela had assured her mother she could cope. There was no need for mother to join her and absolutely no call for her to cancel her evening out. The dressmaker was a Mrs Maureen Crosby, a friend of the family and a well-known local seamstress who worked from her home at No.3, Sycamore Drive; the fitting had been scheduled for seven o'clock that evening and any alterations would be completed in time for the dress to be collected by no later than a week the following Friday, the day before the wedding.

According to statements by both Pamela and Mrs Crosby, the young woman had arrived at the house on time, no one had followed her and she had spent time trying on her dress. A few alterations were necessary, all minor. She had remained in the house for about an hour to ensure everything was right and had then left to walk home, a distance of about three-quarters of a mile. It was a fine evening if a little cool, but it was dry and there was no wind. It was light when she began her walk, darkness not falling until after nine o'clock.

As Pamela turned into Crompton Avenue from Crompton Lane, she was aware of someone behind her, she could hear footsteps and it sounded as if they were being made by someone in a hurry. She took no further notice and did not turn around to look because people were often about at that time of evening, sometimes walking dogs, sometimes exercising or sometimes just enjoying an evening stroll in this quiet part of town. The footsteps came nearer, however, and as she approached her home, she knew the person was very close behind, she could hear his heavy breathing and thought it was someone running for exercise but as she turned up the garden path he followed her . . . .

She turned to see the man now known to be Edward Albert Swainby, then aged twenty-five or twenty-six and the look on his face, and his utter silence, terrified her as she placed the Yale key in the lock of the front door. She hoped to get inside the house and slam the door behind her but as the door opened to admit her, he forced himself into the opening, pushed her into the house and slammed the door even before she could scream. He thumped her on the head and face, dragged her into the living room and beat her about the body with his fists before ripping off her underclothes and raping her while threatening to kill her if she told anyone. She screamed throughout but the neighbours did not hear (it transpired they were out too, at the cinema) and the more she screamed, the more violent he became. It was all over in a few minutes; he ran out, slamming the door and leaving her bleeding on the floor in a dreadful state. With no one to help, and humiliated and tearful, it took Pamela a long time to summon the strength and courage to call for help.

She rang the neighbours but they were out; she tried to ring Dick but he was on duty somewhere and so she rang her parents, apologizing for interrupting their evening . . . and they rang the police.

Shortly afterwards, the first police arrived on the scene, one of whom was a policewoman; a doctor was called and it rapidly became evident that this was indeed a true rape, not a fictitious allegation and so a hunt was launched for the man described by Pamela – a man in his late twenties, with dark hair, heavy black eyebrows, sharp features and wearing a grey shirt with an open neck, a dark blue jacket or blazer and grey trousers. She did not know his name but fortunately, Swainby had been spotted running away by a man working in his garden just along the road, and he recognized him. He even told the police they'd probably find him in the Three Tuns – that was his regular haunt. He must have known Pamela, he must have known her parents were out for the evening and perhaps he even knew the neighbours were absent.

The police began to think he had been preying on Pamela, watching her for some time before committing the crime. Swainby was found in the bar. He was wearing the clothes described by Pamela and his description fitted too. He was arrested immediately and taken to Hildenley Police Station where the police doctor found scratches on his face, blood and fresh semen on his underwear, and fibres which matched those on the carpet on Pamela's parents' house. His clothes were all removed and taken away for forensic examination and he was given a set of prison clothes while he languished in the cell at Hildenley Police Station.

Under questioning, he admitted having intercourse with Pamela but said it had been with her full consent as she had the house to herself because her parents were out. He claimed she had told him they would be out that night. She was a virgin hence the blood on his underpants and he strenuously denied rape. Due to his claim that Pamela had consented, he was eventually released on bail with a requirement to report to Hildenley Police Station daily unless he received a written notice to the contrary.

Pamela in the meantime was examined initially by the police doctor and subsequently by a gynaecologist; her clothing was removed for subsequent examination by the forensic service and she was subjected to the ordeal of having to make a long written statement which described her dreadful experience in considerable and very graphic detail, even recording Swainby's act of ejaculation and his shout of triumph upon doing so. It was all necessary to ensure a prosecution, she was told; rape, not mere intercourse, had to be proven in a court of law when the defence would claim she had consented or that no rape had occurred, merely some rough horseplay.

PC Simpson, as he was then, was located on his beat and allowed to hurry to the side of his fiancée to provide what little comfort he could but there was little he could do. What was not stated in the file, but which Clifton knew would have happened, was that PC Simpson would know the ordeal for Pamela was not yet over, not by a long way.

Even after giving her statements, she would eventually have to appear in court – not just at one court but two (the committal hearing and then the trial at the Assizes) there to relate her experience in more graphic detail but also to undergo the rigorous and highly personal cross-examination by the defence who would do all in their power to destroy her by making her look like a prostitute or a woman of easy virtue or even a woman out for revenge.

The file did contain a note, however, which said that PC Simpson had been a tower of strength to his bride-to-be, so much so that she agreed to go ahead with the wedding in spite of her injuries. The scratches on her face and arms could be covered up, some by the sleeves of her wedding dress and others by make-up, while the bruises to her body were concealed by her clothing. And so the wedding had gone ahead; she would not let a criminal like Swainby ruin her life. As he read the notes, Clifton felt proud of Simpson; clearly he had been a tower of strength on that occasion, and since. To bring up the rapist's son was truly an act of great charity.

In reading the file, Clifton was also sure of two things. First, he was sure that Pamela had suffered a dreadful rape and second, he was sure the guilty man was Edward Albert Swainby. What he could not understand was why Pamela had not been able to pick out her assailant on the subsequent identification parade – in spite of the powerful evidence against him, this had enabled Swainby's defence to cast doubt upon his guilt as the rapist and so the magistrates had found no case to answer.

It was a travesty of justice, a guilty man had gone free to commit further dreadful crimes – until now. Swainby was now dead, murdered by an act of violence equal to that he had used upon his victims. Rough justice? True justice? Or was it really justice at all? An eye for an eye . . . had one of his victims gained sweet revenge? Even after all this time? More than twenty years? Could such a murder be regarded as a good thing, he pondered? But he was not paid to ponder such difficult questions. His job was to find the killer. And now he was sure he knew who it was.

It was time for the two o'clock conference.

CHAPTER 14

THE conference began with Clifton asking the teams if they had learned anything significant that morning. One or two produced snippets of information which were rather more general than specific – for example, several people had seen young men in black clothes around town on Thursday night, but, as someone had pointed out, it was fashionable for up-to-date young men to wear black. This prompted one detective to say he'd stopped and interviewed three young men in black and all had had alibis for Thursday night.

One or two detectives referred to organizations and societies which had had meetings or gatherings on Thursday evening, generally with their members leaving between nine-thirty and ten o'clock but, after tracing most of those members, none could provide any useful information about people they'd seen in town. Pub leavers had also been quizzed but none had noticed anything out of the ordinary and none could be regarded as suspects – all those questioned had alibis for the critical time.

One of the detective sergeants mentioned the drama evening class, adding it had a membership of fifteen, most of whom had been traced thanks to the attendance register; one of them was Ian Simpson, he told them, adding that this was the son of Sergeant Simpson who, after the class, had gone to the home of a friend called Simeon Villiers. He'd interviewed Simeon who'd confirmed Ian had left around nine-thirty that night to walk home, but to date, the sergeant had not located Ian. He had Ian's address but when he'd called the lad was out. He added that it was his intention to interview Ian this afternoon or this evening when he came home.

'Forget it,' said Clifton. 'I've already interviewed him. He'll be at work this afternoon, he's a ladies' hairdresser. He does wear black, by the way, and he could be our mystery man. I'll be delving further into that this afternoon and I'm also considering a search warrant for his flat. He's at work all day. Leave him to me.'

There was no more information of immediate interest but from their response it was clear the detectives were talking to lots of people in town and this pleased Clifton. He praised his teams for their efforts and said they were doing a wonderful job – and updated them, saying he wanted them to continue in the hope someone might be found who could provide the vital clue. Someone walking near the park, for example, over-looking the park perhaps, driving past it, hearing people talk about being in the park on Thursday night, seeing someone rushing away, finding bloodstained clothing or a bloody handkerchief in their back garden or rubbish bin. Some might even recall a previous or unpleasant experience involving Swainby . . . there was a great deal yet to be done.

He asked if there were any questions or further comments and upon being assured there were none, he told Detective Sergeants Huntley and Burrows to meet him in his office in a few minutes' time, then dismissed the other men to their duties, even if he felt they would not turn up anything of significance. He did not remind them that negative news was often as significant and as important as positive news, rather like the famous dog which did not bark in the night in the Sherlock Holmes story, 'Silver Blaze'. In his heart of hearts, though, he felt sure none of the detectives would find anyone else who had been in the park during those critical minutes.

But he must be sure – or as sure as he could be. As the men were head-ing for their respective areas of town, Clifton went down to the enquiry office.

'Is Superintendent Firth around?' he asked the duty constable.

'No, sir, he's gone to a family funeral. He said he expected to be home around eight o'clock tonight. He said he'd tried to find you, sir, to tell you, but you were out in the town. Inspector Burn is in charge of the sub-division during his absence.'

'Fair enough, I'll catch up with him. Tomorrow maybe. He won't work Sundays though, will he?'

'I expect he'll be on duty tomorrow, sir, seeing we've a murder enquiry on.'

'I would hope so. All right, I'll catch him later, it's not urgent.'

Clifton wanted to speak to Firth to tell him about the development concerning the Simpson family, but it would have to wait. Now, he intended speaking to Mrs Simpson and did not relish the idea. But, rather like the words of the famous Gilbert and Sullivan song, one's constabulary duty must be done. He went up the stairs to his office and found the two sergeants waiting patiently.

'Gentlemen, we have unpleasant work to do,' he told them. 'We three. We're going to interview Mrs Simpson. I'm not looking forward to this, it's almost an invasion of family privacy because I'm going to ask some very personal and private questions, but we are investigating a murder. We must put all considerate thoughts and personal reservations to one side during the interview. I thought about doing this enquiry alone, even on a rather informal basis, but I've decided against that. It's so important I can't take chances, it has to be a very formal interview.

'That means I need you, Detective Sergeant Burrows for your usual note-taking skills, and you, Detective Sergeant Huntley for the benefit of your local knowledge as well as providing corroboration of what takes place. I know it looks heavy-handed going in three at a time like this to interview a woman who's been subjected to this sort of thing before, but it must be done. Now, Detective Sergeant Huntley, you know where the Simpsons live?'

'Yes, sir.'

'Good, then you can drive us there. We won't tell anyone else where we're going and we need to speak to Mrs Simpson without her husband being present. It might mean taking her out in the car, I expect he'll be in the house. You, Sergeant Huntley, should take a listening role but if you think I've missed something, or got something wrong, please interrupt. I won't mind, in fact I will appreciate it if it's relevant. And Sergeant Burrows will do his usual expert note-taking. Right, let's get this over with.'

It was quarter to three when they arrived at the house to find Pamela Simpson in the garden, hanging out some washing. It was fine and sunny, one of those warm summer-like days which so often arrive in mid-October and which are known as St Luke's Little Summer. She turned and saw them park their car on the road outside. She recognised Maurice Huntley and ended her pegging session to come and meet him at the gate. She smiled a greeting.

'Maurice, hello. You've come to see Dick, have you? I'm afraid he's in bed, asleep. He was very tired so I suggested he went for a lie down.'

'How is he?' Knowing the nature of their visit, Huntley now found himself profoundly embarrassed and took refuge from his emotions by sheltering behind the dominating presence of the mighty Clifton as he put that question to her. Clifton was now out of the car with Burrows close behind. They were not here to ask after the health of Sergeant Simpson.

'Very tired. He's been working very hard but he's sure he's got leukaemia, Maurice, he's sure about it even if the doctor isn't. He's told me to be prepared for the worst. Dick lost a friend through acute leukaemia, you know, it was very sudden and he's worried because the symptoms were just like Dick's but Doctor Ewart won't be rushed . . . I just hope he's right and Dick is wrong . . . .'

'Er, Pam,' Huntley interrupted her. 'This is Detective Superintendent Clifton from Headquarters, and Detective Sergeant Burrows, his assistant. They'd like a word with you.'

'With me?' she frowned. 'What about?'

Clifton, towering above her said, 'I don't want to disturb your husband, Mrs Simpson, so if you like we can go for a drive, just down the road, and talk in the car.'

'I don't understand.' She had lost her smile now. It had been replaced with a worried look. 'I've no reason to hide anything from Dick, nothing at all . . . we've no need to go away to talk . . . what's this about?'

Clifton paused, then said, 'You knew Edward Albert Swainby, I believe.'

'Not willingly!' she smiled ruefully.

'No,' he said. 'No, I realize that. You know he's been murdered? I'm sure your husband has told you all about it.'

'Yes, Dick did tell me. So what has that got to do with me?'

'I'm trying to build an accurate picture of his life,' responded Clifton. 'I thought you might be able to help me.'

'Oh, well, yes, I suppose I can tell you a little, not that I know much about him. He wasn't one of my favourite people, as you can imagine. I am assuming you know what he did to me?'

'Yes, it's in our records, which is why we are here. That's why we want to talk to you.'

'Dick knows all about that episode of my life. You needn't be frightened to ask me questions in front of him, and I can talk without becoming all emotional and embarrassed, it was a long time ago. I've got over it. You'd better come in, all of you. I'll put the kettle on.'

'No need,' said Clifton. 'We've just had lunch. We don't want to keep you long.'

'Dick's asleep, or he was five minutes ago. He won't hear us, he's in the back room where it's quiet, no traffic noise. Come into the lounge,' and she led them into the house via the front door and into a comfortable lounge furnished with a three-piece suite. She brought in a dining chair and Huntley took it aside for his use, leaving the others to find space on the suite. Clifton told Pamela to use one of the chairs; she did so as Clifton took the other and left the settee for Burrows.

'So, Superintendent, how can I help you?' She looked firmly in control of her emotions even if her mind was dwelling on Ian and Dick. What had they done? Clifton knew that being in her own home and surrounded by her own things would make it easier for her to talk.

'I don't want to pry unnecessarily,' he began in what for him was an almost apologetic manner. 'On the other hand, I do need to establish facts, and I also need to gain some kind of impression of Swainby's character. I might add that I have read the file about his attack on you. I don't think I need go over old ground, I am not going to press you to tell me about it in graphic detail. It is all a matter of record now and the facts are not in dispute, but the case never went for trial and I find that curious.'

'I didn't want it to go to trial,' she was blunt about it. She did not flinch from making that bold and unexpected statement.

'You didn't? But it wasn't your decision, Mrs Simpson!' exclaimed Clifton. 'This was a serious crime, very serious, and the due processes of law should have been followed to a conclusion. There is no way you could or should halt legal proceedings and I cannot see why you should not want Swainby to be tried before a jury.'

'Superintendent Clifton, I did halt those proceedings. I don't mind admitting that now. I said I could not identify Swainby, it was as simple as that. I was not on oath at the time so I committed no offence. Quite simply, I did not pick him out on the identification parade. That meant the case could not proceed; there was very little firm evidence, most of it was circumstantial. And Swainby said I consented.'

'I can't understand why you failed to pick him out, after what you suffered.'

'You are not a woman, Superintendent, but I know you are a very capable and efficient detective and I know you will have examined this case from every angle; you will know, I am sure, that I became pregnant with Swainby's child.'

'You don't pull any punches, do you?'

'Not with policemen, no. I am not a fool, Superintendent. A lot of people knew Dick could not father a child, half Hildenley knew thanks to gossip from the hospital but we managed to keep it from Ian, our son. So there we are. That is why I did not want the case to go to the Assizes. By the time we had reached the stage of holding an identification parade, and then going to the committal proceedings, I knew I was pregnant. I had no wish for my child to grow up tainted with the knowledge his or her father was a violent rapist.'

'That's something I can sympathize with,' admitted Clifton.

'Thanks, it wasn't an easy decision, I can tell you that. So at the identity parade, I said I could not recognize him – they should have held the parade earlier than they did, but because he'd been arrested following my description of him, they didn't think a parade was necessary. My description of the attacker matched him and there was other supporting evidence. However, he admitted being in my house which took the steam out of things rather, even if he lied by saying I'd consented to what happened. The police changed their minds just before the committal, though, and held the ID parade only a week or two beforehand. I think by then they realized they had very little real evidence of rape and Swainby had got himself a good defence lawyer; they hoped the identification parade would provide the necessary proof with me pointing him out as the rapist. But I halted things, I made sure the case didn't go to the higher court. I didn't want to go through all that trauma and have my child brought up with the stigma of being fathered during a rape.'

'So you were happy to allow a rapist to go free, and probably rape again?'

'How could I possibly know he was going to do it again? I was concerned for the future of my unborn child, Superintendent. I'd no idea of his true past but I am sorry for what he might have done since then, truly sorry. I've lost sleep over it, believe me, but prosecuting him wouldn't have stopped him, would it?'

Her openness and blunt honesty had shaken Clifton. He wondered if she was aware there had been two unsolved murders in Garminghamshire and that Swainby was a suspect for each; in any case, he had expected to drag this information from her, to fight a long battle with a tearful and emotional woman but instead he found himself confronted by a very determined person, very controlled and very calm.

'And Sergeant Simpson was happy to bring up the child as his own?'

'Yes he was, Ian's arrival made us into a family. Dick registered himself as father, partly to stop gossip in the town. We do live in a small town community, you know, with the inevitable small town mentality. We both loved him, and still do.'

Clifton adopted one of his long pauses. 'A remarkable story, Mrs Simpson. So how did Swainby react to all this? Did he know he had fathered a child?'

'I think he did, but not at first. It took time. His brother was in hospital at the same time as Dick, he knew the extent of Dick's injuries and when I became obviously pregnant, he must have worked things out. Swainby saw me with my big bump around town, shopping and such, but he never acknowledged me or mentioned the child. He left town soon after I began to show my pregnancy but I think it was because he overstepped the mark with a butcher's wife. I think he thought I might claim maintenance from him, but we had no such thoughts. He's been away for twenty years, until now, and in all that time Ian was ours and ours alone.'

'And Swainby was definitely the father of your child?'

'I don't have to answer that, Superintendent, but I will because this is a murder enquiry and I want the truth to be known. I was a virgin until he raped me as the file will show. Those doctors asked me that time and time again when I was being interviewed. I did not have sexual intercourse with any man before my marriage, not even my husband-to-be.'

'I had to ask that, I'm sorry,' Clifton issued one of his long sighs. 'So Swainby left Hildenley before your child was born?'

'Yes, for a while I had no idea he'd gone, or where he'd gone, and didn't care. When I knew he'd left, I was delighted. I'd not see him about town. He never said goodbye, but he wouldn't, would he? Especially not to a policeman's wife!'

'I think not! But he came back and the question I need to ask is why? Why would he come back here?'

'I have no idea, Superintendent.'

'Did he come to see you?'

'Yes, he did.'

'And you talked to him?'

'At the door, yes, I did not let him into the house, even though he'd found out where I lived.'

'When was this?'

'It would be about a month ago, I can't be sure exactly. Maybe five weeks.'

'Did you tell your husband he'd called?'

'Not at the time, no, I didn't want to re-open old wounds, but he knows now. He was angry with me not telling him at first, but he understood my reasons. I thought Dick would be happier not knowing about his visit.'

'So why did you change your mind? Why did you tell him later instead of at the time?'

'It was because of the murder. Dick told me that Ted Swainby had apparently come back to Hildenley to live but had been murdered and so I told him he'd called at our house some time previously.'

'I'm surprised he has not provided that information to the investigating team,' said Clifton pointedly.

'He's not been into work since I told him,' said Pamela, knowing this was a white lie. 'He would have told you, I'm sure.'

'So why did Swainby call at your house?'

'He wanted to know whether I'd given birth to a child. He'd heard I had and was checking, he wanted to be sure, then he wanted to know where he could make contact with Ian.'

'So Swainby *did* know about Ian?'

'By then he did, yes. I don't know how or when he realized I'd had a child by him. I didn't ask. He might have known for years and done nothing about it.'

'So what did you do?'

'Before I told him where to find Ian, I made him promise he would not tell him that he was his father. We had never told Ian that Dick was not his real father. We had thought about telling him that he was adopted, we thought we might do that when he was little but then we decided not to tell him at all. Later, we had a change of mind and wondered about breaking the news after his twenty-first birthday, once he'd become an adult.'

'That must be soon, is it? His twenty-first?'

'Yes, it's in February next year but in the end we decided not to tell him. After all, Dick's been his father all these years and we didn't want our secret to be revealed to Ian, we felt it would destroy him, he's a very sensitive person. We wanted our nice family unit to continue as it has in the past, happy, loving and trusting.'

'And did Swainby promise that?'

'He did, and I believed him. He said all he wanted was a look at his son, his own flesh and blood as he said; he would do so from a distance, then he would go away. He said he had no one else in the world. He apologized for what he did to me, he said he lost control at times especially when people walked away from him and I'd walked away that night, so he said. He said when people did that, he couldn't help himself growing angry and violent, but he went on to say he was very proud to be a father. He was so nice, Superintendent,' and tears began to form in her eyes. 'I couldn't believe this was the man who had attacked me so viciously all those years ago, he was charming, humble, apologetic . . . so I told him where to find Ian. At work.'

'Did you give him Ian's home address?'

'No, definitely not.'

'And did he go to find Ian?'

She paused, just a fraction too long in Clifton's opinion. He knew she was trying to conceal something. 'I don't know, I've not seen Swainby since then.'

'So has Ian said anything about Swainby trying to make contact?'

Again, there was a long pause and the tears intensified as she made up her mind to tell the truth.

'Yes,' and she was crying freely now. 'Yes, he did go to look at Ian, at the salon where he works, "Style" it's called, but he broke his promise. He told Ian he was his real father.'

'And Ian's reaction?'

'Well, at first he didn't believe it, he thought Swainby was a crank of some kind but Swainby persisted and showed Ian photos of himself when he was Ian's age and, well, he knows the truth now. He's devastated, we all are.'

'Your husband too?'

'Yes, he's devastated that Ian found out in such a dreadful manner, even if it all emerged after Ted had died.'

'We'll have to speak to Ian. I've spoken to him already but he made no mention of Swainby paying him a visit and certainly he said nothing about Swainby being his natural father. And your husband, we must speak to him too, when he's well enough. You realize that?'

'Yes, of course,' and she broke down in tears as she began to realize that her entire and happy world was now beginning to crumble about her.

'Come along,' said Clifton to his sergeants. 'We must go. It's time for another chat with young Ian.'

CHAPTER 15

THE three detectives, a formidable trio, returned to 'Style' and once again asked to speak to Ian Simpson. They were told he was busy with a client whereupon Superintendent Clifton bellowed a response which left the receptionist in no doubt that their purpose was far more important than any woman's blue rinse or permanent wave. They were shown to the upstairs room to wait but no cups of tea were offered. It was Saturday afternoon and the salon was very busy; that was made abundantly clear by the receptionist who said something about it being the busiest day of the week. Clifton ignored her mild protests and said they would wait; Ian Simpson arrived a few minutes later, pale-faced and nervous and he apologized for having delayed them.

'Lady Scramshire is one of our best customers,' he breathed. 'I couldn't leave her just like that, I had to finish her off.'

'We won't keep you long, Ian, so don't look so worried,' said Clifton. 'We just want to clear up a few matters, things which have arisen since our chat this morning.'

'Well, if I can help in any way . . . .'

'The dead man, Ian. His name has not been released to the press yet but I'm sure most of the people in town know who it is. As you do from our previous visit. Your parents knew him well. Were you aware of that?'

Ian was now thinking fast, switching from a nervous hairdresser to a more confident character whom he drew from his small repertoire of strong fictional people. This would have to be another faultless performance.

'My dad told me his name but I didn't want to get him into trouble with his bosses, so I didn't tell you I knew his name. It hadn't been in the papers. You didn't ask if I knew Mr Swainby.'

'All right, point taken. But Swainby was known to your parents, Ian.

Did you know that?' Clifton had to clarify that vital point.

The young man paused as the three detectives waited and then he lowered his voice in a very dramatic way, moving his head and looking down at the floor as he replied, 'Swainby himself told me that, he came here, to the salon. A few weeks ago. He hung about outside, waiting for me to leave. I didn't know him then, of course, and had no idea what he wanted or how he found me, I'd never seen him in my life before, never, and no one had mentioned him to me. He was a total stranger.'

'So what did he want?'

Ian knew there was no way he could pretend Swainby had been haunting the salon because he was interested in one of the girls; clearly, the police had more information than they were revealing. Their demeanour told him so. And his dad had warned him they would discover the truth of his parentage, adding one should always tell the truth to the police – or at least imply the truth through relating facts which could be checked. Now was the time for his best performance so far. And hadn't he rehearsed this speech so many times already?

'He wanted to talk to me, so he said, he asked me to go for a drink so we could talk. Well, I mean, he looked an awful sort of person, Mr Clifton, really awful, if you know what I mean, and I said I had no idea who he was or what he wanted, so I didn't go with him. I hurried off. He was older than me and out of condition so I could leave him behind, I ran off. I made sure he didn't follow me home, though, but the next day he was waiting outside the salon again. He was very insistent, he said he must talk to me and when I asked him what he wanted, he said he was my father, my real father.'

'So what did you say?'

'Say? I didn't know what to say, Superintendent Clifton, I was speech-less, quite speechless. Well, you would be, wouldn't you when somebody comes up to you like that, a complete stranger and says he's your father, quite out of the blue, a rough-looking person, more than a bit smarmy. He tried to be charming but he couldn't fool me. I thought he was awful, mentally ill even. I told him not to be silly and ran off then thought no more about it. Well, you wouldn't, would you? I mean, I had a father and a mother so how could that man be my dad?'

'So that was during his second visit to your salon?'

'Yes, it was, but he kept coming back, he wouldn't take no for an answer. We were getting worried about him turning up every day at closing time; my boss said I should find out what he really wanted, to stop him pestering us. It wasn't nice, not good for business having a man like that hanging around outside the salon.'

'So you decided to talk to him?'

'Yes, in the hope he'd stop pestering me. I didn't want to be alone with him, Superintendent, he made me uneasy, so I chose somewhere in public where people could see us all the time. We just walked along the street.'

'A sensible choice. So what happened?'

'He insisted he was my natural father. I said he must be confusing me with somebody else because I had a dad who was a police sergeant and he said he knew that. He said he and my mum had been lovers, years ago before she married dad, and he'd made her pregnant. With me.'

'Did you believe him then?'

'No, I couldn't see how it made sense, knowing my parents, but then he said dad couldn't father a child due to an injury. I still didn't believe him, I thought he was crazy, honestly I did. I was thinking he'd got me mixed up with somebody else but when he began to explain things, giving mum's maiden name, where she lived as a young woman, the dates and all that, I began to wonder if he was telling the truth. He knew a lot about her, and about dad. I looked at my birth certificate. Mum keeps it at their house but I go every Friday evening for a meal and sneaked a peep. It says Richard James Simpson is my father and that is good enough for me. Swainby said the certificate was worthless, and he'd take a blood test to prove it. I said I didn't want him to do that but he insisted he was my natural father and kept arriving at the salon, Superintendent, night after night. He began following me, all the time insisting he was my real dad, saying I'd soon be twenty-one and I was all he had in the world, his own flesh and blood as he put it. He said he had no one else, no relations, no family, which was why he'd come to find me. He was pathetic, really.'

'And did you ever believe him?'

'I began to wonder if he was telling the truth, I must admit. Everything sounded right. Then he showed me some photographs of himself when he was younger. I looked in the mirror and began to see a likeness but I wondered if I was imagining things and then, only last night – after I'd heard about the murder, I ought to stress – I mentioned him to mum but all she said was she'd known him when she was younger, she never said anything about him being my dad. So I asked my dad, at first he said

Swainby was a convicted rapist and sex offender and when I said Swainby had told me he and mum were friends, dad said it wasn't a case of being friends. We talked, just me and dad alone, and after a while he told me how Swainby had raped mum, and other women, with extreme violence. I was the result of her rape, he told, and said he'd brought me up as his own because he couldn't have children and wanted a family . . . well, Superintendent, I was devastated. I cried and cried, I don't mind admitting, I still cry when I think about it . . . I might cry now if I'm not careful . . . .'

'So Sergeant Simpson told you this last night, Friday? You weren't aware of any of this before Thursday?'

'Well, Swainby had told me before Thursday but I didn't believe him. How could I believe such a tale? It was only yesterday when the awful truth began to sink in. Dad confirmed it last night, yes.'

'So you accept that Ted Swainby is your natural father?'

'After what dad told me, yes I do. It's awful, Superintendent, really really awful but Richard Simpson is my true dad, the best dad anyone could have . . . I've really tried to cope with all this . . . oh dear, I'm going to cry . . . I'm sorry . . . .'

They let him cry quietly for a few minutes before he managed to gather himself together again and after taking a few deep breaths, wiping his eyes and standing to stare out of the window for a little while, he turned to face them again.

'Sorry,' he said. 'Sorry, I'm not much of a man, am I? Breaking down like this. Not like my dad . . . the sergeant, I mean . . . .'

'It must have been devastating, Ian, really devastating.'

'It was, but I'll get over it.'

'Devastating enough for you to kill him, to kill Swainby?'

Ian knew he was putting on a performance of a lifetime as he said, 'Devastated enough to *want* to kill him, Superintendent, I don't mind admitting that, but I couldn't kill anyone, I even open windows to let flies out. But he was already dead, wasn't he? When I learned the truth, when I knew he wasn't lying, he was already dead and there's no way I'd want to kill him just for pestering me. I mean, he must really have wanted to get to know me after all these years. I am his natural son after all, his flesh and blood as he kept telling me.'

'All right, I follow your logic. So let's go back to Thursday night, shall we? You've admitted being in Latima Park between nine-thirty and about quarter to ten, but were you aware that you were followed there by Ted Swainby? From Simeon's to the park?'

'Yes, I know, I should have mentioned that but I was worried you might think I had killed him. Besides, his name was not made public so I wasn't supposed to know who was dead, was I? Anyway, Superintendent, that night I saw him waiting outside Simeon's. I could see him from the kitchen window, so I sneaked out of the back door but Swainby saw me and shouted for me to stop for a chat. I hurried away and said I wasn't interested, I said I didn't want to change things, then he became angry and said he didn't like people walking away from him and if I'd been a woman, he'd have hit me for doing that. By the time we reached the park, he was quite a long way behind me. I'd got well ahead of him by then. There were other people around, fortunately. The pictures had just turned out.'

'And you were still a long way ahead when you turned into Latima Park?'

'Yes, I knew I could lose him in there. It was dark, I was in dark clothes and knew my way through the paths and trees. I didn't want him to follow me home. He'd never found out where I lived and so once I got through the gate I ran and concealed myself behind trees and bushes, making my way across the lawns and away from the paths to the top of the slope, to Gate No. 2 as you called it last time we talked. And then I hurried out. I was shielding my face just in case he did see me, but he didn't. I know my dad saw me come out but because I had my hands over my face, he wouldn't recognize me. I daren't stop to talk to dad, the sergeant dad I mean, in case Swainby caught up to me, I didn't want him and Swainby to meet. Swainby was nowhere behind me when I left the park. I've no idea which way he went . . . well, now I know now, of course, because of what happened, but I never saw him there.'

'I must ask this again, did you see anyone else in the park? Or hear anyone?'

'I saw a young couple making their way towards a bench some distance behind me, I think they'd been to the pictures. I saw them when I stopped to look back, to see if Swainby was following me. I don't know if they saw me, probably they didn't in the dark, especially as I was trying to hide from Swainby. I didn't see anyone else.'

'And, as you told us before, you left the park by that top gate and went straight home?'

'Yes, I did, you can ask my landlady.'

'And did you kill Ted Swainby?'

'Superintendent, I know and you know that I was in the park at the time, and you might think I had a motive of sorts, but I did not kill him . . . I couldn't, I just couldn't do such a thing. I had no reason to anyway. Not then. I had no idea what he was like, what he'd done to mum, all that stuff came out afterwards.'

'All right, Ian, that's all for now. We'll let you get back to work, but might want to speak to you again.'

'If I can help, I will, you know that, Superintendent,' and Ian left the room to make his way downstairs.

'What do you make of all that?' Clifton asked his sergeants.

'It sounds right to me,' said Burrows, who had been taking notes. 'Everything seems to tally.'

'He tells a good story,' smiled Clifton. 'It's almost as if he'd rehearsed it. Maybe he did, but that doesn't necessarily make him a liar or a killer. Come along, we've more work to do. That's two of the Simpson family interviewed. We need a chat with Sergeant Simpson next. Before I talk to him, though, I need to go through all the statements, word by word. So it's back to the police station for another reading session. I wonder if anything's happened in our absence?'

Nothing dramatic had happened and as he dismissed his sergeants to go about their follow-up duties of preparing statements about their chats with Pamela and Ian, Superintendent Clifton called for the main statement file. It was maintained by one of the secretaries and comprised typed copies of every statement taken during the investigation, all filed in chronological order and each indexed with the name of person who had made it. Even after only less than three full days, the file was about six inches thick and so he bore it into his office with instructions to the staff not to put through any telephone calls or admit anyone, unless it was something very important indeed. He wanted to read the statements without interruption.

There had been a development at the Simpson household. It began with a telephone call to Dr Ewart who was on call that weekend. It meant the surgery phone and all emergency calls were put through to his home. For that reason he could not leave the house and occupied himself in his greenhouse, available to deal with any problem which might arise.

'Don,' his wife called. 'Telephone. It's the hospital, they say it's urgent.'

Calls of this kind were part of life in a busy general practice and he ambled indoors to deal with it. One did not panic and rush about like a headless chicken, for it was in the best interests of everyone that he remained calm.

'Dr Ewart,' he announced.

'Hello, doc,' came the male response. 'It's John Preston here in the lab at the hospital. That blood sample you sent, the one you wanted dealt with urgently. Name of Simpson.'

'Yes?'

'You need to get him here as soon as you can, our tests show it's leukaemia, it's very advanced. He needs to come immediately doc, and I mean immediately. We need further tests. I suspect he's suffering from the acute version.'

'That's dreadful! You'll send an ambulance?'

'I'll have it sent direct to the house. We have the address. Can you warn him?'

'I'll go straight away, yes.'

When Doctor Ewart arrived to warn the Simpsons before the arrival of the ambulance, he found Pamela in the garden; she was tidying one of the borders as her washing was fluttering in the mild and gentle October breeze. She smiled a welcome, even if her face showed concern at his unexpected arrival. Another shock for her.

'Doctor?' she greeted him. 'I wasn't expecting you.'

'No, it's rather sudden, I'm afraid. I've just had the results of Dick's tests from the hospital, they treated it urgently as I asked, and I'm afraid it's very bad news.'

'Oh my God . . .' she put her hand to her mouth. 'Oh my God . . . Dick kept saying it was serious . . . he must have known . . . .'

'The blood test indicates leukaemia, Pamela, probably acute. He'll need further tests and a transfusion straight away. He'll feel much better afterwards but that will only be a temporary improvement, it's not a cure.'

'Oh my God . . . he'll need pyjamas, toothbrush, shaving gear and things,' she was trying to be calm and practical. 'He's asleep now, Doctor, he was very, very tired this morning and he's got a purplish rash on the back of his hands . . . .'

'Then wake him, now. I'll come with you.'

And so it was that Sergeant Simpson, white, feverish and very, very tired, was whisked off to Hildenley Hospital. Pamela rang Ian at work to tell him, but there could be no visiting until the specialist gave his authority. All they could do was sit and wait, and ring the hospital from time to time for a progress report.

Late that Saturday afternoon, Superintendent Wilf Clifton sat alone in his office, isolated from the men who were still out and about in Hildenley trying to gather more information about the murder of Edward Swainby. He found himself sitting and staring at the pile of statements, while deep down not wanting to believe what they suggested. He got up from his chair and walked around the tiny office, peered out of the window, then sat down, got up and sat down again.

He had made a time chart, a piece of foolscap paper with the names of the people known to have been in Latima Park on Thursday evening between nine-thirty and ten o'clock. As near as he could, he had broken the times down into single minutes and from what that had revealed, he had then made another list, a list of what might be termed circumstantial evidence. He knew the legal definition of circumstantial evidence – it was *evidence, not of the actual fact to be proved, but of other facts from which that fact may be presumed with more or less certainty.*

There were several factors which might fit that category and, as a senior detective with years of experience, he knew that most, if not all, murderers were convicted on circumstantial evidence. That was because so few murders were witnessed. Very rarely was a killer seen in the act of committing the crime and for that reason, to prove the guilt of the person responsible, circumstantial evidence had to be gathered for presentation to the jury, albeit supported by real evidence in ideal conditions. Often, though, it was the circumstantial evidence which helped them make their decision guilty or not guilty. just as he was doing now. He knew, however, that before taking any further action, he needed to discuss this with another experienced police officer. The most senior officer at Hildenley Police Station, Superintendent Firth, was away at a family funeral and was not expected back until eight tonight.

Firth's deputy was Inspector Burn but, as Clifton knew, he had no CID experience and he did not feel like discussing what was a very sensitive matter with a uniform man of that rank.

On the other hand, Detective Sergeant Burrows, Clifton's partner in these investigations, was of a lower rank than Inspector Burn but he was a highly experienced and very bright detective; if only he would take and pass his promotion exams, he would be promoted to Detective Inspector within a very short time indeed. Clifton had every confidence in him. He was the person with whom to discuss his awful theory. He picked up the telephone and when the duty constable answered, he said, 'Clifton here. Find Detective Sergeant Burrows, will you? And send him up to my office. As soon as you can. And I wouldn't say no to cup of tea! For both of us.'

'Yes, sir,' said the constable.

Fifteen minutes later, the two detectives, differing greatly in rank but partners in many similar and successful investigations over the years, were sitting with cups of tea before them. The duty constable had even found some chocolate biscuits, probably pilfered from the station tea fund. Clifton had the files spread before him along with his time chart and notes of matters he considered to be important circumstantial evidence.

'I've been thinking, Sergeant,' he began, and Burrows knew this meant he had reached a conclusion, albeit one he wished to discuss before implementing any action.

'Sir?' Burrows knew he must wait as the big man decided how to present his theory.

'When you were at Detective Training School, Sergeant, what were you told about the person who reports finding the body of a murder victim?' he asked.

'They become an immediate suspect, sir, in the frame immediately. Some people report finding their own victims because they hope it will place them in a good light with the investigating team, that is, throw the scent off them because they appear to be so co-operative and helpful. It happens a lot.'

'Right, Sergeant. All detectives know that, consequently we closely investigate those who report finding murder victims. In many cases, we can eliminate them because they are genuine, but from time to time, one turns out to be the killer. Am I right?'

'Yes, sir.'

'Good. So who found this body?'

'Sergeant Simpson, sir. But he was on duty . . . .'

'He was indeed, but he found the body, Sergeant. You've read the statement file, so what else did he manage to find?'

'The stone on the roof, sir, the murder weapon.'

'Right again. And before that?'

'Well, er, yes, the hole in the rockery where the stone came from.'

'Right again. Very observant of him, wouldn't you say? Or very convenient? Rather like finding the body itself . . . he's been very good at finding important clues that everyone else had overlooked and his behaviour since the murder has been decidedly odd.'

'He's ill, sir.' Burrows found himself acting almost as devil's advocate.

'Is it genuine, Sergeant, or is it psychosomatic? A self-induced illness in other words. I accept he is not well but has his mental condition, mental strain perhaps, contributed to it?'

'I've had no idea, sir, but finding the body was nothing more than good but routine police work, and so were those other clues he led us to . . . you can't seriously think he's the killer?'

'Can't I? Why not? Suppose he got a fatal illness which will get him off the hook? Suppose he dies before he can be tried at the Assizes? Suppose he knows he will never stand trial? He leaves this world without an official stain on his character but he's got his own back on the villain who raped his wife. Having said all that, I do think he is very seriously ill, Sergeant, I've seen that sort of thing before. I knew a man with acute leukaemia, I think the sergeant knew the same chap, a policeman's father. I reckon he'll know what's in store for him because that other fellow died within days of being diagnosed. And that knowledge, and his involvement in this crime, might have exacerbated his condition. Now listen to this – think "motive" now. He's been enjoying a really nice life here, he's approaching pensionable age – police pension that is, at a young age; he's got a lovely wife who's got over an awful experience at the hands of a rapist and *wham*! Suddenly it all goes wrong. If he's as ill as I believe, what's he got to lose by getting rid of Swainby, the man who could threaten family happiness even when Simpson's dead and gone? Swainby appears on the scene, a man from the past, from the very unpleasant past, and he starts by visiting Mrs Simpson and reminding the family about the rape, then telling the son he's Swainby's, not Simpson's . . . suddenly, and very dramatically, Sergeant Simpson's life has changed, and changed for the worse. And think of this. When did Sergeant Simpson become aware of Swainby's return? We don't know, he might have known for some weeks and that could have provided a motive, or caused him to confront Swainby for some reason at a pre-determined place and time. Might an argument have developed between them? There's been ample time for that. An argument about Ian perhaps? And his real paternity? Is this the result of something that's been festering for weeks? I think we'd all agree that the planet will be a better place without Swainby, but that's not the point. You can't go around killing people.'

'I can't think Sergeant Simpson would have killed Swainby for that reason alone, sir, he's lived with the knowledge of Swainby's rape for years and brought up his son. He's not a vindictive man, he's got no violent temper, so I'm told; everyone here at Hildenley, police and public alike, love him. That's come over loud and strong during our time here.'

'I agree with all that, but something happened in the park that night, Sergeant. It was something none of us knows about and as a result Swainby got himself killed. It was probably not pre-planned as our pathologist friend has suggested and I'm sure it was very spontaneous. A sudden lashing out with a handy lump of stone. Even the calmest of people can react violently if they're pressed hard enough. Don't forget Swainby had been secretly visiting Ian – to the point of being a nuisance – to tell him about his fatherhood, to break the family secret. Did Simpson know that? Was he aware of Swainby's presence but keeping it to himself? Was it some way of protecting Ian? Or protecting his own family image? Was he struggling to persuade Swainby to leave town? To leave his family in peace? Simpson would not want his happy family ruined – try to imagine the trauma caused by the family secret being revealed by his wife's rapist who turns up after all that time . . . when it had almost been forgotten. Was it more than a reasonable man could take perhaps? And so Simpson stopped Swainby from ruining the family. That makes sense to me, it's a bloody good motive.'

'Even if that was the case, I still can't see that he'd resort to murder, sir, not Sergeant Simpson, not after living with this for such a long time.'

'There's more, Sergeant. Remember this is a murder enquiry with the deceased having a previous association with Mrs Simpson, not voluntarily on her part but a connection nonetheless. So why didn't the sergeant volunteer that information in the early stages of the enquiry? He should have told us. It is material to the investigation and yet Simpson hasn't mentioned it, not once. And Simpson didn't tell us of Swainby's visits to his wife or Ian. He's been covering up, that's how I see it. So we have to ask why? Did he hope we wouldn't learn about his wife's rape? He must have known it was relevant if only for elimination purposes, and he must have known we'd discover it. Damn it, he's a very experienced and intelligent police officer.'

'It does seem odd, sir.'

'Odd? It's most odd, Sergeant, criminally odd in my view. And there's more. When I interviewed him about his presence in the park, how he found the body and what he did there, his pocket book was not up to date. The last entry was nine-thirty on Thursday. I know he was busy that night, I know he was under pressure but you know and I know it is a policeman's prime responsibility always to have his pocket book bang up to date. The fact it wasn't up to date could suggest – and I use the word could – that he was going to write something in it which would explain or cover his movements at the critical time. In other words, he could have committed the murder, and then made up his pocket book to cover his tracks during the criticial time. And he did divert through the park on his way to book off duty, telling the constable he needn't check the park. Did he do that for a reason, do you think?'

'It sounds bad for him, sir, I must admit.'

'And what about the mystery man he reported seeing? I must admit that at first, I thought he'd made up the sighting to throw us off the scent. When I first began to suspect him, that made sense. Having committed the crime, he could claim to see a mystery man fleeing from the scene and we'd all go hunting some chap who did not exist. But in fact, the mystery man was genuine. By one of those flukes, it happened to be his son, even if he says he did not realize it at the time. I doubt that, I think he knew. I did think, for a time, that Simpson and Ian had been in this together, but I'm veering towards the idea that Ian is innocent. After all, Simpson did describe him as the mystery man. In doing that, he put his son firmly in the frame.'

'But we did well, sir, to trace the mystery man.'

'Yes, but think of it like this, Sergeant. If Simpson had committed the murder, which I am beginning to believe more with each passing minute, then he was trying to throw the blame on to that mystery man. He was trying to create a wonderful red herring by which our attention would be diverted on to the mystery man, and his description was vague enough for it to fit anyone. From our point of view, the mystery man was indeed our prime suspect. But things didn't work out because we learned it was Simpson's own son, even if Simpson didn't tell us that. He'd already mentioned the sighting to Stalker for reasons best known to himself – to set up a red herring perhaps – and couldn't retract it which meant he almost got Ian blamed for killing Swainby. I must admit the lad was my prime suspect. But it was a clever ruse, finding someone to blame – but we scuppered that plan by finding Ian. Although he was in the park at the material time and doesn't deny being there, his story stands up. The ball's firmly back in Sergeant Simpson's court. He was the only other person in the park at the material time and he was one person whose presence there would not be questioned or considered suspicious. He had time to commit the murder – and he has a motive. He's got to be our prime suspect, Sergeant.'

'I'm sure you're right but I'm still not totally convinced of Ian's innocence, sir. Bearing in mind what we know, it's too much of a coincidence, him being in the park at that critical time and with so many links to the dead man.'

'We'll never be completely sure of his innocence unless Sergeant Simpson coughs to this one. But there is another nail in the Sergeant's coffin. Those bloodstains on his uniform.'

'Yes, sir, but he accounted for those by saying they came from Swainby when he was attempting to revive him.'

'And what a marvellous way of explaining the bloodstains he'd got when smashing that stone into Swainby's skull! Simpson is not a fool, Sergeant, and if he killed Swainby with that stone, he would know his uniform would be bloodstained, with small splashes more than likely. Just by rubbing his hand down his uniform and making sure there were more stains after tending Swainby would be enough to cast doubt upon how the stains got there. Of course his uniform was bloodstained – he made it bloodstained! Quite deliberately, and with a purpose. Surely you can see that?'

'I can see what you are driving at, sir.'

'Good, because we're dealing with a very clever man who has a knowledge of how police investigations are run. Which reminds me, having reached this conclusion, I now need that uniform of his. For evidence. I asked him to keep it but we need to have the bloodstains analysed, just to prove they were from Swainby, we'll need that for a prosecution. Now think about this as well, Sergeant. Was Swainby still alive when Simpson "found" him? Simpson was alone with the body for some time before Stead arrived, and Stead's statement says that Simpson insisted Swainby was dead and did not attempt any first aid. He made absolutely no attempt to revive or care for the dying man. Simpson insisted he was very experienced in such things and he maintained all along that Swainby was dead and beyond medical aid. Simpson is not a doctor, Sergeant, he is not medically qualified, he had no right to say such a thing. And, of course, we don't know what transpired in those few minutes before Stead turned up. So did Simpson kill Swainby and then return to 'find' him? If by any chance Swainby still had a flicker of life in him when his attacker left, it was snuffed out by the time medical aid reached him. And remember, Simpson made sure Stead did not return to base through the park. He said he would check the park and museum himself. I think he knew Swainby would be at the museum – perhaps he'd arranged to meet him there, for a chat? About their unfortunate family business?'

'You'd think Mr Stalker should have noticed whether there was blood on his uniform or hands, sir?'

'He said he couldn't be sure one way or the other because it was dark. The bloodstains wouldn't show in the darkness and besides, he wouldn't be looking for them, would he? And if Simpson shone his torch towards Stalker, as he did, it would temporarily blind him. I'm not sure what he could see of the sergeant's features but if his hands were bloodstained, Simpson would be sure to keep them out of sight. Now, consider this. Simpson *knew* Stalker would be walking past at that time. Stalker walks his dog each night at the same time along the same route, an ideal alibi witness. I think Simpson killed Swainby only moments before returning to No.1 Gate where he saw Stalker; Stalker would unwittingly provide him with an alibi and then Simpson could return to the park to "find" the body.'

'There's the time element to consider, sir. We know Sergeant Simpson was talking to PC Stead at nine-thirty, at West End.'

'We do indeed. It takes ten minutes to walk from West End to the No. 1 Gate of the park. I've checked that. Simpson could have arrived at the park at twenty to ten; if he went directly in to check the museum, as he claimed was his regular task, it would take a minute, no more, to reach the museum from No. 1 Gate. Nineteen minutes to ten. The confrontation with Swainby broke out – who knows what it was about – and how long does it take to rain six or seven blows with a stone? Six or seven seconds? A minute is a long time in these circumstances. He could have done that, thrown the stone onto the roof, and been back at No.1 Gate by quarter to ten – as indeed he was because we have a witness to say so.'

'It's possible, sir, I'll agree to that.'

'There is another scenario, Sergeant, which has never been propounded, and if I go down that route, it might mean another chat with the pathologist. We know Swainby had a very thin skull which means brain damage and even death can easily – even accidentally – be inflicted. Suppose Simpson had been going about his normal duties, calling at the museum to check it and unexpectedly encountered Swainby coming out of the gents? Quite a likely scenario, I would say. Imagine Simpson expressing his anger at Swainby's recent behaviour, calling on his wife and pestering his son; is it likely a sudden and violent argument developed, with a thrown punch? Did Simpson punch Swainby and knock him down? To smash his head on the ground . . . and Simpson then took the opportunity to smash his head with a handy piece of stone and finish him off, then set about covering his tracks? Could that have happened?'

'It could but he might have used his truncheon, sir, to beat Swainby about the head.'

'Too risky, truncheon marks would be too easily identified by the pathologist which is why he didn't do that. And blood, skin and hair would adhere to it. No, the stone was an ideal weapon and it happened to be handy enough to use and then dispose of. And being an experienced policeman, he would know a rough stone would not bear fingerprints.'

'I can understand there may be alternative scenarios, sir, but in spite of all that we've no real evidence against Sergeant Simpson.'

'There's the blood on his uniform reinforced by plenty of circumstantial evidence. And a strong motive. As I said, I don't think Simpson and Ian were in this together. In my view it's all down to our highly respected sergeant acting alone. Right, I've said my piece. What we've discussed is not for the ears of anyone outside this room, understand?'

'Yes, sir.'

'Right, postpone this evening's conference. We're going to arrest Sergeant Simpson.'

CHAPTER 16

WHEN Clifton and Burrows arrived at Sergeant Simpson's house, they found Pamela in the garden. She was trying to find something useful to occupy herself and was tidying one of the borders, removing dead flowers and plants which had provided her with colour and pleasure during the summer and early autumn. Many were dead and it was time to clear them away. It was difficult concentrating on her work after Dick had been rushed off to Hildenley General Hospital but the doctor had suggested she did not accompany him or visit him, not just yet. There was no point; he'd be whisked away almost immediately for a thorough examination and then into the theatre so that a sample of marrow could be abstracted from his breast bone and he'd also be given a blood transfusion. The transfusion would make him feel better within a very short time even though he would be really no better at all, she was warned, and if she rang at, say, seven this evening, they would tell her whether she could visit him. The answer would almost certainly be yes. She had rung Ian at work to tell him the news and he said he would come home once the salon had closed. It was due to close at half past five, he reminded her. She said she'd have a meal ready before she checked with the hospital. It was with some surprise therefore that she heard the car ease to a halt outside her gate; she thought it must be Ian in his new sports car, but it was an unmarked police vehicle and it discharged Clifton and Burrows.

'Hello, Superintendent,' she smiled. 'And Sergeant Burrows. Back so soon?'

'Sorry about this, Mrs Simpson,' said Clifton. 'We've seen Ian and spoken to him and now we'd like a word with your husband.'

'Oh, dear, you've just missed him.'

'Just missed him?' Alarm bells began to sound in Clifton's mind – had this man done a runner? Fled the scene? Realized his guilt had been so apparent and taken the opportunity to make himself scarce?

'He's been rushed into hospital, Superintendent. He's got leukaemia, it's been confirmed, it's shown up in his blood test, they're treating it all very urgently . . . I'm so worried . . . .'

'Leukaemia? Are you sure?'

'I can only go by what the doctor said, Superintendent, but he insisted Dick was admitted straight away, he said there wasn't a moment to lose, so the ambulance came for him. They told me not to ring just yet, not until they've had time to do whatever's necessary. I have to ring about seven this evening.'

'I wanted to speak to him as a matter of urgency . . . who's your doctor?'

'Doctor Ewart. He's gone to the hospital as well, to be there while they treat Dick, but I think they've called a specialist in. So is it anything I can help with?'

'I'm afraid not, Mrs Simpson – ah, yes, well, there is one thing. His uniform, the one he wore on Thursday night, the one that got stained with Swainby's blood. Is it still here?'

'Yes, he put it in the garage, I couldn't bear to have it in the house, being stained with Ted Swainby's blood. He hasn't had time to deal with it.'

'I told him I'd authorize a replacement, so I'll take it with me,' Clifton said. 'It'll get it out of your way.'

'Would you? I'd appreciate that, you'd better come in, I'll show you where it is.'

Clifton did not tell Pamela it was his intention to have it analysed to prove formally that the bloodstains had come from Ted Swainby, but when Sergeant Simpson was charged with murder, it would be a vital piece of evidence. It would prove there had been personal contact between suspect and victim, and that Simpson had been at the murder scene – maybe twice – should he later try to deny it. The blood should also match that found on the piece of stone. Pamela led them into the garage at the rear of the house where she showed them a uniform tunic, pair of trousers and a shirt on a coat hanger. The tunic bore the sergeant's stripes and his service number was on the epaulettes. The stains could still be seen, albeit now dry.

'Give Mrs Simpson a receipt, Sergeant,' said Clifton as he carried his trophy back to the waiting car.

And so they left the house, with Clifton saying he would check at the hospital to see when he might be able to have a chat with Sergeant Simpson. He could conduct his chat at the hospital if necessary. He was told to ring again at seven o'clock, but when he insisted in his most pressing way he did not want to speak to the sergeant while his family were in attendance, they suggested he rang an hour earlier, say six. He responded by saying he would despatch a uniformed constable to sit outside the ward until further notice.

He did not want Sergeant Simpson escaping but he did not explain this to the matron. He said the constable's presence was necessary because Sergeant Simpson was an important witness in the investigation of the murder of Edward Swainby and he had vital information which they needed to obtain from him. The constable was there to write down anything he might say while under the influence of the anaesthetic or other medication, and also, of course, to protect him against any other unstable witnesses who might arrive at the hospital. It was not quite the truth but the matron was not to know otherwise; she said she understood. She assured Clifton that the constable's presence would be no trouble; after all, the presence of a police officer at a patient's bedside was not all that unusual, especially in hospitals in the bigger cities and towns.

Clifton and Burrows then returned to Hildenley Police Station where the sergeant's uniform was listed as an exhibit and prepared for its journey to the Home Office Forensic Science Laboratory at Harrogate in the West Riding of Yorkshire. The two detectives then adjourned to the little office near the billiard room where the big man sifted through the thick file to identify those statements which were vital to his case.

Clifton quickly read each one, marking in red ink with a large capital letter 'E' (for exhibit) all those he wished to be entered in what would become the prosecution file. In due course, a file would be prepared and sent to the Director of Public Prosecutions so that his authority to proceed could be granted, and a Crown prosecutor would be appointed to oversee progress of the case.

The police did not prosecute cases of murder. It did not take long for Clifton to scan the statements because he had read them all several times and knew which ones were vital to his case. Those were the ones he now marked for retention. Then, after dismissing the detectives and uniform constables until nine o'clock the following morning and following a quick supper of fish and chips, it was time to ring the hospital. Except that

Clifton did not believe in ringing people when a personal call had much more impact. So at six o'clock he and Sergeant Burrows arrived at the hospital complete with a brief case full of documents and papers, and made their presence and purpose known.

'I cannot sanction an interview with Mr Simpson.' The matron was a large blousy lady who must have struck fear into the nurses under her control; she was just like the stereotype of a competent matron but it was clear the hospital was efficiently run and it was also scrupulously clean. A good matron was essential – just like a good station sergeant.

'So who can?' demanded Clifton. 'I am prepared to wait until I can speak to Mr Simpson, however long it takes. All night if necessary.'

'The specialist is here, Superintendent, he's from Leeds, a Mr Buxton. He has been especially called in to deal with Mr Simpson so you will need to speak to him.'

'Be that as it may, my business is extremely urgent and important, Mr Simpson is a key witness in the murder enquiry which I am currently conducting in the town and it's vital I speak to him now. I will not interfere with the family's needs and have no wish to create anguish; his wife is aware of his condition, and she has just told me. So I know the state he is in. My chat will take only a few minutes, five perhaps. I cannot stress how important and urgent this is.'

'I will go and see what Mr Buxton says,' she said. 'Go and sit down in the waiting room and I will be as quick as I can.'

When she had gone to see what could be done, Clifton said to his Sergeant, 'You see, lad, if we'd rung to fix this, we'd have got nowhere, that matron would have put us off, delayed us, tried to say she couldn't help but because we're here, sitting right under her nose, she has to do something about it. She knows we won't go away until we get what we want. Remember that when you're in charge.'

'Yes, sir.'

'And don't let petty self-important officials run rings round you. Present yourself in such a way that they have to do something about it – and they always can! And if you've problems, always ask to speak to the boss.'

'I'll remember that, sir,' smiled Detective Sergeant Burrows.

The matron returned about ten minutes later and announced, 'Mr Buxton will see you now, Superintendent and Sergeant, follow me please.'

She led them through a maze of clinical corridors with shiny floors and pale natural coloured walls until they came to a door marked, 'Consultants.'

'He is not resident here, he's a visiting consultant,' she whispered. 'So he has to share an office,' and then she tapped on the door and opened it. 'Detective Superintendent Clifton and Detective Sergeant Burrows, Mr Buxton.'

'Come in gentlemen,' and Buxton, a tall 50-year-old with thick iron grey hair, rose from behind the desk in the large and airy office. 'Roger Buxton, please sit down. How can I help you?'

They settled on the two chairs before his desk and Clifton said, 'I am in charge of a murder enquiry here in Hildenley, Mr Buxton. You might have read a little about it. A man called Swainby was attacked in Latima Park on Thursday night and died from his wounds. Sergeant Simpson, the man under your care, found the body and is a vital witness, not only now but during the future of my investigation. We need to speak to him urgently. I might add he was taken ill after finding the body.'

'I can assure you his finding of the body in no way contributed to his illness, if that is what is going through your mind, Superintendent Clifton. This is not a case of self-induced illness or anything which has developed through nerves or stress.'

'I'm not suggesting it is, I do know he has leukaemia, and am aware of its potential. His wife has just told me.'

'In that case, I can tell you the sergeant has been seriously ill for some time, several weeks I would estimate even if the problem has unfortunately just come our notice. I fear we are too late to be able to provide any effective permanent treatment, Superintendent. He has acute leukaemia. Normally, I would not discuss his medical condition with you but I accept these are very unusual circumstances and I know his family has made you aware of his condition. You can understand, I am sure, why I need to be very careful who speaks to him just now.'

'Does he know how sick he really is?'

'Yes, I have told him, it is terminal. I felt it better that he knew some time before his wife, he needs time to come to terms with his condition. He took it very well, in fact I don't think my news was totally unexpected.'

'So how long has he got? I need to know so that I can make the necessary arrangements for the continuation of my investigation.'

'One of my patients died within eight days of his condition being

diagnosed, Superintendent. Five weeks is not unusual because acute
leukaemia is extremely rapid in its effects; to survive five months is excep-
tional but a lot depends upon how early we are made aware of the condition. There are other types of cancer which take longer to manifest themselves and some which can be held at bay. In this particular case the
patient was suffering from the disease for some time before we were
alerted. It is my considered opinion that Sergeant Simpson will be dead
within two weeks, three at the outside. I am telling you because it is
clearly important to your investigation; you might wish to be aware that
he might not survive to see the case in court. I would ask that you do not
repeat that outside this room, you do not inform his colleagues. His wife
and son are coming to see him later this evening. I will have the awful
task of giving them this dreadful news.'

'This is awful,' Clifton spoke quietly. 'Truly awful. He is a good police
officer and popular around town. I respect your trust in me.'

'Good, so how can I help you?'

'I need to speak to him, in confidence and in private. It is very important, otherwise I shouldn't be troubling you – or him – like this.'

Burrows thought Clifton was putting on a most caring act; it was most
unlike him, but it seemed to be producing the right effect.

'He has had a blood transfusion, Superintendent, and that will give
him a temporary boost, he will feel better and look better, and he will
think he has improved. You can see him in, er . . . fifteen minutes from
now. Will five minutes be long enough with him?'

'That's long enough for my purpose.'

'If you would like to return to the waiting room, I'll call you. Is he
expecting you?'

'Not to my knowledge.'

'Leave it with me, I'll call you shortly.'

Back in the waiting room where they were alone and safe from being
overheard, Clifton said to Sergeant Burrows, 'I'm going to formally arrest
him for the murder, Sergeant, and then charge him.'

'Isn't this a bit premature, sir? We haven't much evidence . . . .'

'We'll never have enough evidence to convict anyone of this crime,
Sergeant. This is as far as we can go. Simpson is going to die soon which
means he will never stand trial, and the story will not get into the newspapers. Once I've charged him, though, I can write off the case in our
records. For Home Office statistical purposes, it will appear as a detected

murder, even if it doesn't get to court and we don't get a conviction. It means all enquiries can now cease and the teams can be dismissed. The investigation is over as from this moment. We've only the loose ends to tie up.'

'There'll be an inquest, though.'

'There will, but it will return a verdict of "murder by person or persons unknown". I'll make sure of that because I shall have to prepare the evidence. I have no intention of revealing Sergeant Simpson as the guilty person, not to the press and not to anyone else, not even to his wife and son – because he will never face a trial. His secret will be safe. And I shall instruct Sergeant Simpson not to tell anyone he has been charged, not even his wife and son.'

'But the press will have to be told, sir.'

'I shall make an announcement tonight, Sergeant. It will be too late for the Sunday papers and by Monday, other news will have superceded it in the nationals. It will be a minor item of news for the big papers because I shall say a man has been arrested and charged with the murder of Edward Albert Swainby and in due course he will appear in court on remand. That will keep them quiet for a few weeks. I shall not give his name; that action is not in the least unusual and it will serve our purpose for the time being. I can cope with any enquiries they make in the period after remand and before the trial – we say nowt. We don't have to tell them anything we don't want but some time later I shall announce that the suspect has died on remand. That will take suspicion away from Sergeant Simpson.'

'Obviously, sir, you want this kept secret?'

'Got it in one, Sergeant. The charge sheet will be kept in the file and not in the charge book in Hildenley's general office which is there they're normally kept; the reason for that is because the arrested person has not been placed in the cells or remanded in custody; he is in hospital. Quite normal procedure.'

'Pending his release from hospital, in theory?'

'In theory, yes. Only you and I know of this development and neither of us will reveal this information to anyone. I shall take the entire file back to headquarters with me and it will be lodged in our secure safe, sealed with wax and placed among other highly sensitive files, including several top secrets ones held over from wartime – suspected traitors and so forth. It will be destroyed after thirty years. There will be no record of the case in Hildenley Police Station – it wasn't their enquiry, it was mine. Due to the development with Sergeant Simpson's illness, I shall stand down the teams as from this evening, allowing them time to complete their outstanding paperwork. Tomorrow, each will get a message to say a man has been arrested, no more. No name will be given to them, they don't need to know that; that action is not unusual. I am sure they – and everyone else including the press – will think the arrest was made in Garminghamshire. I've already made it known that enquiries were being conducted in that area and see no reason to make a contrary statement. I shall ensure the matter is brought to a very satisfactory conclusion. If the members of the press ask why a man has not been brought before the court, they will be told he is on remand but too ill to attend court. I can keep them at bay for a while with that story and then, after a further period, if they persist, I will say the suspect died of natural causes. As there was no trial, he cannot be named. Due to the very unusual circumstances of this case, I do not want them to know our suspect is Sergeant Simpson. I need to protect the image of the police service, Sergeant. We don't want Joe Public thinking policemen go around bumping off villains who evade justice in the courts, do we?'

'But sir, forgive me if I appear stupid, but I don't understand why you are doing all this . . . you're not convinced Sergeant Simpson is guilty, is that right?'

'I am not one hundred per cent sure, Sergeant, that's all I want to say; I think Sergeant Simpson is a very clever man who has brought this upon himself for reasons which may be clear later, but that is not important now because this action will halt the investigation into the death of an evil villain. I suspect that is what the sergeant wants, although he will never say so.'

'So no further enquiries will be made?'

'Right, Sergeant. It all stops with our impending visit to Sergeant Simpson. Our files – which cannot be seen by the public or press – will record the murder as detected. Our 100% murder detection record will be maintained. As a detected crime, we do not need to keep the file open. So it's all neatly tied up and soon to be forgotten, eh?'

'And so this investigation will become nothing more than a figure 1 in the detected murders column of our crime returns?'

'Absolutely right, Sergeant.'

Then there was a knock on the door. It was Mr Buxton.

'Sergeant Simpson can see you now, gentlemen. Five minutes.'

They dismissed the constable on duty at Sergeant Simpson's bedside, telling him to take five minutes for a cup of tea. After a preliminary chat during which Clifton asked after Simpson's condition before revealing his full knowledge of the family secret, he said, 'Sergeant, I have been examining our files about Swainby's murder and it is my duty to tell you that the available evidence, circumstantial though most of it is, suggests that you killed Edward Albert Swainby.'

'Suppose I say I did not?'

'I will record that on the charge sheet, Sergeant.'

'It doesn't really matter what I say, does it?' smiled Sergeant Simpson. 'I'm going to die soon, Mr Clifton, very soon in fact. Too soon to stand trial.'

'I am aware of that, Sergeant. Now listen carefully – I would wish to add, off the record, that there is no evidence to suggest anyone else is guilty of this crime.' He paused to let the import of that statement sink in. 'It is my proposal that I charge you with the crime, under caution, but, again off the record, I shall ask that you do not tell anyone of this, not even your wife and son. No one outside this room will know you have been charged. The file will then be closed. The investigation will cease at that point. The file will be kept in the secret safe at the force headquarters, along with war records and other highly sensitive material, the disclosure of which is considered not in the public interest. The file will be sealed and it cannot be opened without a court order. Rest assured it will be destroyed in thirty years' time without anyone seeing the contents. You understand what I am saying, Sergeant?'

'Yes, sir.'

'Good,' and he formally cautioned Sergeant Simpson and charged him with the murder of Edward Albert Swainby.

Simpson said, 'Thank you, sir.'

'The Swainby file is now closed, Sergeant,' said Clifton. 'Permanently.'

Sergeant Simpson died a month later, his last words to Pamela and Ian being, 'I love you both, you were my life.' Both were in tears. He was buried in Hildenley churchyard with hundreds of townspeople attending his funeral. The body of Ted Swainby was eventually returned to friends in Garminghamshire for burial.

Three years later, Ian left his profession as a ladies' hairdresser to become a very successful actor, intially on the stage and eventually on television.

Pamela got a part-time job in the library at Hildenley.

According to the local newspapers which appeared some time after the murder, the suspect, who was never named and who was thought to come from Garminghamshire County, had died of natural causes while on remand and before he could be brought to trial; therefore the case was closed.

In detecting his first and last case of murder, Sergeant Simpson considered his sacrifice worthwhile.